I0665350

EXIST

Jennifer Cazey Daniels

Exist
First Edition

Copyright © 2015 by Jennifer Cazey Daniels.

Published by Happy Lil Book Nook Publishing
www.existthenovel.com

Book & Cover design by Happy Lil Book Nook Publishing
www.happylilbooknook.com

Printed in the United States of America

ISBN 978-0692535585

Dedicated to the **dreamers**, **lovers**, **believers** and all who dare to run into the unknown with an unshakeable faith that requires courage and boldness. You will reach the end of this race and while the road my be long and hard, don't lose hope or focus; your destiny is worth the fight.

Dare to exist!

"*All that is gold does not glitter,*
Not all those who wander are lost;
The old that is strong does not wither,
Deep roots are not reached by the frost.

From the ashes a fire shall be woken,
A light from the Shadows shall spring;

Renewed shall be blade that was broken,
The crownless again shall be king."

-J.R.R. Tolkien
"All That is Gold Does Not Glitter."

CHAPTER ONE

"Em wait!!!" He ran after me, but I didn't know why he did. I hated that he did it and at the same time it was exactly what I needed and wanted him to do. He didn't want me anymore. In a split second of rash decision he gave me away; pushed me back into the world alone. I wanted to keep running. I wanted to run forever until my heart stopped beating and I didn't have to feel it break anymore. But I could hear his thoughts and I could feel his heart and I stopped. I didn't turn around though I just stopped dead in my tracks as if I had just walked right into a brick wall and had no where else to go. I had always been far too forgiving and too nice for my own good, but I loved him more than I knew was possible and I couldn't avoid that. That undeniable, unexplainable, unavoidable love is what made me stop and hope in the tiniest of ways that he had changed his mind. Aden put his hands softly on my shoulders and turned me around to face him. I could feel my body wanting to collapse. "Em, please don't try to block me." I narrowed my eyes trying to focus but it's amazing how much strength it takes to block all thought and emotion from yourself. It's like trying to stop the ocean from having any current; it's nearly impossible. I tried to avoid his deep brown eyes because they were like pools of quicksand that could pull me in and I would drown and never have a chance of escaping. I guess I secretly was hoping I would either succeed in blocking him so we could have this conversation or that I would pass out before he could reach me. My body began to fall and he grabbed me right before I hit the ground. He had strong arms and even when I was heartbroken by him, they were still the safest place in the world. "Em, look at me. Please, Em, just look at me." I didn't want to open my eyes. I didn't want to look at him and face reality. I didn't want to accept that this could be the last time I'd ever be able to look at him again but I was too weak to fight him, so I did.

I opened my blue, green eyes and stared directly into his chocolate brown eyes that literally sucked me in and made me feel defenseless, obliviously happy and content all at the same time.

"I have to do this Ember, please you have to understand." He was pleading with not only his voice but his eyes for me to understand.

"Why?" I meant to make it sound harsher and stronger, but it came out as a sad whisper.

"It's what is best for us." He gently moved a strand of my fringe behind my ear and I felt tears well up in my eyes. It was bad enough to feel my own pain but I could feel his too and I could hear the thoughts that ran through his mind that were very different than the words he spoke.

"But it's not best for me or you. You know this, why are you doing this?" I didn't want to beg for his love but I did deserve to understand why he was choosing this. He appeared so strong and almost cold on the outside.

It was as if his mind were truly made up and I suppose to people that were different than us, they would see this as final, as what he truly believed and wanted, but I knew differently and he did too. "I'm sorry Em. I have to do this."

I looked up and directly into his eyes making the connection only we could and allowed him to feel me, but he quickly closed his eyes severing the deep connection we had. I instantly lost all strength in my legs and began to fall again. He caught me and helped me back up to my feet and held my hands for a brief moment. "You're going to be alright. I know you'll be safe and okay." He said it to me more to convince himself of this truth he so badly wanted to believe than to actually ease my heartache.

All I could do was shake my head, no, but why couldn't I find the words or the right expressions to tell him this was all wrong? He knew it and I could hear it and feel it from him, but he was trying to fight against who he was and what he believed and it didn't make sense. I did what I knew I had to do and I kissed him. I took in every single minute feature of his I could. The way his dark brown hair felt slightly in his eyes and danced in waves along his shoulders. His lips that were soft and tender. His chocolate skin that felt so smooth and soft to the touch. I ran my hands down his arms that were toned and safe. I placed my hand on his chest, right in the center near his heart and I could feel his internal warmth ooze out of him. I could feel his heart take fast, irregular beats and I could feel him fighting with every ounce of strength he had within him to remain composed and unaffected by this moment. He placed his hand on my chest right near my heart too. The soothing, intoxicating warmth that leaked off of him began to take over inside me. I could feel the pain disappearing, the sadness turning into happiness and it was as if nothing bad had ever happened. I quickly took his hand off my chest and blocked him. "Don't try and use your ability on me now. It's too late." He looked down at the ground and I knew he was only trying to help but it wasn't permanent and only having him in my life forever, like we had planned, would make this better. Somewhere in the back of my mind I wondered if this would be the last time I'd ever see him, but in my heart I knew it wouldn't be. He returned the kiss and if nothing else it was the way I wanted to remember him.

I walked to my car and as I drove away I couldn't dare look back at him but I could still feel him and hear him and somehow as heartbreaking as that was, it gave me hope and comfort because deep down inside he still cared and wanted this too.

I drove home and found my way quickly to my bed. It was the only place I felt I could just let myself cry and still feel somewhat held together. I clutched onto the stuffed rabbit Aden had given me and cried as if I could fill up an empty river bed. I lived alone in a small, one-bedroom apartment. I didn't have any family, that I knew of, and my parents had died at the hands of the government before I was born and I was raised inside a government facility; alone. For a long time I lived supervised by agents but it didn't last long; I managed to escape them…but that's a story for another time. What it all equaled up to was I was alone then and once again alone now. I had always been okay being on my own. It's all I knew and although I had made friends with some of the kids in school, I wasn't encouraged to get close to anyone, ever. Aden and I met in high school and had just graduated. We had our future planned and it was going to be incredible. Our lives were anything but normal; we are supernatural. People called us psionics and based on fiction and role-playing games I guess that's what we are. The government calls us a threat and Aden called us extraordinary. I preferred to call us Ember and Aden, our names, because we weren't defined by what we could do, but rather who we were and would become. Regardless, who we were made us "dangerous" to the world and in most cases made us resident aliens. It was all right by me because it's all I've ever known. Aden knew a much different life than I did, but having him in mine made it all seem worth it, made it all seem okay.

Everything around me was silent tonight and I wasn't in control of my thoughts or my emotions. I was in a bad place and I wanted it all just to stop hurting. I wanted to not feel anything and yet despite my ability to change others thoughts, I couldn't change my own. I couldn't do anything to make the memories fade from earlier tonight or make myself believe the multitude of lies I was flooding my mind with. Suddenly the light that hung above my bed began to crackle and before I knew what was happening a massive spark blew out from the light above my bed cascading glass onto the sheets and floor. I covered myself with my hands and stuffed rabbit and managed to escape without getting hurt. I carefully looked around and noticed the glass everywhere but thankfully nothing was on fire. It wasn't the first lightbulb that had ever blown-up around me but I still wasn't sure if it was coincidence or me that did it. In that moment I didn't really care. If I was capable of blowing things up with my mind all the better. It distracted me, even if momentarily while I cleaned up the broken glass. For a moment I leaned over the broken glass and looked at all the sharp pieces spread around the floor. I was caught in a mindless moment of no thoughts, no feelings; just nothing. This glass was my life, heart and soul right now and maybe it was symbolic that the light broke above me, especially if it was my fault. I broke things and I was broken and maybe I was a fool to believe I could ever be put back together again, or that a man like Aden could ever truly love me.

As I swept up the last pieces of glass I noticed I cast no shadow over them. It was odd at first but I realized it must be due to the lack of light now. I dropped the pieces into the trash and then walked over to the sink to wash my hands. As I passed by the microwave on the counter it turned on making me stop and stare at it completely confused. "That's impossible." I pushed the stop button and as I leaned down to turn it off I noticed I couldn't see myself in the plastic door. I always could see myself, was the lighting that bad I couldn't? I avoided major appliances for the moment and walked over to the mirror in the main room. I was curious if my mind was just playing tricks on me or if something was happening to me. I could feel my nerves kicking in as I walked slowly to the mirror in the entry way. A part of me really didn't want to know but the other part of me had to know. Every step I took closer to the mirror the more nervous I became. As I finally got closer I heard a cracking sound and stopped walking. I noticed the mirror beginning to crack and shatter in the middle and before I could look away the glass blew out in a violent explosion, as if the mirror was laced with dynamite. I fell to the floor trying to protect myself from the blast. Once the sound of glass trickling around me stopped I looked around the room and sparkling pieces of mirror were everywhere. I was a telepath there was no way I could be effecting all these things unless my emotions were causing my abilities to go off the wire. I noticed some blood on my arm slowly flowing out from a clean cut that had been caused by a piece of falling glass. I sighed and walked into the bathroom to clean myself up with the emergency kit. I went straight for the medicine cabinet. I opened it mindlessly grabbing the emergency kit and then closed it. I was pulling out bandages from the kit when I looked at the mirror in front of me. There was no reflection. I waved my hands in front of my face and the mirror but there was nothing reflected back. I touched my face with my hands to make sure it was still there and it was. I pinched myself confirming that I was very much awake, but I had to be dreaming, people don't just disappear. None of this could be real. I had to wake up. How could I wake up? How could I find myself when I didn't appear to exist anymore?

I walked back to my bed and sat down pulling the pillowy comforter around me. I had to be dreaming. Any minute now I would wake up and realize all of this had been some horrible nightmare. I sat there for a few minutes just rocking back and forth slowly wondering when this dream would end. It definitely didn't feel like a dream but being a telepath made dreaming a very vivid and real experience some times. As a little girl I used to long for just one silly dream to appear but it never came. No, I was always inside someone else's dream or seeing something that was yet to come. I didn't get the luxury of dreaming about pink elephants and flying. The silence in the apartment was deafening so I decided to turn on the television for a welcomed distraction. Maybe I just needed to quiet my mind, fall asleep in the dream so that I could wake up back in reality. The television turned on to a breaking news report. "Reports are flowing in about another major earthquake, this time in Malaysia that has claimed the lives of at least 150, but first responders expect the number to grow. This is the third major natural disaster to strike the globe within two weeks. Scientist are calling it the effects of global warming, religious sects are calling it the end of times, and conspiracy theorist believe it to be the work of aliens. Whatever the cause of these awful events may be, we must be prepared and do what we can to help our fellow humans. The Red Cross number…" The anchor woman's voice began to fade out as I found myself lost in the footage of people injured and surrounded by debris. Their homes and lives destroyed. The other two events before this were a massive tsunami and a tornado. There wasn't a clear reason as to why these random natural disasters were occurring but it definitely had the world on high alert. I turned the tv off quickly as my heart could withstand breaking any further tonight and laid down in bed. The events of the night were finally hitting me hard and I welcomed the sleep. Hopefully the next time I opened my eyes, this would all be over.

+ + + + + + + + + + + + + + + + + + +

"I exist. I'm alive. I exist. I'm alive. I exist. I'm alive." This is the mantra I repeat throughout the day to myself just to make sure I don't forget. I'm afraid if I stop reminding myself I really will cease to exist. Since the night Aden broke my heart life has become a chain of unfortunate events that have caused me to run for my life. The irony is it's a life long forgotten and yet a life that I fight for everyday.

I stop momentarily to catch my breath and lean against the cool exterior of the New York brick building that is next to me. Its cool feel helps me to calm down for a moment. A moment is all I ever have. I watch people walk past me and inside my heartaches wondering what it must be like to be them, to be loved and to exist. They walk around unaware of the world they actually live in, taking everything for granted. Unaware of what dangers and evils surround them constantly and they don't seem to mind at all. I wonder what that would be like, to live without the constant fear of being hunted? To wake up every morning and only have to worry about what I want to eat or what outfit to wear. But that's not my reality, no, I barely sleep and I find myself being hunted every second of everyday. Sometimes I swear that should have been my middle name; hunted. Maybe that's why I was never given one because it would be far too cruel to name a child that and predict such a horrid future. There was nothing ordinary about my life, as I had spent every year since I was born on the run in search of hope. A hope I desperately held onto that allowed me to believe there had to be a version of my life that was better than the one I was born into. Unfortunately for me, I'm never allotted much time or able to remain in one place for long. Except right now I decide to take a few moments, not to rest but to search. I guess the benefit of being invisible is that I can people watch and no one will accuse me of being strange or staring at them. People watching was something I used to enjoy back when life was a little simpler. It's actually how I taught Aden to use his abilities more. We would go to the park or a shopping mall and just sit on a bench. We'd then watch all the people, young and old, walk by and rather then try and guess who they were or what kind of life they lived we'd read them. Aden would practice reading their emotions and I would then read their thoughts and intentions to see if he was right. Sometimes we would just sit and try to be like regular people, at my request of course, and guess without our abilities who all these strangers around us were and where they were going. We would then check if we were right or wrong and use our abilities afterwards. Being normal and like all the other sleeping, unaware people seemed like fun at times, and was a life that I was envious of. Once Aden learned to use his abilities more and got stronger he preferred to use them all the time if possible. He kind of lost out on what it meant to be like everyone else…ordinary.

Right now though this wasn't a leisurely game of people watching and ability practicing time. I was looking for specific people and I had spent the past two weeks scouring New York for them. Aden and I had discovered through some research he had done, that there was a group of psionics living in New York. I didn't know their identities but I had to follow any lead, no matter how small it may be. I looked around the city before me and sighed, this was like trying to find a needle in a haystack. In that moment, watching all the people I was suddenly hit with the feeling of deep despair and hopelessness. What was I thinking believing I could find people to help me? Even if I found them I wouldn't be able to talk to them. I had spent every night sleeping on cold park benches because I couldn't get a room somewhere else, couldn't work, couldn't even get a spare bed in a shelter. Finding food was a whole other story. I found myself sliding down the wall until I was sitting against it on the cold cement pavement below. It was an unimaginable feeling knowing you were completely lost and alone in the world. You could see the world but would anyone ever be able to see you? Was this a permanent thing? I had no idea how it started in the first place or what was causing this. Trust me, invisibility wasn't an ability I ever hoped to have or wanted. I dreamed of being able to teleport or fly, not disappear.

I dropped my head into my hands and could feel the darkness consuming me. I just didn't have the strength or energy to keep going. *Ow*. I looked up to see a man in a business suit looking around him to determine what he just kicked, but of course, there was nothing to be seen so he continued walking. I looked at my leg as it throbbed from the point of his dress shoe and just sighed. How does hope turn into despair so quickly?

Oh no...

I jumped up to my feet and immediately took off running. They were getting closer and this was exactly how they worked. They knew they could override the block I had placed on my thoughts and somehow my emotions had become a vulnerable spot too. They used my abilities against me. They hunted me by making me want to give up. Placing thoughts inside my head and heart that knocked me into the deepest chasm of despair and depression a person could find themselves in.

I hadn't realized this at first, until I saw them. They showed up at my apartment about 2 months ago. It was when I first began running. My heart was already broken and I had noticed my abilities were going on the fritz. I had locked myself up in my apartment until I could gain control over them. I had spent the time trying to wake myself up from this horrible, endless, nightmare only to discover that I wasn't dreaming and I was definitely invisible. When Aden showed up he proved my worst fears were true. He was knocking on the door and as I opened it he looked right through me. I talked to him and he didn't respond. He just walked into the apartment and looked around and began to make phone calls. He was worried about me and trying to find someone who knew where I could be found. I tried to comfort him, I tried to touch him and I could feel him. I could hear him. I could smell him. Yet he couldn't see me at all. He couldn't feel me or hear me. He called all our friends and they all said they hadn't heard from me in quite awhile. He placed the last call and then slammed the phone down. "Aden, I'm here. Don't you see me?" I was crying now as I screamed out to him. How could the love of my life not see me? I panicked and grabbed some paper and a pen. I wrote on it a message to Aden. *"Aden, my love, please know I am with you. I love you. Please see me. Love Always and Forever, Em."* I placed the paper down near him and waited. I saw him begin to look around the desk and he saw the note. He picked it up slowly and I noticed his hand began to tremble slightly as he read it. He sat there staring at it, touching the paper as if somehow it was apart of me he could reach and tears filled his eyes. "I'm so sorry Em. I'm so, so sorry." I wrapped my arms around him to comfort him and he just continued to cry. I was nothing to him anymore. Just a memory. Words on a piece of paper. Yet I knew by the way he worried and the tears that fell from his eyes somewhere, no matter how deeply tucked away it was, he still cared and I wanted more than anything to reach that part of him, but I couldn't even reach him at all anymore.

I watched him get up and walk into my bedroom. He ran his hands along the bedding and I smiled. We had napped there together many times. Spent hours sitting on the bed watching movies and TV. We would dream there together about the world and future we wanted. Was he remembering those moments too? Suddenly I knew how I could reach him. I closed my eyes and began to reach out to his mind. When I made the connection, his mind was nothing like I remembered it being. His mind was now foggy, darker and confused. It was a chaotic mess. I could see the waves of thoughts that were not his own. It was as if his mind had been taken hostage by a terrorist and it was now a dangerous place to be. His mind used to be a beautiful place, a safe place and a place that I loved. Now it was like walking through a dark war zone. My head was beginning to throb as I tried to navigate through his mind. I knew this was dangerous for me but I wasn't going to leave him like this. I was beginning to understand, even in the smallest way possible, why he left me after seeing the change that had occurred within the landscape of his mind. As I moved through the noise and chaos that was his mind I looked desperately for him. He was hiding in there somewhere. How terrible must it be to have your mind taken over and not to even know where you are inside yourself anymore? I felt bad for him. I wanted to rescue him but even I could only do so much. I telepathically called out to him and I could faintly hear his voice respond back but quickly I was pulled away. There was a force within him that was stronger than I had ever known in my life. It terrified me and I began to feel tears stream my face as I wondered if he could be rescued. Aden used to tell me that I was the only one who could save him from himself, rescue him if he ever was too far-gone. Now I wondered if that had been just some romantic idea he had dreamt up, because from what I could see there wasn't a way for me to reach him. He had shut me out and I could die trying to rescue him, but it wouldn't make a difference.

Somehow knowing I couldn't get through and recognizing the danger before me didn't make me stop. Love is a powerful force that I still believed could and would conquer all. Aden wouldn't have left me in this state and I wasn't about to leave him this way either. I continued to push past the pain in my head and try to find him inside himself. The further I got the harder he fought to keep me out. His mind created endless amounts of walls to protect what it was trying to hide. It was like an infection that knew antibodies were coming to rid it from the host and it would do anything to win. I continued to push in deeper and then I saw him. He was in the corner of a dark room. His knees were up to his chin and he looked deathly afraid. I saw him look at me and suddenly our connection was made. "Run Em, Run!" I didn't even have a chance to ask him why or get to him, I was thrown out of his mind, the connection was broken and I was knocked onto the floor and blacked out.

When I woke up Aden was no longer in my apartment. I couldn't tell how long I had been passed out for but I was weak and had an incredible pressure, as if someone had filled me with lead, inside my chest that made me feel like remaining on the floor forever. My thoughts were desperate for hope, desperate to know what happened to Aden, but in a way that wasn't going to fight, it was in the way of knowing that you had failed and wondering how it happened. The overwhelming feeling that you lost the one you love. The kind of awful, heart crushing feeling that you couldn't protect the person who needed you more than ever. It was a desperate feeling of failure and hopelessness. It was as if someone was whispering thoughts into my head and I couldn't fight them from coming. I wanted to surrender to it. I wanted to give up right then and there, after all, Aden couldn't see me; I was nothing to him now. I managed to sit up and lean against the doorframe and noticed a piece of paper move across the floor from the breeze of the air conditioner. It blew towards me and I wanted to just watch it and not engage in trying to stop it, but it stopped when it hit my side. There was a picture of me on the page and the words MISSING at the top in bright read letters. My heart for a brief moment leapt thinking that Aden was looking for me. That despite the chaos and darkness that had overtaken his head that he still cared. He was still fighting for me. Then I noticed the name and number of the contact. "James Addison." My heart dropped and froze in fear. He was the commander of the government agency who had raised me. He had been looking for me since I managed to break free from them. How had he gotten this close? How did he find me? Did he taken Aden? Then I noticed the sun that had been piercing through the windows was cut off quickly. I looked at the window and it was covered in Shadows. The whole apartment suddenly felt like a steel prison. I could feel the pressure in my head and chest as if someone were trying to hijack me and take control. I fought against it and used all my strength to get up. I got onto my feet and looked for an escape. I could see the Shadows everywhere and I could feel them, I could hear them and it killed me to read them because there was nothing good or pure inside them. It was destruction and death that radiated out of them and it was an energy that sought to take me apart from the inside out. Like a tugboat pulls a giant ship, I could feel myself being pulled in all directions but my own.

I heard the front door open and knew that exit was gone. I had only one hope, one chance of escaping, and I surely wasn't going to be taken by whatever this force was, without a fight. I closed my eyes and used every bit of energy and strength I had left to block them out of my head and heart. I was vulnerable and it was harder than ever to block something so strong, but this was life or death and my abilities were the only defense I had. I could feel the inner war rage on inside as I fought between surrendering to the darkness and fighting against it. I used what little bit of strength, will and energy I had left in me and blocked them. It was like a sonic boom had emanated from me and I could see the energy waves fly from me across the room and outside. In one loud, thunderous sound, the glass in all the nearby windows blew out and shattered to the ground. The Shadows were blown away and disappeared. I didn't know how long they would be gone for. All I knew was that I didn't have time to stop and collect anything. I just had to run. I had to go. I grabbed a necklace that Aden had given me that was on the table next to me. It was a heart made of clear crystals and I placed it quickly around my neck and jumped out the window and climbed quickly down the fire escape. I made it to the ground and heard the words Aden had said, "Run Em, run!" I did just that; I took off running in no particular direction. I wasn't safe here anymore.

That was the first time I had ever experienced such darkness and felt a force, stronger than myself, overcome me like that. I had no idea where the Shadows came from or who was controlling them but I knew they could find me. It was the type of force I knew I would never be able to run from, but I wasn't going to surrender and make it easy to be taken either. If I was going down, I would go down with a fight. Commander James obviously couldn't see me either and that's why he claimed I was missing and hadn't taken me right then and there. I could only hope that Aden was safe from him. As far as I knew no one knew what Aden could do except for his parents and I. People knew Aden was unique and special, but they had no idea how true that was. I never did stop to check on Aden physically but it was safer this way. I did connect with him briefly, telepathically, and he was still as lost and broken as he was before, but he had a strange sense of being content. The greatest danger to any person was just laying down and accepting life as it is and being content with it; to become indifferent. Not wanting anything more or hoping for something greater, just taking life as it came and for what people told you it would be. That wasn't who Aden was, not at all, but that's who he was becoming and I didn't know why.

Since the first assault I had been running and finding my way around trying to avoid slowing down for too long. Whenever I would slow down the Shadows would attack. The worst part was my own shadow was now my own worst enemy. My shadow was now a constant reminder of the enemies that were just a few steps behind me at any given moment. I was slowing down and the feeling of despair and hopelessness was overtaking me. If I remained there the Shadows would surround me and I wasn't about to let them win. Without anyone being able to see me, I wasn't sure how I would begin to seek help. It's incredible how much we take for granted the ability to scream, to talk, to just interact with people. Even with all the gifts and abilities I had it was all useless. My only hope was to find another psionic so hopefully I could make a connection with them and they could help me.

I finally had to stop running again as my lungs began to burn. New York was fairly cold this time of year and the cold, crisp air, ripped through my lungs like mini razor blades. I stopped to catch my breath and noticed people who appeared out of place amongst all the others. There was a look in their eyes, a posture about them that made me feel at home. They appeared as if they were on guard and at any moment the world was going to close in on them and expose them. I smiled for the first time in months and muttered to myself, *psionics*.

CHAPTER TWO

As excited, as I was to find people I assumed to be similar to me, I also knew that I had to approach them with caution. One thing I had learned through Aden's research is that not all psionics used their abilities to better the world, so to speak. There were factions around the world that sought power and control and they fought against the peaceful psionics, the ones who just wanted to exist and live their lives. To the unsuspecting world we were just ordinary people and to those who hunted us we were seen as threats and dangerous. It didn't matter what side we chose or didn't choose to stand on in what was quickly becoming known as the psionic war. We all were marked, even those who didn't recognize their abilities yet. The first time I heard about the war was on the first night I arrived in New York. I managed to over hear some people talking at a local deli, who clearly were on the team that sought control and power; the Opposition as they referred to themselves. According to the two men I eavesdropped on, somehow the forces that sought to control us or destroy us had discovered a way to find us. No one was safe. I hadn't been able to gain much information since then because finding psionics wasn't as easy as I had hoped it would be. All I could assume was that a war waged by psionics would be a war waged on the world as well.

I approached the two standing around Central Park with caution. I had to laugh at myself because it was kind of silly being so covert considering they couldn't see me and therefore they wouldn't know to block me out either. Once I determined their overall demeanor and motives I would have a small window of opportunity to reach them and possibly connect. I watched them from a nearby bench for a second to see what abilities they might have. If one of them was a telepath I probably would be discovered the minute I tried to read them but if they were something else I might be able to read them without them even knowing I was there. I suppose being invisible in this moment had its perks, but being unskilled and uneducated in the ways of the psionic world left me at a great disadvantage. I watched them talk to each other and suddenly I felt a pang of sadness inside my chest. The realization hit me that I hadn't been able to have a real conversation in months. I craved human companionship and I had a deep longing to just connect with anyone. I talked to myself all the time but I had gotten used to listening to the voice within my head that I wondered if I would even recognize the sound of my own voice anymore or if I still had one? I decided that out of desperation I would throw caution to the wind and would approach the two in the park and see what the situation was. At this point this was my only hope. All I could now was pray they were friendly and not foes.

As I slowly approached the two psionics they appeared to be harmless. They both looked to be somewhere in their early 20's at best. The guy had sandy blonde hair that fell just a bit into his eyes and his build was fairly athletic and rather tan. He almost looked as though he belonged on a beach in Hawaii or California. New York did not look like his scene at all. The girl on the other hand had a simpler but beautiful look. She was dressed in nice jeans with a waist length military green coat covering her. Her hair was a light brown that almost bordered blonde, like her counterpart, but her skin was softer in tone. She wore her hair in a side swept, long ponytail that was partially hidden and held in place by a black knit beanie. I continued to move closer to them and observed what they were doing and hoped to get close enough to hear part of their conversation. I found a large rock nearby the lake in Central Park and quietly took a seat. I sighed as I sat down and rolled my eyes in frustration. I have no idea why I was still worried about being quiet or stealthy when I was invisible to the world, but I suppose it was the eternal hope inside me that believed someday, someone would finally be able to see me again.

I focused my attention on the two as they appeared to be admiring the lake. "Sam, don't do it here. It's too public." "Ah, come on Liz it's just for fun." Liz giggled and looked at him with a warning glare but I could tell she was just doing it for a show. The benefit of my abilities meant I didn't need to read minds in order to discern a person's intentions and spirit. Her intentions and spirit were carefree and filled with excitement. Nothing about Liz gave me the impression that she was part of the Opposition in the psionic war and Sam didn't appear to be apart of the Opposition either. They were either apart of the Resistance, trying to fight the good fight, or not aligned at all like me. I watched them both look around to make sure they weren't going to get caught and then they focused back on the ducks in the lake.

Sam kneeled down and before I knew it ripples were forming in the pond and the nearby ducks began to scatter in concern. Liz giggled and then I noticed her begin to focus and suddenly the climate around us began to change from a crisp day to freezing. This part of the park began to drop drastically in temperature and suddenly the pond water began to freeze. My mouth felt as though it had fallen onto the ground. I had never seen these abilities before and it blew my mind. Aden had done a lot of ground research for us once and we had read about what other psionics were capable of but we had never met any like this, then again we had never met any to begin with. In that moment I felt the hand of sadness grip my heart wishing he was here with me witnessing this. He would be beyond excited to know others were out there and to be experiencing this as well. Aden enjoyed the use of our abilities more than I did. He was constantly wondering what he was capable of and how he could further his abilities. I, on the other hand, just wanted to use them to help people, but at this very moment I had to admit I was really excited to see them in action. The ducks flew back to the pond and slid a bit on the newly, unexpected, frozen ice. They looked as confused as the mother and child walking by. Sam and Liz laughed and began to walk away. I couldn't let them get away so I got up quickly and followed them.

After their display at the pond I was confident that they were safe to read and connect with. As we walked I began to explore Liz's mind first. Her mind was an array of colors, images of Sam and memories, both recent and old. I left her mind and looked into Sam's mind. His was a bit more complicated and protected. Although his exterior displayed someone who enjoyed mucking around, he definitely was much more serious on the inside. His mind held what could only be described as vaults. He kept the things he felt were worth protecting locked away I suppose. Whatever his life experience was he knew to keep his mind safe. So I left his and moved back to Liz. I mentally reached out to her asking for help, *"Please, help me."*

Liz immediately stopped and grabbed hold of Sam's arm. The smile on his face quickly disappeared and was replaced by instant concern.

"What is it?" Liz silenced him and began looking around. "A telepath." They both began looking around but even with me jumping up and down, flailing my arms in front of their faces, they couldn't see me.

"I don't see anyone. What do they want?" Liz shrugged and listened, "Help." Sam looked confused and pensive. It was a look I knew all too well from Aden. Maybe psionic men were just that way, where everything seemed to be a life or death situation. "Well find out where they are." Liz closed her eyes and I heard her ask me where I was inside her mind. I replied back, *"Right in front of you. My name is Ember and I'm invisible as strange as that sounds, but please I need your help."* Her eyes shot open and she looked straight ahead. I hated how people looked right through me. I wasn't one to enjoy being the center of attention, but I really didn't like feeling as though I didn't exist. Liz then extended her arms out in front of her. Sam looked puzzled by her actions but didn't interrupt as he continued quietly observing. I could feel her arms touch me briefly and then she grabbed onto my arms holding me in place. She shook her head in disbelief and looked at Sam. "This is strange. Her name is Ember and she claims she's in front of us but we can't see her because she's invisible. What ability makes people invisible?"

Sam thought for a moment, "If she's a telepath then she could alter our minds to not see her."

Liz shrugged and leaned in closer to Sam, whispering, "You think she's part of the Opposition don't you?"

Sam sighed and his face was hard and difficult for me to read, "It's hard to say. We can't be sure of anyone anymore, Liz. We have to look out for ourselves first now."

Liz looked straight through me but it felt oddly comforting to pretend for a moment she could see me. "But what if she really needs our help? If she were part of the Opposition I would think she would have attacked us by now."

Sam looked straight ahead deep in thought for what felt and seemed like too long before he spoke again, this time directly to me. "Show us who you are. We'll know if you're lying or not." They were both silent for a moment and I decided all I could do is try and show them who I really was...or used to be.

I closed my eyes and suddenly all of Central Park began to fade away. I could feel and see the intersection between Sam and Liz's minds as they came into focus allowing me to show them the exact same thing at the same time. I took them back to my apartment and showed them Aden showing up and then me passing out. I showed them Addison showing up and the Shadows that now followed me. I wasn't a strong empath, that I knew of so I couldn't make them feel my heart in this but I could convey my intentions to them and I did that the best I could. I opened my eyes slowly. Using my abilities this much in public made me extremely anxious, as I knew, the Shadows would have already tracked me down and be close behind, but I had to take the risk. Liz and Sam glanced at each other silently and then nodded. "Alright, you can come with us but we have to figure out a better way to communicate with you so we can help you." I smiled as Sam spoke and grabbed hold of Liz's hand. His voice still rang clearly of hesitation and I knew he didn't trust me, but I was thankful that they were giving me a chance at least. I felt a pang of heartbreak in my chest as I watched Sam and Liz walk hand in hand. That's how Aden and I used to be. He was my best friend and I have no doubt if we were together right now, using our abilities like they did, we'd be doing silly things too. We used to enjoy laying in the grass at the park near home and reading each other. It was so simple and fun and sometimes truly frustrating. Aden was the only person who could ever truly see me and knew me. He saw all my fears, flaws, failures, dreams, hopes, desires and everything in between. I had hidden for so long from the past I had run from and yet somehow he saw me for who I was and didn't run away. The more he saw me the more it pulled him closer to me. I shook my head to try and erase the memories because right now I needed to focus and thoughts of Aden were only going to distract me.

I managed to keep up with Liz and Sam. From time to time they would ask if I was still with them and I would telepathically say, "*yes*". Every time I had to use my ability to communicate I felt a sense of paranoia rush over me. My abilities were a honing beacon for the Shadows and the less I used them the safer everyone would be. I knew the Shadows were close and I knew they would be honing in on me any second. I just tried to keep my focus on moving forward and not allowing anything to get inside my head that didn't belong inside there. Although we had been walking for awhile we didn't appear to be getting very far. I realized I should have probably asked them how far we had to go before we were going to arrive at our given destination. I didn't dare use my ability right now though, especially not in public. The last thing anyone needed was a fight between the Shadows and myself. Two things that couldn't be seen and that could cause everyone around us massive destruction. Liz stopped momentarily at a nearby shop to purchase some fruit. I stayed as close to Sam as I could while we waited outside. Out of the corner of my eye I saw a shadow from behind me and I grabbed him out of fear. He jumped, surprised by my touch, and then laughed it off knowing people thought he must be crazy. "What's wrong?" He asked quietly. I let go of him and responded back telepathically, *"There are Shadows coming after me and I thought they might have found me. They hone in on me when I use my ability."* "Are they here now?" *"I don't think so. I usually feel them coming."* "How?" *"I'll explain more later, it's not safe here."* I saw genuine concern in his eyes, but was it for me or him? I didn't know about the

Shadows until I became invisible. I was like everyone else, unable to see the world beyond my own until I was forced into this new world. I was apart of the unseen world now and that was a much different world then I was used to knowing. There were so many things people didn't know existed beyond what they could see and in some ways I wasn't too excited that I knew about those things now myself. Aden used to tell me everything happened for a reason and that we all had a purpose in this world. I'll be honest sometimes I loved to romanticize the idea that he had, that we were needed here for a reason and nothing happened by accident. Other times I found myself not able to believe that at all. I didn't feel I had much of a purpose in this world, except to the government who wanted to study me and use me. I suppose to some people the government's plans would be acceptable, because to the world we were portrayed as enemies, but I actually cared about people and didn't want to see them get hurt because of the knowledge my existence could bring.

"*Sam?*" I whispered.

"What is it?" He tensed up and looked around as if he somehow would finally be able to see me or at least see what was wrong.

"They're close." I said quickly trying to
minimize using my abilities.

"How close?" Sam began looking around as
if he could see the impending doom coming.

"I don't know. I can feel them, I have to go."
My initial response was to run because the further
away I got, the less the Shadows could effect me,
and possibly hurt the Statics around us.

"Don't go. Let me get Liz. Stay right here."
Sam ran into the shop and all I could see was the
world around me fading. I hated this part, I felt like
I had absolutely no control over my mind or body,
like I was fading out of existence altogether. I felt
as though I were merely a puppet and and the
master was pulling on my emotional strings and the
more he pulled, the more everything became dark
and hopeless. It was the kind of feeling that you
would give anything to make stop. I guess this is
why people claim to sell their souls to the devil, to
make the unimaginable desperation for relief end,
but that's not who I was. I was a fighter and I
wasn't going to go down without a fight. I looked
around at the busy street before me and saw
hundreds of people gathered for an arts and crafts
show. I could feel my stomach seize up knowing if
any fight ensued here it would be disastrous for all

of us. Whoever these Shadows were they had no concern for life, except the lives they hunted. I may be the only one who can see the Shadows and therefore knew to be afraid of them, but I would fight to the death if I had to because I didn't want others to get hurt, especially when it wasn't their fight. I knew if they got close enough and tried to take me they wouldn't let anything stand in their way and I wasn't going to go willingly with them either. There had to be another way to resolve this.

Liz and Sam rushed out of the shop looking around, "Ember, you here?"

"*Yes! Run!*" We took off running and every time my feet hit the cement I could feel a burst of pain shoot through my nerves. Dang, they were powerful and it was taking every ounce of my energy to fight against them. "*STOP!*" I cried out telepathically and saw Liz and Sam skid to a halt and turn around.

"Why?" Sam asked wrapping his arm protectively around Liz.

"*They're here.*" I could see in front of me the wall of ominous Shadows that now surrounded us like a cage. I closed my eyes for a moment and shared the vision I was seeing with Liz and Sam. I wasn't very good at it but I was trying to help them see what we were up against. "Oh, this is bad." Liz said as she shared my vision. Suddenly the ground began to shake as the Shadows began to move in all at once towards me. I broke my connection with Liz and Sam as we stumbled to keep standing and watched people around us run in fear. I could feel my heart racing as I fought to regain control from the Shadows. "What do you want?" I yelled out to them. I couldn't tell which one said it, but I heard in a low, guttural voice, "You!" "No! I'm not going anywhere with you!" Suddenly I was knocked on the ground as my heart ached as if someone had their hand gripped around it and was steadily squeezing tighter and tighter. It was as if the entire world's population of pain and hurt was placed inside me. I couldn't move. I couldn't get back up and worst of all, I couldn't fight back. I was curled up in the middle of the New York street in fetal position trying to fight the pain, and losing hopelessly. I looked around and saw Sam and Liz on the ground nearby and they weren't moving. I couldn't tell if they were feeling what I was or if something else had happened to them. Seeing them like that, my only friends in the world right now, I felt a fire inside ignite. As I worked on standing to my feet the ground continued to shake and pieces of building and sidewalk were cracking apart. People were running in a panic, yelling, "Earthquake!", but it was far worse than that. I finally made it to my feet, with a strength inside me I didn't recognize. I closed my eyes and used what little energy I had left within me and shut it all off. All my feelings went away and my thoughts stopped as well. I blocked all thoughts and emotions out, even that which were my own, and just focused on becoming completely empty and numb. Focused on creating a telepathic shield and a massive gust of wind forced me to open my eyes.

The Shadows were gone.

I breathed a sigh of relief and rushed over to Sam and Liz. "*Are you alright?*" I asked them.

"Yeah, what happened? What are those things?" They sat up and we looked around New York. People were injured from trying to escape falling debris and running during the shaking. Buildings were cracked and falling apart in places. Street vendors were hurriedly trying to recollect their goods that had rolled into the street.

"*The Shadows. They did this.*" I said painfully as I found myself helpless to what was happening.

"Are they still here?" Liz asked looking around defensively, as if she could somehow fight this invisible invader.

"*No. They're gone for now.*" I replied a few stray tears from my cheeks and turned away from the scene before me.

Sam helped Liz get back onto her feet and took a long look around. "So this is what it's going to be like?"

"What is Sam?" Liz touched his face gently as it wasn't hard to see the fear and concern in every line on his face.

"The war. This is what will happen. Innocent people who know nothing about us will be hurt or worse." Liz's face fell into sadness as well and Sam pulled her close.

"*It doesn't have to be this way.*" I said to them.

"Really? You've got unseen forces coming after you, Casper that will decimate an entire street, how else is it going to be once this war happens?" Sam's voice was cutting and laced with anger and I didn't blame him at all.

"*I don't know enough about it. I just discovered it a couple weeks ago. But there has to be something we can do. I don't want to see people get hurt as much you don't and I'm on your side to end this before it gets worse.*" Sam looked angry and I didn't dare open myself back up. I felt in that moment he may be regretting his offer to help me. That somehow he was blaming me for what happened and saw me as more of a threat than anything. I just hoped somehow he realized this wasn't my fault and I didn't want people getting hurt anymore than he did.

Sam ran his hand through his hair and looked like he was about to fume smoke out of his ears. Liz looked into his eyes with a soft, loving expression and it seemed to melt Sam in his tracks. She reached out for both of his hands and kissed them gently and he smiled. "Thank you." He smiled a tiny bit.

"We're going to be okay, Sam. Let's get back home and we can all talk, get on the same page, and we'll go from there, okay?" Liz had a soft, soothing voice and whatever it was about her, it could reach Sam when I don't think anyone or anything else could. I watched them enviously wishing I could have had that effect on Aden. Sadly, no matter how deep, real or strong the love between us was, I couldn't save him, but that didn't mean I would give up on him. I couldn't give up on Aden

48

because I knew if the roles were reversed he wouldn't give up on me. Aden had spent many years fighting for me first and now it was my turn. I didn't know what I was doing or if the answers I was seeking would even help me, but I had to try. My hope, my determination, my faith that a miracle could happen is what kept me moving forward. "Come on Ember, let's go." Sam called out to me as he walked ahead with Liz leading the way.

As we began walking again I took one more look at the scene we were leaving behind and whispered, "*I'm sorry.*"

I followed Liz and Sam a few more blocks through the busy streets of New York to a third floor walk up. It was above a Chinese restaurant and I had to laugh at how stereotypical this seemed of New Yorkers in movies. Once we got to their place it was really nice inside. Their place was simple but it felt homey and cozy. This was the first semblance of home I had felt or seen in months. I stood in the middle of the front room and just inhaled a massive dose of air as if I could take in the moment forever and never let it leave me. I didn't know how long they'd let me stay or if I'd even be welcome to stay long once the Shadows came again, so I was making sure to take in every bit of it while it lasted. Sam and Liz moved about the place kicking off their shoes and removing their jackets and scarf. I noticed Liz had scrapped her elbow during the Shadow encounter earlier. Sam, also noticed, and immediately pulled out a first aid kit and headed straight over to Liz. I noticed Liz smiled as she sat down on a bar stool in the kitchen as Sam was preparing to tend to her. I moved in further and took a seat on a nearby chair and watched them together. I felt almost guilty watching them but I couldn't help myself. Life was like watching an endless reality show and I was seated in front of the television watching life happen before my eyes without anyway to be apart of it. I wanted what they had and for some time I actually had it and there was a part of me wondering when it would all fall apart for them too. I used to be a hopeless romantic and I believed that love was stronger than anything in this world. That there wasn't a force or establishment strong enough to break it when it was real and pure. I believed with all my heart and soul that what Aden and I had was forever and that aside from one of us losing our lives, nothing could break us apart. There was something about our relationship that didn't seem as if it could have been formed by earthly conventions and a part of my heart that knew from the moment I met him I was destined to be his. After everything that has happened between us and seeing him let me go and not seem to care what happened to me once I was gone, I was starting to wonder if what I believed about love and destiny was ever real at all? Watching Liz and Sam gave me some shred of hope, but it wasn't enough for me to fully believe again. Apart from Aden coming back to me, I don't think much would ever make me believe again in love like I had before. I missed who I used to be and I wished more than anything I could go back in time and rescue her. But time travel wasn't something I had come across so I had to find a way to deal with the loss of her and accept who I was becoming.

Sam finished tending to Liz and they looked around the room, obviously for me. "Ember?"

"*Here! I'm sitting in the chair.*" I responded telepathically to them.

Sam laughed to himself, "Okay, I don't know how this is going to work." I felt my heart freeze in fear for a moment wondering if I had already become too much of a burden for them and if they were planning on sending me out to the streets again.

"Sam don't be dramatic. We're doing just fine with her. It's just different." Liz playfully nudged Sam and he relaxed and put the first aid kit back. Being in this place made Sam seem less intense and for whatever reason, being home made him calm down and relax.

"Just so you know Ember, you're safe to use your abilities here. No one can track you." He couldn't see the shocked and confused expression on my face but I wished he could have. That didn't make sense at all.

"*How is that possible?*" I responded anxious to hear his answer.

"We have another friend, his name is Dylan, and he was able to get ahold of some tech that allows a shield to be placed over this immediate area and no one, not even others, like us, can track us. We're completely off the radar. You're free to use your abilities here to communicate with us, which should make this easier and less life threatening." I felt truly bad for what had happened just a little while ago and I really hoped people weren't too badly hurt. How could I, just one girl, become such a problem and have my life put so many other lives at risk?

I sighed and relaxed a bit trying not to think about what had happened. *"Thank you for letting me stay here and putting up with my....odd situation."*

Liz giggled and her bubbly, warm personality came out again as it always seemed to. "It's definitely an odd situation and one I have never encountered before. Are you sure you can't become visible again? That this isn't just a telepath trick?"

I closed my eyes for a moment and focused with all the energy and will power I had inside of me and then opened my eyes, *"Can you see me?"* Sam shook his head along with Liz and said, "No."

I slumped down in the old, but comfy, chair and looked at them both, *"Then yes, I'm sure this isn't a trick and I can't become visible again."*

Sam walked around and took a seat on the couch. He was examining the chair where I sat as if he could see me but I knew he couldn't. "Were you always invisible?" He asked leaning forward until Liz came to take a seat next to him and he sat back putting his arm around her.

"No. I was definitely visible my whole life. I didn't even know for sure I had become invisible until people showed up at my apartment and

couldn't see or hear me." It felt good to finally share my story and I was hoping with everything inside of me that they would be able to find an answer to this problem.

"I've never heard of anything happening like this before." Liz said intently listening to my telepathically communicated story and playing mindlessly with a strand of her long hair. "Did something happen to trigger this maybe?"

"*I don't know. I can't think of what would have happened. My abilities went on the fritz after Aden, he was my boyfriend, broke up with me. So I stayed inside my apartment for weeks till I could control them.*" Sam sat up for a moment with a smirk on his face, "Well that's it then, your abilities must still be on the fritz."

CHAPTER THREE

It had been roughly two days since I had met Liz and Sam and had been staying with them. I didn't dare leave their place because I knew the Shadows were waiting for me to re-emerge and I wasn't interested in meeting them again any time soon. I had yet to meet Sam and Liz's friend Dylan, who supposedly lived with them. Although I was beginning to wonder if he was real or imaginary since I hadn't seen him or heard him. Then again I spent most of my time sleeping lately. I was exhausted and finally having a soft, warm place to sleep; even if it was on the old oriental rug in the corner of their place, was a dream for me. They

55

even allowed me to eat with them, which Liz and Sam found rather amusing. Sam had affectionately named me "Casper" because I reminded him of the friendly ghost in the cartoons. When I eat or touch things it's as if a ghost is doing it because it just floats through the air, well at least what they see. On my side it looks completely normal. I was thankful to have people around me who weren't scared of me or afraid to help me. After what had happened with the Shadows I was sure that they would ditch me and leave me to my own battles, but they didn't. We hadn't really had much time to talk over the past two days. Sam and Liz worked jobs in the city and that meant I was home by myself. Well at least it seemed I was alone. I noticed from time to time that dishes would be moved or things were a bit out of place when I'd wake up, and I assumed that meant Dylan was milling about as I slept and I was determined to catch him in the act eventually.

Noon. I had gotten used to sleeping in and had to admit I didn't want it to end, although I knew eventually it would have to. I got up and folded my blankets and placed them, along with my pillows, off to the side and moved into the kitchen to get something to eat. As I was rummaging through the cupboards and fridge I heard footsteps. Immediately

I froze to silence myself and grabbed the nearest weapon I could find; a large kitchen fork. It wasn't exactly my finest moment of possible self defense but I didn't have a lot of options. The footsteps were coming from inside the apartment, which meant that either someone had gotten in or Dylan did exist. I moved quietly from the kitchen towards the living area keeping my eyes on the closed door at the other end of the place clutching my large fork for protection. I could hear rustling coming from the room as if someone was looking through papers or searching the place for something. Step by step I moved in closer and closer to the door and the wood floor below me creaked loudly. All the noise in the room stopped and everything went suddenly silent. I quickly moved my back against the wall and ceased to breathe anymore. This was the kind of moment you'd find in a movie when big bad trouble is about to ensue and the brightest idea anyone has is that somehow not breathing will keep them hidden. Wait a minute, I'm invisible. *Stupid Ember, stupid.* I guess being around Sam and Liz was making me forget, my greatest advantage; no one could see me. So I hid the large fork in the back of my sweats and crept closer to the door. I laid my ear up to it just to see if there was really someone inside and before I could hear anything the door opened and I fell over creating a large thud on the ground.

"I'm so sorry, I didn't know you were there." I looked up to see a hand extended to me. I reached up for his hand and he grabbed mine. He was strong and he had no problem lifting me back to my feet, as my own strength replaced by utter shock, failed. I stood there looking at him unable to speak, unable to move, unable to read him even. This was the first time in months anyone had helped me or let alone managed to interact with me.

"H-H-How?" My words stuttered out as if I had suddenly forgotten how to use words at all.

He smiled and leaned against the doorway. "How what?"

"How did you know I was there?" I couldn't see his eyes because they were hiding behind his sunglasses, which at the time I should have considered odd to have on inside, but I was more interested in whether he could see me or not. It seemed to take him far too long to respond to me but when he did I didn't expect his response.

"I can see you, Ember." He didn't seemed alarmed or confused by my questions.

"What? How? Am I visible again?" I looked at my arms and hands and body to see if there had been some change but there was nothing I could see.

"No, you're still invisible." He walked right past me with such confidence that it frustrated me. It was the kind of confidence and arrogance that irritated you so much you had no choice but to follow after them because you had to know what made them seem so important.

"How can you see me?" I leaned against the counter in the kitchen as he moved about grabbing a glass of water.

"I've always been able to see you." I had no idea how to respond to that since this was the first time we were meeting.

"We've never met before." I replied getting tired of his game of riddles.

"Not formally." He took his glass of water and proceeded towards the living area and sat down on the couch. There was nothing about him that made me think he was anyone I should be worried about, but there was every reason not to trust this stranger.

I took a seat in the oversized chair that was across from him and leaned forward examining him for a moment. He was dressed in a black t-shirt and jeans. He had dark brown hair that was fairly short but still managed to hang down a bit. It was hard to make out most of his features with the sunglasses blocking his eyes and parts of his face. His skin was pale which made me think he didn't get outside much. "Who are you?"

"I'm Dylan. It's a pleasure to finally meet you." He spoke casually and un-guarded as if I were just a friend stopping by for tea and not the invisible girl being hunted by Shadows.

"Oh, it's nice to finally meet you as well. I wasn't sure if you were just a myth or not." I could feel myself relax a bit as I realized he was safe and I definitely wasn't in any danger.

He smiled with that confident, almost arrogant smile again, "You've been sleeping an awful lot."

"You watch me sleep?" I wasn't sure how to feel about that. I was sleeping in the main part of the living quarters but having some stranger watch me sleep made me a bit uncomfortable.

He smirked and I began to get a bit irritated. "You can stop probing my brain. All it's going to get you is a nasty migraine." I could feel my face

EXIST

narrow in as I scowled at him and pulled back from trying to read him.

"You better start explaining now or I'll make your head explode." He didn't seem afraid or shocked by my outburst, but I'll admit, I was. That was so unlike me to threaten anyone. People had told me over the years I was too emotional. Makes sense I suppose why I ended up with an empath who could control emotions. Aden always found a way to calm me down when no one else could. Although I don't attribute that to his gifts, it was just who he was; special.

"You can't harm me." He said kicking his feet up onto the coffee table.

"Says who?" I asked in my most intimidating tone I could muster up, which wasn't all that intimidating at all.

He leaned forward and smiled. "Well first of all you don't seem very strong or intimidating," he pointed to the t-shirt I was wearing, "just because you wear a superhero t-shirt doesn't make you a hero."

Now I was getting pissed off. "I'm not trying to be a hero. I just want everything to go back to normal. I'm just trying to exist again and survive." His face fell into what I can only describe as pensive, but there was a softness to it. "What are you?" I asked as I moved back into the chair and crossed my legs keeping myself as strong looking as I could. Although I suppose this was more like a kindergartener sitting on the rug for story time than an almost adult trying to keep herself alive.

Dylan's mood changed to something calmer and not so arrogant. He seemed to be feeling compassion for me now and I got the feeling he realized I was scared even though I was trying very hard not to let it show. I wanted to believe in that moment he somehow understood that while this might be a joke to him, this was serious to me and I had no idea what was happening to me or going on around me. Whether I was right or not, I couldn't tell, because I couldn't read him. I just hoped I was right and that he'd finally start answering some questions. "I'm a See-er or as the proper term would be, a pre-cog."

"A pre-cog?" I had never heard that term before in my life and I suppose my confusion rang through loudly.

His nose crinkled up and his mouth went sideways, "You don't know much of anything do you?" I shook my head, no. "A pre-cog, meaning precognition, can see the future but things are always changing so I can't know for sure the ultimate outcomes but I get most things right."

"Oh. So is that why you can see me?" I pretended for a moment to understand everything he was telling me.

He smiled softly, "Not exactly."

"Then how is it possible?" All I could think of doing at this moment was finding out how he could see me, in the hopes, that others could as well. "By birth I am a pre-cog but over the years I developed a telepathic type ability that allows me to see people in a unique way." His explanation was very matter of fact but left much to the explored.

I nodded as if I understood but my mind immediately was jumping into thought overdrive wishing I could read him. "So you can read me?"

"Not exactly, but I can see you." He replied, again giving me an answer without an actual answer.

I dropped my head into my hands out of frustration. "You lost me again."

I laughed slightly out of frustration and he did the same but this time he reached out and touched me softly. It was the kind of touch that was reassuring and comforting. A touch like that I had only ever felt with Aden and it sent chills throughout my body. I hadn't realized how much I missed physical touch. "Don't worry Ember, we have plenty of time. I'll answer all your questions in due time, I promise."

I exhaled slowly and nodded, "Thank you." He sat back on the couch and I watched him for a moment wondering if I was allowed to ask him another question. I decided it couldn't hurt. "Why do you wear those sunglasses inside?"

He smiled and his arrogant attitude returned, "Ah, I"m a cyclops therefore it's best you only see me this way." I felt my mouth drop open and I was left speechless as I processed the probability of that, but his loud laughter let me know the joke was on me. "There are no real cyclops, only in comic books."

I rolled my eyes and sighed, "Funny! In this world you never know what is real or what isn't anymore."

He shrugged, "That is true. In our world anything seems possible, but there will always be limitations."

The sound of the front door being unlocked made Dylan jump to his feet. "I have to go, but we'll talk later okay?" I nodded even though I had no idea why he wasn't allowed to be around Sam and Liz. Dylan hurried back to his room and closed the door. I watched Sam and Liz walk inside holding onto each other. It made me smile seeing two people so in love and as if the dark world around them couldn't dim their light for anything, but it also made me intensely sad on the inside knowing what it felt like to be them and then having it taken away from you.

I telepathically said *hello* to them and they smiled and waved, "Hello Casper, wherever you are today." "*I'm in the chair and do you have to call me that Sam?*"

Sam smirked and winked, "Yes, I do! It fits you. Maybe if you find a way to become visible again I will call you by your real name." I stuck out my tongue at him and laughed to myself enjoying the fact he couldn't see my reply.

"So what have you been up to today?" Liz asked as she set down the grocery bags and took a seat on the couch.

"*Not much. Just hanging out.*" I wanted to ask them about Dylan but seeing how he responded I didn't know if I should. As much as I trusted Sam and Liz I didn't know them all that well and I definitely didn't know anything about Dylan. So I assumed keeping quiet for now was the safest bet.

At least I would remain silent about him and I talking until I had had a chance to talk with him more. Dylan was the only one who could see me and somehow I had a feeling he knew more about me than anyone ever would.

Liz broke my train of thoughts, "You know eventually you're going to have to go outside, Ember?"

I thought about that for a moment and then responded to her, "*No. It's too dangerous for everyone. I'm better staying in here where I'm not a threat.*"

Liz always managed to have this pure softness to her expressions and it made me feel comforted even when it didn't seem possible that anything could truly comfort me. "I know you've been through a lot lately and you have every reason to be afraid, but I don't want to see you, well I apologize for the bad choice of words, but I don't want your life to end up being locked away somewhere. You have so much life ahead of you Ember." I bit my lip listening to her speak. It was a terrible habit of mine and if she could see me she'd know I was deep in thought at the moment. I always somehow managed to bite my lip when I was thinking. Thank goodness for my trusty lip balm or else I might not have any lips left.

I looked straight ahead at Liz and responded telepathically. "*I really appreciate everything you are doing for me. Even more so, I appreciate the fact that you and Sam are looking out for me. You're like the big brother and sister I never had. But my life has always been locked up somewhere and the only break I had, the only moment of pure happiness or freedom was with Aden. He kept me safe, he showed me a life that was full of possibilities and he believed that anything was possible. Everything I had ever dreamed of or been told was too far fetched wasn't when I was with him. I saw that beautiful future before me and I wanted it more than anything, but he took it away from me Liz. I guess it's like Cinderella, she got her chance with the Prince and had this wonderful time but all the fairy dust in the world couldn't make it last.*"

Liz listened intently and it was nice to have some girl talk for once. "What are you two talking about?" Sam asked from the kitchen. He was making himself something to eat and Liz barely acknowledged him back. She waved her hand at him letting him know he needed to butt out and he did. Liz continued our conversation,"Even Cinderella eventually had her dreams come true. She was locked away but she found a way out and she got her Prince and the life she longed for. Don't you believe you could have that too?"

I laughed slightly, *"I used to. I used to believe as a child and even into my teens that those kind of things really did happen. That life wasn't just some sad chain of events. That people could actually be happy and live their dreams. Now I'm not so sure."*

"You can't let one guy take all the hope for your life away from you. If Aden is everything you seem to believe he is, then this surely can't be the end." Liz spoke gently to me as if she somehow could sense that this wouldn't be the end for Aden and I.

I wiped my eyes and was truly, truly thankful no one could see me crying right now. I hated when people saw me cry and it was something I tried very hard to avoid at all costs. Thankfully, as far as I could tell my emotions weren't necessarily conveyed in my telepathic thoughts. *"Aden is...was... an incredible man. He had so much fire inside of him, so much faith and passion for his dreams and life. He believed in destiny and that it was worth fighting for, no matter what. He believed that dreams really could come true and that who we were...are...was for a greater purpose and we would change the world. I had never met someone like him before. When we talked it was like talking to myself in a mirror. We just connected and never once thought of each other as strange or weird. In our hearts and minds it all made sense and suddenly I knew that I was home. That all the cheesy cliches in romance novels were true, we were meant to be together, and I saw forever with him. Every time he looked into my eyes sparks flew and I could feel all the love he had for me. I could tell there was not a single bad bone in his body and that come hell or high water he would do anything to protect me. That we would love each other till the end of time and maybe even beyond that."*

I looked up at Liz and now she was wiping her eyes. "Wow." She sat there captivated by what I was telling her and I realized it wasn't that my words were eloquent, what captivated her were the images, the memories, attached to those words that she also saw. She saw everything I held inside my heart and mind.

Sam took a seat next to Liz and placed his arm around her, "Are you okay babe?"

She nodded and reached for a tissue, "Yeah."

"What did I miss?" She smiled and kissed him softly on the side of the cheek. "Girl talk."

"I can do girl talk." Both Liz and I laughed at Sam and she just patted him on the leg. "I know you can baby."

"Ember, you can't give up on him. I don't know why he was such an idiot to let you go like he did or why he would change so much in an instant, but what you two have is rare and I don't think it's worth letting go of. At least not yet." Liz continued our conversation despite having Sam join us.

I let my head fall over the back cushion of the chair and I stared up at the ceiling. *"Doesn't it make me a fool though for loving him? For holding onto hope with him, when he's clearly left me for good?"*

Liz was quiet for a moment. "No. Not at all. It means you are a heart designed to love relentlessly. You are one of the rare people in this world who actually believe in going after what you know is true. You're stronger than most people because if I were you, by now I would have given up all hope in everything. I'm amazed that you're still fighting to save yourself, trying to protect everyone in this world from the darkness that follows you and still able to love Aden through all the hurt he's put you through."

Sam's normally deep, hard face softened and he spoke up, "Casper, most men dream of finding a woman who will love them when they are at their dumbest and darkest. A woman who will forgive them a million times plus one, even when they don't deserve it. A woman who will still see them as their hero, when they clearly fall short of that title. I don't know what Aden was thinking but I'm sure he had a good reason for what he did. You are special and I really hope that Aden wakes up and realizes that before it's too late. I can promise you if you open yourself up again to others, you'll see he wasn't the only who will love you."

I was overwhelmed by their hearts for me and in that moment I began to feel as though maybe Aden wasn't the only one who would protect me and believe in me. Maybe I had been led to Sam and Liz for reasons I had yet to understand. *"Thank you guys. I won't give up, I promise!"*

CHAPTER FOUR

A couple days had passed since I had seen Dylan for the first time. As much as he annoyed me to the bone with his cocky and arrogant attitude, there was a part of me that was anxious to see him again. There was just something about Dylan that made me want to dive inside his mind and expose the secrets he kept hidden away. I walked around the living area pacing holes into the rug hoping he'd come out to see me again. I even had woken up earlier the past two days hoping to catch him. Sam and Liz never spoke about him and something wasn't adding up with the whole thing of him living there and yet acting like a prisoner. Thankfully, I trusted them and I knew there had to be a logical reason for his behavior and why he was so secretive. After 15 minutes of pacing and almost tripping multiple times into the hole I had worn into the rug I walked up to Dylan's door and was about to knock when it swung wide open. He was leaning against it with his arrogant smile and sunglasses on, as usual.

"You can't surprise me." I rolled my eyes and sighed as I watched him smirk casually at me.

"Well then why did it take you two days and me coming to your door if you knew I was waiting for you?" I turned away and headed over towards the couch to take a seat.

Dylan closed his bedroom door and followed me over to the couch, "I've been busy."

"Doing what? You never leave your room." I took a seat with a huff as he replied, "You never leave the walk up, so what difference does it make?"

I grabbed onto my head in frustration. "Do you always talk like this?"

He smirked and leaned back on the arm of the couch. "Yes. Does it bother you?"

"Yes. Greatly." I replied openly sharing my frustration.

He sat there examining me from the couch for a moment before he responded. "It bothers you not being able to read me doesn't it?"

"Slightly. I just don't get you. I mean why did you bolt when Sam and Liz came home the other day and why do you never come out of your room?" He nodded and I could tell by the way his lips formed a hard line he was thinking of an answer. "I want the truth."

He smiled softly, "Did I ever say I would give you anything but?"

"No, but so far from our time together I have good reason to doubt your willingness to give me the truth. I can't read your mind to know if what you say is in fact true and your snarky expressions don't really help either." I exhaled slowly and leaned back on the couch watching him carefully.

Dylan sighed quietly before he decided to answer my question. "It's complicated with Sam, Liz and I. My living here is more of an agreement than anything else."

I waited for him to continue with his story but he didn't. "What kind of agreement?"

"The kind where I offer them protection and they offer me a place to stay and work." His voice lacked emotion and I couldn't tell how he truly felt about his living situation.

I nodded, "What kind of work do you do?"

"I work for the Resistance. Think of me as Homeland Security but for your people." He smiled slightly at the end indicating he was proud of his work.

"My people?" The response came out kind of snarky and I didn't mean for it too but there was something about the way he said that that made me feel like he believed we were better than everyone else. We weren't better, we were just different. And wasn't Dylan one of us?

"I mean Benders, or as some might call you psionics." His response didn't answer my initial gut feeling but over the years I had learned to trust my gut instincts and I had a feeling that this was only the beginning of a much larger world than I had previously realized existed.

I tried to read Dylan's body language as usual and couldn't get much from him so I decided I would stick to basic questioning. I would have to do this the normal way and I kind of liked it. I had grown far too dependent on using my abilities and it was nice to remember what it was like to not use them for once. "Alright you said it's complicated with Sam and Liz, why?"

Dylan's face for the first time ever crinkled up and I could tell this was not a topic he wanted to discuss. "You promised me the truth." His lips pursed together and I could tell he was deciding to either stick with his promise or go back on it. Finally, after what seemed far too long, he sighed and nodded. "Fair enough. You call people like yourself, psionics and it's the technical, governmental term, for what you are. In the real world though psionics are called Benders. Humans are called Statics and..." his voice trailed off and I could feel something emanating from him, something vulnerable and on the verge of defeat, "and anyone who is born of both sides is called Lost."

"Lost?" The word escaped my mouth as if it were the most completely absurd word I had ever heard in my life. He nodded and I waited for him to explain this whole thing further but of course he didn't so I had to pry more. "What do those names all mean?"

"Benders are what you are. It simply implies that you can bend the laws of psychics and what is natural in this world. Statics, the normal humans, they can't do anything special, they remain static and live by the natural laws of the world. The Lost are anyone born of both Static and Bender blood. Meaning one parent was static and the other was a bender. They call them Lost because they don't belong to either side and tend to find themselves very lost in this world, lost in the in between. In most cases the Lost are looked at as dangerous because their allegiance can't be defined to either side and the Benders worry that they will expose this world to the Statics or that they will align with the Statics and hunt down the Benders."

"Wow." Pathetic answer but it was seriously all I could say. The more I began to discover about this world the less I felt I actually knew. I guess I could understand the reason for war a bit more now knowing that everyone was segregated. "Dylan, you're a Bender right?" I don't know why I asked and honestly I was beating myself up mentally for it, what a stupid thing to ask, but something inside me wanted to make sure.

He shook his head slowly, no. "What are you then?" "Lost." He said it looking straight at me and with such an overwhelming sadness that I could have sworn my heart broke and shattered in a loud crash all over the floor. "Lost?" He nodded. "My Dad was a Static and my Mom was a Bender. She also was a telepath much like you." He seemed to relax a bit now that the truth was out and I leaned back further into my seat taking it all in.

"This is why it's complicated with Sam and Liz huh?" The words came out slowly as my mind began to process everything I was hearing.

He nodded. "We're family. Cousins actually and they took me in because I had no where else to go."

"Well if you're family then you shouldn't have to hide from them." He sighed again and I could tell things were about to get more complicated.

"Technically I shouldn't even be talking to you." "Why?" "The Lost aren't supposed to really interact with Benders or Statics. We're supposed to keep our distance and only be useful if needed or called upon. It's a hierarchy system and you happen to be at the top. Benders stay with Benders. For those who fall in love with Statics it's complicated because it looks as though their loyalties are changing, that they are aligning with the Statics and denying who they are. But even the Statics have rank above the Lost. We just kind of float in and out of existence and aren't really supposed to be seen or heard."

I took in his words and wondered why he was willing to take the risk talking to me. "So it's kind of a risk for you being my friend then?"

He smiled and nodded. "Yes, but I know I can help you and I want to, so I took the risk. This is why Sam and Liz can't know."

"They're your family though, would they really treat you so badly?" He nodded, "They don't have a choice. Ember, in every culture, every civilization there are rules and guidelines that have to be followed and adhered to. Our world is no different and in order to remain safe and alive we have to follow those ways of life very carefully."

"It doesn't seem fair though and what if I don't agree with it?" I could feel my inner warrior awakening wanting to fight for the rights of a group of people I didn't even know existed until now.

He leaned forward a bit taking my hand into his and it felt wonderful to be comforted and touched. "You have to my little Bender. At least for now." "For now?" He got his arrogant, confident smile back. "I'll explain everything to you I promise. Just know that you're special." I could feel myself blush and my cheeks grew warm and I had no idea why. I was in love with Aden and I couldn't possibly be feeling anything for a man I didn't even know all that well. There was just something about Dylan that made me feel safe and connected and right now it was everything I longed for and needed. The moment was interrupted when we heard the keys jangling in the lock of the front door. Dylan winked and ran into his room shutting the door behind him leaving me alone on the couch. "Ember, you still here?" I heard Liz ask as she and Sam entered carrying in bags of groceries. I reached out to them, "*Yeah, I'm still here.*" My brain was running a million miles a minute and I couldn't seem to process everything Dylan had said but I knew the second I got another chance I would talk to him again and pick his brain.

The next night Sam and Liz were running around the apartment in what could only be described as a frenzy. Clearly they were running late for something but I got the feeling whatever they were trying to get to it was serious because neither of them seemed very excited and rather stressed over it all. Liz was showing her frustration with the situation more than Sam and I wasn't sure if I could ask them whether they were okay or not. I watched Liz for awhile and then decided I would try my hand at questioning her. I could read her but somehow it just felt wrong. I had this personal policy that I wouldn't use my ability on friends and family. This policy was how Aden and I built such a deep trust and respect for each other. We knew that we could easily get inside one another's heart and head but we didn't. *"Hey Liz, you okay today?"* She looked up in surprise as if she had forgotten I was there, which I found odd. This wasn't like her at all. "Yeah, just been one of those days." *"Anything you want to talk about?"* "No." She was quick to answer and she moved from one place to the other in such sharp and erratic movements that I knew something was up. *"So you and Sam have a hot date tonight?"* She stopped moving around and put her hands on her hips. "No. We just have somewhere to be. We'll be back late tonight just so you know." Without another word she slipped into the bedroom and closed the door behind her. Moments later both her and Sam rushed out of the bedroom stuffing folders of what appeared to be documents into a messenger bag as they raced for the front door. I immediately stood up and followed them. Whatever they were up to it was serious and not just relationship drama serious either. No, this was bigger than the two of them and I had to find out who they really were.

81

I followed them for about 5 blocks as they quickly darted from one place to another keeping a very low profile. They didn't talk to each other the entire time they were walking and that wasn't like them at all. I began to get that deep sinking feeling in my stomach that Liz and Sam weren't who they appeared to be. Knowing what Dylan had shared with me about how the system worked had opened my eyes to a lot and made me question everything I knew and Sam and Liz were no exception to that. Finally they slowed down as they disappeared into an alleyway. I followed them into the dark, dank alley and noticed others converging towards the same doorway at the end of the alley. The door was open with one guard standing on the outside checking each individual as they passed through. No one spoke or exchanged pleasantries, they just kept looking ahead and moving towards their destination. Sam and Liz disappeared into the building followed by a few other people. I waited outside to watch the different people going inside in the hopes that it might give me a clue as to what was going on. The guard began doing a last check for any possible stragglers and I knew I had to get inside before he closed the door. I ran ahead and slipped in as the guard followed behind me and the thick metal door slammed shut. I jumped at the sound of the door closing and a gust of air swept over me. The hall connecting to the door was dark and the only light that could be seen came from a room directly ahead. As I moved forward slowly I found it odd that for the amount of people that had walked into the building there were no voices to be heard and very little movement in the room at the end of the hall.

The light grew brighter around me calling me forward into what I assumed was a large meeting area. I stopped at the entrance to peer inside and discovered a long wooden table in the center of the room surrounded by an arena style seating filled with people. A few people around the edges whispered quietly to one another and the twelve people I counted seated around the table remained silent awaiting the beginning of whatever was about to happen. I moved into the room further and positioned myself against the wall closest to the exit. Even though I knew no one could see me I still managed to get the feeling I was an intruder and what I was doing was wrong on so many levels. Plus, not knowing exactly what type of meeting this would be I wanted an easy way out. Without warning, or much sound, every head in the room turned towards my left facing a small door hidden within the far brick wall. From behind the door walked an older gentleman dressed in a crisp three piece suit. As he walked towards the center table he didn't meet eyes with anyone and came across rather robotic. If it weren't for the movement under his suit indicating that he was indeed breathing I would have believed he wasn't human. He took a seat at the head of the table and was handed a stack of papers in a nondescript folder. He carefully looked through them as everyone silently gave him time to do so. After what felt like far too many silent moments he closed the folder, set it down in front of himself and looked at the twelve people around the table.

The gentleman stood up and looked around the room slowly, as if he could somehow make personal eye contact with every individual in attendance. Could this guy be any more dramatic? I suppose he wanted to build the intensity but it wasn't needed considering everyone was on edge already it appeared. "Welcome to the third Guild meeting of the year. I'm Drake and I will be your moderator tonight." I waited for people to clap or give some verbal response but it was silent. How could they all remain so quiet? It was either they were afraid of making any noise or extremely reverent in their respect for the happenings tonight. Watching the meeting begin the reality sunk in that these most likely were Benders and if so, I had far more to learn about this world than I could have ever imagined.

"Before you are the Leaders of the Guild. I will quickly introduce the twelve to save time so that we may continue on with our proceedings. Guild Leaders please raise your hand as your name is called. I will begin to my right. Tevon, Liz, Sam, Ryan, Deva, Kix, Ummi, Zaniel, Rilo, Villiam, Kate and Michael." Everyone that was introduced maintained a straight face and did not give into vanity whatsoever or maybe they just knew they were important and didn't feel it was necessary to give into grandstanding, I personally found it rather eerie. Everything about this meeting had an ominous feel that left me wondering if this was a foreshadowing of what my life was to become. "Let's begin this Legacy meeting of the Guild. As everyone is aware all members on the Guild represent the Opposition or the Resistance. In this room we are all Guild members and will uphold the beliefs and honor of that position regardless of which position you have chosen to take and represent." The Guild members exchanged challenging glances with one another and then looked back to Drake. "Last we met we were discussing possible solutions for a compromise to appeal to both sides to prevent a war. We did not reach a compromise but agreed to adjourn to allow both sides time to discuss options. Who would like to begin?"

Looks were exchanged amongst the members of the Guild and papers began to shuffle until Rilo raised her hand. "The Opposition would like to begin." "The floor is yours." Drake took a seat and Rilo stood up facing the Guild. She had a hard look to her and it wasn't because of the all black ensemble she wore either. Her face formed hard lines and her eyes narrowed naturally as she peered across the table to the side Sam and Liz were on. I assumed that side was made up of the Resistance. "Our requests have continued to remain the same, we believe that full disclosure and exposure will allow our people to live in freedom. We've been forced to live in hiding and fear because of who we are and that needs to end. The government agencies hunt us like animals but if we expose our world we will gain the power we need to control this situation and not live under the fear and oppression of others. Unfortunately, not everyone in the Guild agrees with this decision and although we have tried to reach a compromise the Opposition has not been able to find a middle ground after many hours of discussion and thought. The only options are exposure or war to decide which side will have the ultimate say in what happens." Sam raised his hand and Rilo respectfully nodded her head and took her seat as Sam stood up. "Fellow members of the Guild, I am saddened that we have reached this pinnacle in our situation and had hoped we would have been able to reach a resolution before now. The Resistance has discussed all foreseeable futures and we still believe that exposing who we are is a non-negotiable issue. As we discussed at our last meeting if we allowed for Benders to choose to reveal themselves it puts everyone in danger, even those who choose to remain hidden. The proposed war goes against everything The Guild has stood for and we are horrified that trusted members would even suggest it. Given though that it appears to be a stark reality of what we are facing we have reached what we believe to be an acceptable compromise." Sam glanced down at Liz and the Resistance members with a look that seemed uncertain and concerned as if he were trying to decide right then and there if the decision they were making was right or horribly wrong. Yet somehow he managed to keep his demeanor strong and confident on the outside. He exhaled slowly and began to share the decision they had made. "We have come in contact with an extremely powerful telepath who has abilities far greater than any of us. Her parents founded The Guild prior to their capture and then death at the hands of the government. She is unaware of this intel we have on her and we believe once she is made aware of this she will then be in a position to choose her own side of this debate. We would like to issue the compromise of giving us time to talk to her and reveal her past with her and then allowing her to make the final decision as to whether war will occur or not, given that she is a Legacy by birth right."

I was frozen in shock, disbelief, horror and every other emotion a person could feel. How could Sam and Liz betray me like this? My first instinct was to run and never look back. To go somewhere remote where no one could find me. Yet deep inside I wanted to know about my parents, I wanted to know about my past and something told me Sam and Liz wouldn't do this to me if they didn't have a good reason. I chose to stay, at least till the end of the meeting, to hear the rest of the story before I jumped to any assumptions. Zaniel stood up clapping sarcastically, "Good show mate. You really gave this a good go but you have to be kidding if you think we'll buy that load of rubbish." Sam sighed and ignored Zaniel's mocking, "This isn't a joke Zan, we're serious. All of you should remember Arya and Ash, leaders of the original Guild." Everyone was silent for a moment as if they were paying their respects. "Ember is their daughter. She's been through a lot and by chance she found us, we've been trying to help her and haven't wanted to expose all of this to her just yet. She has the most at stake here, more than any of us do. The government, Statics, killed her parents, our founders, because they found us threatening and wanted to put an end to us. I think that allowing her to decide what happens is only fair because she will either seek revenge or take a higher road and choose against war." Kate stood up looking stoic and unreadable, "Please allow us time to talk this over. We will have an answer for you within the next two days." Sam took his seat to imply that he agreed with the terms. Zaniel stood up again and looked at Sam as if he were challenging him, "If we agree to this compromise will we be allowed to meet Ember?" Sam nodded, "Yes." "Her abilities are far stronger than any of ours?" "Yes. She isn't fully aware of what she is capable of yet but with training she will be." "In essence she's like a weapon for either side?" Zaniel's eyes glowed with eager anticipation at the thought of holding within his hand the super nova to win the war his side wanted badly.

Sam stood up breaking his calm character and leaned over the large wooden table towards Zaniel, "She's a Bender not a weapon." "I understand that, but you do see what I am implying, do you not?" Sam was rendered speechless and I assumed he did understand, heck even I understood. "Let us know what you decide." Sam took his seat and Liz linked arms with him to help calm him down again. Zaniel took his seat and gave a sneer at some of the Opposition members he was with and my stomach sank wondering if it was too late to go back to just being the invisible girl.

Drake stood up and although he was speaking to everyone I could no longer hear a single word he said. My life was flashing before my eyes. For the first time in 18 years, I knew my parents' names and a little bit about them. I knew a little bit more about myself too and as wonderful and exciting as that was, I also was faced with the foreseeable future that people saw me as a potential weapon and chess piece to their war game. I was wrestling with the reality that to this world I wasn't just Ember, no, I was a bargaining chip, a missing piece in their hierarchy and a prize to be won, nothing more. Much like everyone else in my life, Sam and Liz had only kept me around because they had something to gain, but I was no longer going to allow them to use me.

CHAPTER FIVE

As much as I had promised myself I wouldn't run, that's exactly what I did. I ran out of the building before anyone would possibly discover I was there. Before anyone could decide my fate without even telling me the truth. Before Sam and Liz would have a chance to track me down and pull me back into their web of lies. How could they do that to me and lie to me? At what point did they discover who I was and why have they played along as if they knew nothing? A million thoughts were running through my head and I couldn't seem to shut them off or make the storm raging inside of me go away. I just allowed my feet to continue moving underneath me. The freezing air hit my face like nails flying out of a nail gun and somehow I was thankful for the feeling because it was the only distraction I had at the moment. Eventually though my lungs began to give out on me and I couldn't keep going. I fell down onto a sidewalk bench and my body went weak beneath me. I took a moment to allow my breath to return and took out my phone. Scrolling through the contacts I passed by Aden's name and my heart came back from the dead. The feeling wasn't a good one, it was like dying a horrible death for the millionth time knowing I needed him and wished he was here right now, but I wasn't allowed to reach out to him. I kept on scrolling and stopped at Dylan's name, he must have placed his number in my phone when I wasn't looking. I was truly thankful for his foresight to do so and sent him a text "Help!" He was quick to respond and I was honestly thankful for him being in my life right now and I couldn't overcome the feeling of needing him next to me. After what had happened with Sam and Liz, I had no reason to believe Dylan was any better or that he could be trusted either. Yet from what he had disclosed to me before about who he was and the world I found myself in, he was my only hope now. So far, he was the only one telling me the truth. Plus he made me feel safe and even though it felt like a completely irrational way to feel my heart told me it was real. "I'll be right there. Stay where you are, I have your phone tracked." I took in a deep breath and exhaled slowly allowing the world to slow down for the first time in what seemed like forever, but had really only been a matter of minutes.

Dylan ran up to me and immediately began looking at me as if he were expecting to see wounds or broken limbs. I didn't care though I just loved that he could see me.

"What's wrong? Are you okay?" His lack of arrogance and cockiness that was replaced by care and concern threw me off. I hadn't seen this side of him before but I really liked it.

"I'm okay I guess. I'm not physically hurt if that's what you mean." I took his hands into mine and moved them away from me since there were no wounds to be found. His shoulders relaxed and he exhaled. "What happened?"

"Sam and Liz are using me as a bargaining chip for the war." The words came crashing out of my mouth as if I couldn't hold the secret in any longer.

"What?" Dylan sunk onto the bench next to me as his face dropped in horror and anger.

"I heard it myself Dylan, I was there when Sam presented the compromise to the Guild." I could never see Dylan's eyes but his mouth showed his emotions and he looked furious. "I can't go back there. I have to leave."

"Leave to where?" His words were sharp and harsh but I knew not to take it personally. He was just as angry as I was.

"I don't know but I need to get as far away from here as possible." He sighed and looked off into space, "You are safer here with me than you would be anywhere else."

The words escaped his mouth so effortlessly and as much as my heart wanted to fight the feelings those words evoked in me I couldn't. I turned to face him and could feel my heart racing, "With you?"

He turned to look at me and moved a bit closer. "Yes. I want to protect you. I mean I will protect you."

"Why?" He laughed sarcastically and I felt relaxed knowing he was still himself despite the serious moment we were in. "You would ask why. You can't just accept that someone may actually want to take care of you. Were you like this with Aden too?"

My lips instantly went into a defensive pout, "No." His eyebrows arched up and I sighed, "Fine, yes, I guess I was."

"Wow, I'm impressed you actually let him take care of you then. What magic did he do to make that happen?" Dylan was clearly trying to distract me from what had happened tonight and redirect my thoughts somewhere else.

"Nothing, he was just him." I didn't really want to think about Aden right now, but it was helping me to calm down a bit.

"What about me? Am I enough to do that too?" I shrugged as I thought this through and before I could respond he took my hand gently into his and said, "It could be a matter of life or death for you."

My head dropped down and I fought back tears, "You are enough. I'm just not sure I am." Dylan stroked my hand and it was comforting but I couldn't find any words to say beyond what I did, it was the most vulnerable I had ever been. I don't think I had even admitted that to Aden before. Maybe if I had he would have understood me better. There were times he felt that he wasn't enough, but it wasn't that he wasn't enough, it was that I didn't feel I was enough to deserve him and all he was to me. Now it was happening with Dylan and I didn't want that.

Dylan stood up and held out his hand to me, "Let's go somewhere private." I took his hand and followed him. I hoped he didn't mind that I wasn't ready to let go of his hand because it felt nice to know I wasn't alone anymore and that for the time since being on the run I was safe. Aden used to be a leader and he was the kind of man who had the heart of a leader and he did it well when he'd allow himself to lead. I loved that about him and for the first time in my life I enjoyed allowing someone other than myself to make decisions and take the lead. I trusted Aden with all my heart and soul and I missed having that kind of connection in my life. I looked over at Dylan and smiled a bit knowing that I may have found another person that I could trust again. At least I certainly hoped I did.

We walked in the Shadows which felt safer to me because somehow I knew that's where I would always belong. We didn't really speak as we walked and the further we got away from the places I recognized the more curious I got. "So a few blocks away wasn't private enough?" I asked Dylan curiously.

He gave a snarky side laugh and stopped in front of an old stoop of an apartment building, "We're here. I have a good friend that can help." I looked up hesitantly at the building and followed Dylan in. I didn't have much to lose at this point did I? Besides I trusted Dylan in a way I didn't usually trust people and as dangerous as I knew trust could be I gave in and went with it. Dylan walked up a few flights of stairs and stopped outside a bright red door. All the other doors were painted a plain dingy white and this one stood out amongst the rest. "Come in, it's unlocked." A female voice inside rang out sounding in a hurry moving about the apartment. Dylan turned and smiled widely as he opened the door and walked inside. I followed closing the door behind him. The apartment was simple in design but full of chaos as it was engulfed with paintings and notebooks everywhere. "This places belongs to my friend Jade, you're going to love her."

When Jade first walked up to Dylan and I there were no words for my first impression of her. She had a presence that made you stop in your tracks and just look at her with awe. Jade was beautiful with her warm brown eyes, long wavy, blondish brown hair and tall, slim build. Yet it wasn't her outer beauty that pulled me in, there was truly an aspect of her presence that commanded the room and gave her power. I didn't know what to say and then I realized I didn't have to worry about that because she couldn't see me. I was beginning to feel a bit cocky like Dylan and sat back on her couch with my arms folded and crinkled my nose up.

"Wow, someone isn't social at all." Jade said taking a seat on the arm of the couch next to Dylan. He laughed and nudged her with his elbow. They seemed really close and their relationship, whatever it may be, made me smile because for the first time ever I saw Dylan. Meaning I truly saw Dylan, not the fake, arrogant side he tried to show all the time, but the real vulnerable Dylan and it was sweet. Jade had a way of altering the atmosphere around her and I wondered if that was an ability or just a beautiful personality trait she was blessed with?

"You can see me?" I said sitting up straight and on guard even though I knew it probably wasn't necessary.

"Yes." Jade replied confidently, as if seeing another person wasn't unusual.

"How can you see me?" I looked from her to Dylan and back. He just gave me his usual cocky smirk with his eyebrows raised and laughed quietly. Jade also laughed as if they were apart of some inside joke.

Dylan obviously could read my expression and he quickly found his composure and said "Jade is also a pre-cog, like me. She can see beyond what most can see." I relaxed a bit but still wanted to know more. "Plus, she can read auras too, which always helps." Dylan added that extra point proudly as he glanced over at Jade. Jade smiled at me and I had to admit I wanted to instantly trust her, but being who I was, it was difficult. The more people who found out about me, the more I had to lose, and the greater the risk became.

"We need to go somewhere less public." She said as she took out her car keys and stood up. "

You make a valid point." Dylan stood up and reached out his hand to me. "I thought we were already somewhere private?" I asked taking Dylan's hand.

"You can never be too safe." Jade said grabbing her coat and opening the door. I hesitantly moved through the door and walked with them to Jade's car that was parked on the side of the street.

I watched Dylan relax more once he was in the car with Jade and I liked this side of him. When he was at Sam and Liz's he was always so tense and on guard and seeing him relax was nice for a change. I had to admit when he was like this, rushing in to save the day, and protecting people, I really found myself drawing closer to him. But I couldn't get close to him. Not in this way at least. My heart belonged to Aden and I knew that without doubt, whether I always admitted it or not, that we were soul mates. It amazes me that every moment of our lives we are filled with indestructible truths about ourselves and what we believe and yet we live in denial of these very truths. We are walking contradictions and honestly it's not much of a surprise as to why we feel so lost in our own skin. Why we spend an entire life trying to discover who we are when in actuality we already know.

”So how do you both know each other?" I asked leaning from the backseat towards the front. Jade drove and gave Dylan a side smile and he began to answer. "I saved her life and now she owes me her friendship for life."

Jade playfully punched Dylan, "That is only partially true." Dylan smiled and shook his head as he leaned it against the passenger seat. "Alright, what is your version of the story then?"

She smirked and pulled some of her hair behind her ear as we waited at a red light. "I was trying to buy lunch and didn't have enough cash on me. I didn't realize that till it was too late. Dylan was behind me and he offered to pay for my meal."

I snickered, "Wow, that is a heroic story."

Dylan remained calm and shrugged, "There are always two sides to every story." "Actually three sides; your side, my side and the truth." Jade completed his statement.

"I don't mean to sound like a brat, but if you can see the future wouldn't you have known ahead of time you'd be short on money?" I saw Jade smirk in the rearview mirror and if I read her expression right, she had set Dylan up that day. Dylan laughed loudly, "Good call out Ember!" I enjoyed the interaction between the two of them. I liked seeing Dylan free to be himself, it filled me with warmth and joy, the kind that could keep you warm on the coldest of winter days without ever reaching for a blanket. He didn't deserve the life he was forced into living, no one deserved to be treated that way, and I wanted to see him have a choice and live the life he was destined for.

Jade pulled the car up to another apartment building, "Wait, where are we now?" I asked as I got out of the backseat following Jade and Dylan. "At my apartment." Jade said casually heading towards the stoop with her key. "I thought that's where we had just been?" Dylan placed a hand on my shoulder, "That was her work studio, this is where she really lives." I nodded as Dylan walked with me onto the stoop and then inside the old architectural building.

We arrived at Jade's apartment, that from the outside didn't appear to be much, and walked inside quickly. Walking into the apartment it became clear that it shouldn't be judged by its ordinary exterior. Inside everything about the place screamed of Jade's eclectic and artsy style. The apartment was beautifully decorated in varying shades of color and patterns. The space gave off a very warm and welcoming feel that couldn't be ignored and called you in. Once the door was closed Jade placed her bag on the entry table and Dylan walked in making himself at home. "Just so you know Little Bender, you're safe to use your abilities here. I have this place blocked too." I felt better knowing we were slightly protected but I still didn't feel completely comfortable yet in Jade's place. Dylan looked over at me as I stood in the corner of the main room and I saw him motion for me to join him on the couch. I walked over slowly and sat down. Jade brought over some cups of warm tea and took a seat across from us.

"So what has you two on the run?" I looked at Dylan because I wasn't sure yet what to tell Jade and honestly I hadn't had time to process any of this myself. Thankfully Dylan spoke up before the silence became awkward.

"Sam and Liz offered up Ember as a compromise to the Opposition." Jade's face quickly turned from content and relaxed to tense and angry. "Why would they do that?" Dylan shrugged and looked at Jade but the look they shared seemed as though they were speaking telepathically, but I'm sure only telepaths can do that right? Jade exhaled slowly and took in the news as she sipped her tea. Dylan glanced at me with a small smile and then connected eyes with Jade again. Suddenly Jade stood up without warning, as if her and Dylan had already discussed their next move, "I'm going to head to bed. Please make yourselves at home. I'll see you in the morning and we can plan out our options." Whatever had happened silently between Dylan and Jade, she wasn't going to stay and get to know me better tonight. She walked off with a look in her eyes that I was having a hard time reading, but I would get to the bottom of it.

Dylan turned on the couch to face me. "Are you tired?" I shook my head, no. Being with him in this current situation made me feel like a child. I was dependent on him because there was so much I didn't know and worst of all so much I didn't understand. I felt vulnerable and I wanted him to hold me in his arms now and let me know no matter what everything was going to be okay. It's what Aden would do and as that thought of him holding me crossed my mind tears began to form in my eyes.

I looked away and Dylan took my hand. "It's okay to cry if you need to."

I wiped my eyes and gained my composure, "I'm fine."

Dylan laughed in his usual cocky manner and pretended to act appalled, "that is the biggest lie ever told by the female species." I crinkled my nose up in frustration at him and held back my response.

Dylan obviously could sense I was in a sensitive state and he moved himself a bit closer to me. "Why don't we go outside and get some air?" I nodded and stood up. Dylan let me lead the way to the balcony. We could see the bright lights of the city that looked like stars from up here. It amazed me how all cities ended up looking magically beautiful at night. It was their cover, their disguise, because beneath all that beauty and light was darkness and danger, but most people only saw all that glitters around them.

Dylan sat down next to me and was silent for a while until he finally turned to face me. "Are you okay Ember, I mean really okay?" I thought about that for a moment it felt as though any answer I would give him would be a loaded one, but the best I could give him was the truth. "No, I'm not." He inhaled in a slow but deep way and I don't know what his pre-cog mind was seeing but it made me wonder if the future ahead wasn't very bright.

"I'm not a telepath Ember so you're going to have to tell me what you're thinking." I looked at him trying to see his actual eyes behind his dark sunglasses but I couldn't.

"I don't want this anymore." My words came out as a soft protest. "You don't want what anymore?" He was gentle in his approach but I could feel him somehow, I could feel his concern that bordered fear. I suppose he thought I meant him, but I didn't.

"I don't want this life. I don't want to be hurt all the time. I don't want these memories. I want go back to how life used to be when I felt like a normal girl and not someone fighting for her life. I used to be happy." He gently reached up and touched my face gently as he placed a piece of my fringe behind my ear. I couldn't help but lean my head into his warm hand and enjoy the simplicity of the moment.

"I wish I could make it all go away for you, but that would mean losing you and I'm too selfish to let that happen." I lifted my head up from his hand and processed what he just said, "Too selfish?" "I've grown very fond of you Ember and being what I am, I've seen the future, the destiny that lies ahead for you and it's important that you remain who you so that you get there."

"So this is all just about who I'm supposed to be and this unknown future that everyone seems to want for me? What about what I want? What ever happened to people consulting with me first before deciding how my life should turn out?" Dylan remained calm and listened even though I was beginning to raise my voice and for the first time let out all the frustration and pain that had been locked inside. "You always have a choice." "Do I? I didn't have a choice with Aden and I didn't have a choice with being "this" whatever it is that I am." Dylan smiled softly and his tenderness in this moment made my heart race faster than it should. "You are special. That's what you are. Everything else is just icing on the cake, attributes, but who you are as a whole is special." His words disarmed me and I didn't like it. I sighed and turned to face the city again. "Did I say something wrong?" I guess he could sense my frustration and this time I couldn't look at him. I wanted to block everything and I wanted most of all to stop getting so attached to him, to stop feeling anything for him, because this couldn't last. Everyone always left eventually, for one reason or another.

"I know I'm not the world's best communicator and that no matter how hard I try, all my intentions, words and heart get lost in translation somewhere. I've spent my life believing in love and that it would one day come for me. I thought there was someone out there looking for me and waiting for me as much as I was looking and waiting for him. I used to spend every night looking up at the stars wondering if he could see them too? The sky was the only thing I knew we shared collectively and as vast and wide as it is, it made me feel like he was close to me all the time. I know it's going to sound crazy but I swear I could feel his heart crying out to mine. There were nights I would just stay awake looking at the stars feeling him searching for me and wishing I could respond and let him know I was right there, that I could hear him and feel him and that I wanted just as badly to find him too. This feeling of knowing he was out there brought me comfort and torment all at the same time. On one hand I was relieved to know that somewhere in the world he existed and on the other hand it broke my heart knowing I couldn't be with him because we couldn't find each other. Then I met Aden and suddenly my heart found its home. I wasn't lost or searching anymore I knew my heart could finally rest because it found the one it had been equally crying out to. When he left everything became so empty. I've longed to feel that way again, to know that there is someone out there, whether it be Aden or someone else, who hasn't given up on finding me. But I don't feel it anymore. It's just silence and emptiness now and it's a horrible feeling and I don't want to believe in love or feel it anymore if this is what it leads to. And at the same time I don't understand how I could go from being that girl who just desperately wanted to love someone else with a reckless abandon to now wanting to shut it off because the world won't let me be her." It felt good to get all of that off my chest and to just verbal rant what I had held inside for a long time now. I looked up at the sky and the New York City lights made it impossible to see stars and I laughed to myself quietly and sarcastically knowing it too was symbolic of how I felt. My safe sky was now empty and it was as if the darkness had come in and swallowed all the stars leaving only a dark, empty void in its place.

Dylan was silent for a while and I suppose it should have made me nervous because he wasn't usually this quiet but with him I just enjoyed having him near me. "You want to stop loving?" Those were the only words that escaped his mouth quietly and almost on the verge of sadness. "Yes." "Don't." I looked at him again and this time made sure my whole body was facing him. "Why?"

He stared straight at me, "It would be the greatest loss this world has ever known if you took your heart away from it. Your ability to love the way you do separates you from everyone else. It makes you who you are; it's what will save everyone you love. I know it's a lonely road and that it must seem impossible to live with, but please think about this before you make any rash decisions. I love your heart and the way you love and again it's selfish of me to ask you to live with this pain and hurt because I don't want to see you lose yourself. I don't want to see what you would become without your beautiful heart and soul. I don't want to lose you. I know that it appears as though this world you've been thrusted into wants you to be nothing more than a vessel for it's cause. That no one cares who you are as Ember and what matters to your heart, but it matters to me."

"You won't lose me, Dylan." I tried to reassure him, but how could I be sure what I was saying would always remain true?

"Yes, I would. We all would. You wouldn't be the same without your ability to love and honestly I don't know that you'd ever be the same again if you let it go, even if you were able to get it back somehow."

Somehow what he was saying made sense to me and it was not what I wanted to hear. "Being able to love isn't an ability Dylan. It's an innate feature we're all born with. I make just as big a mess of love as the next person." I still could feel the rebellion in my heart wanting to shut it all down and live like everyone else. I wanted to love and leave. I wanted to disregard others feelings and worry about only my own. I wanted to not worry about everyone else and just focus on me and most important of all, I wanted to stop feeling everything. Feelings were Aden's thing and it wasn't mine and every time feelings of any sort crept up on me I thought of him and my love for him. That love was too much to hold onto and I wanted to just forget I ever loved him at all, even though I knew it would always be impossible to do.

"You're right love is something everyone is capable of doing, if they choose to. There are some people born into this world with a greater capacity to love than others can. Most see love as a need to fulfill or satisfy, not a gift to give. People claim love as their own and take it from others without care because they don't know what true love really means. Ember, love in it's purest form is a very powerful weapon. Love has caused wars and men of great power to fall. Love in its truest form has saved us all and yet we still choose to corrupt it and make it into something its not. We hoard it for ourselves and make it conditional, but not you. We may not have spent a lot of time together yet but I do know your heart and you just want to love the world for all that is and all that isn't. You don't seek personal gain or power, you just want to love people where they are at. Even a boy like Aden who can rip your heart out and still you choose to love him despite his digressions. It may not mean much to you because this is just who you truly are, but for those of us on the outside, it's special." Dylan's words held a lot of weight and I knew there was truth in what he was saying. I just couldn't seem to find it within myself to believe I was the person he made me out to be. I was just an ordinary girl consumed by the notions of fairy tale love. In all this time I hadn't taken a moment to consider the destruction happening around the world that the news kept reporting on or tried to seek out a solution to get rid of the Shadows that haunted me and were hurting innocent people. No, all this time I was selfish and focused on my own needs and I didn't deserve Dylan's view of me.

I decided to change the conversation because I didn't think I could handle it anymore. I touched Dylan's sunglasses and he quickly took my hand away. He was gentle but I could tell he was protecting something. "Why can't I ever see your eyes?" His lips closed tightly together and formed a firm line where his relaxed lips used to be. He wasn't answering me and I could tell from his body language and overall expression he was trying to make up an answer, "The truth." I said sharply.

He frowned as he sighed and it seemed to take him far too long to move or breathe again, let alone answer me. He took both my hands into his and lifted them to the sides of his sunglasses. "Take them off." He said with no emotion reflected in his voice. I slowly wrapped my fingers around the sides of them and slipped them away from his face. My mouth fell open with a gasp that was unintentional but I couldn't help myself. Behind his sunglasses were gorgeous hazel eyes but they weren't looking at me. They moved on their own it seemed and it was as if he couldn't see me right in front of him.

He was tense and quiet but he finally spoke, "I'm blind Ember."

"H-h-how is that possible?" He smiled softly and nodded, "I was born blind."

"But you can see everything?"I asked incredulously.

He laughed quietly, "Yes, but not the way you can see everything. My ability to see the future gives me images and visions of people, the world, and I use those images to base everything else off of. That's why I can see you. I don't rely on my physical ability to see but my inner ability."

I was still completely dumbfounded and trying to make sense of this in my mind, "So you've only ever seen me in visions?" He nodded, "Yes, basically."

I smiled for a moment, "You like live in the future then all the time don't you?" He nodded, "In theory. I see possible outcomes before they happen and then remember what I saw and when one of those outcomes happens I know which one I am apart of and can then base visuals off of that."

"That is incredible." My previous anger and rants had completely vanished now.

All I could do was look at his gorgeous eyes and face. "I love seeing you this way."

"Why is that?" His eyebrows arched up as if he were excited that I had noticed him at all. "Because it's you and you're not hiding anymore." He got his cocky smirk back on his face, "Admit it, you think I'm sexy?"

I burst out into a fit of laughter and playfully punched him, "No." I said through my laughter.

He laughed with me, "I know you think I am." I leaned in and kissed him on the cheek. He smiled softly and I sat back looking at him as I lost myself deep in thought, letting silence drown us both. "Thinking about how adorably sexy I am?" I laughed and shook my head.

"No. I'm thinking about how I want to read you and see what you see." His face lost its humor and he got serious. "Oh." I pretended to be overly dramatic in my response, "Gasp, are you at a loss for words?"

He smirked. "No. Just surprised." "Why?" "No one has ever read me before except my mom." Reading someone was an extremely personal experience. I couldn't imagine that there was anything more invasive or revealing then having a telepath skim through your innermost thoughts, dreams and visions. Most people didn't willingly let someone read them, and it usually had to be done without permission. I wasn't sure how to respond to that.

He stared out at the city lights without expression and I gave him time to process what I had asked. He then turned to face me again, "You can read me." I smiled and was anxiously, nervous to see inside his mind. "You sure?" He smiled and nodded. "Yes, just be gentle." I laughed and turned to face him and got a bit closer to him and looked into his eyes. It was easier for me to use my ability and make a strong connection when I could see into the person's eyes.

When I entered into Dylan's mind I arrived at a scene I couldn't make sense of at first. I stopped for a moment and took in the scene and noted the bright array of small colorful flowers that bloomed from the bright green grass. They were purple, blue, white and yellow. The sky was the most vibrant, electric blue one could ever imagine and there were puffy white clouds scattered softly throughout it. I carefully moved through the meadow looking for signs as to why this was an important place to him. What memory, what moment did this place hold? Or was it something that was yet to happen? I had never read a pre-cog's mind before and I had no idea how this worked. My best guess was to move slowly and carefully and pay attention to as many details as possible. I finally heard someone walking softly through the grass behind me. When I turned around, I was surprised to see Jade, but I stood still and watched her every movement. Her hair was hanging down softly in loose, wavy, curls on her shoulders and she wore a yellow gauze sundress. The breeze blew her hair softly and the sheer gauze made her appear almost angelic. She walked slowly and carefree and her arms dangled by her side indicating she didn't have a care in the world. I watched her walk through the meadow admiring all the bright flowers before she disappeared into the trees. I kept my distance and followed closely behind. She stopped after a short walk and sat down on a mossy tree trunk that formed a bench on the forest floor, as if it had been designed by faeries themselves. The sound of branches breaking could be heard coming from behind me and as I turned to see what was coming a shadow began approaching her. She didn't seem scared but I was. Shadows creeped me out and I was afraid somehow they had found me here too or maybe Dylan was working with them. My heart froze for a moment, until I saw the shadows revealing Dylan emerging from the trees and I exhaled with immense relief. "Hey beautiful." He kissed Jade softly and took a seat next to her. "What took you so long?" She looked up into his eyes showering him love and affection. He shrugged and pulled out a handful of wild flowers from behind his back and handed them to her. "I stopped to pick these for you by the river." Jade's face lit up as she smelled the flowers and held them in her hands carefully. "They're beautiful. Thank you." "Anything for you." The way Dylan spoke to her and looked at her made my heart seize up. I could feel everything he was feeling. He was deeply in love with Jade and he saw a future with her. He saw somewhere in the infinite possibilities a life like this where they didn't have to live in fear and could just exist and be one with each other. This life was a simpler one and one where all that mattered was each other. I could feel my eyes tearing up as Dylan wrapped his arm around Jade and pulled her close to his chest. I could feel the deep, powerful, intoxicating love that lived inside him for her and only her.

I was pulled out of the memory quickly and noticed Dylan standing up and half way into the apartment. "Dylan, are you okay?" he nodded slowly as he messed with a thread hanging from his shirt, "Yeah, I just need to get some sleep. Have a good night Em." Dylan rushed inside and I could tell that reliving that memory pulled deeply at his heart strings but I couldn't understand why he'd just hide all of that inside? Seeing how he had responded let me know that his feelings for Jade were something that only existed within himself and I was now privy to one of his deepest held secrets. Feeling and seeing everything that Dylan held in his heart for Jade made me wonder why he didn't share those feelings publicly with her and didn't she have a right to know? Dylan's thoughts stayed with me and I couldn't seem to shake it no matter how hard I tried. Venturing inside another person's mind was always a risk. One could never be sure they would leave the same as when they entered depending upon what they saw. Knowledge can be a very powerful thing in the means that it can awaken a fire within to change the world or cause the world to burn. I looked out again at the lights of the city pretending they were stars hoping to get lost in them. Thoughts of Aden kept nagging away at the back of my mind and my heart kept aching for him. It didn't ache in the sense that I wanted romance or for him to love me, but it ached in the deepest of ways when you miss someone terribly. When you miss the sound of their laugh or the way their eyes crinkle up when they smile. I searched around in my pocket for the burner phone Dylan had set me up with. It allowed me to text him and Jade or make calls if needed without being traced. I began writing a text to Aden…again.

9:08 PM

Aden, I realize that I might as well be talking to the wind, because while you read my messages there is no reply. What am I supposed to do when I miss you so much? How do I just carry on about my day as if I never knew you at all? I always said that I didn't want to live in a world where you didn't exist. Ironic, that I never considered the alternative would be that I would cease to exist, huh? I suppose somewhere in my heart I believed you felt that way too. But here we are, strangers just passing by. When did everything go so wrong? Please Aden, know that I'm wanting nothing more than to just hear from you, because I really, really do miss you.

Read 9:09 PM

I waited for a reply but it never came. As with other short texts I had sent to Aden prior to, this was ending up very much the same. He always read my messages but he never responded. In the beginning I had messaged him to let him know that I was in fact okay and asking if he was alright as well. I had messaged him silly observations or jokes I had heard while on my journey to New York that only he and I would appreciate, still no reply. Sometimes all I would send was a short three word text of, I miss you, attached with the wild fantasy that somewhere inside him those words would pierce his heart and he would reply.

After a few more minutes on the balcony waiting to see if he'd reply this time, I put the phone back into my pocket and headed inside to get some sleep. I kept trying to remind myself that Aden was a guy who needed time to process things and while my mind told me he would never reply, my heart kept trying to tell myself maybe this time he would. After all, no reply had to be better than a reply wishing me away forever right?

CHAPTER SIX

The next morning I woke up still feeling exhausted from a restless night of sleep. I immediately pulled my phone out from under my pillow and cringed as I turned it on to find, NO NEW MESSAGES, across the screen. If I was being honest with myself I was extremely disappointed that Aden could be so cruel, but on the other hand this is what I had come to expect from him and I hated that I still believed he was better than this. I couldn't help but wonder how long would I hold out until I had no other choice but to give up on him completely,

123

as it appeared he had done with me? I put the phone back under my pillow and laid still for awhile just staring at the ceiling trying to wake up and process everything that had happened last night with Dylan. If nothing else it was a great distraction from the lack of Aden contact.

Logic told me that what I saw in Dylan's mind regarding Jade was none of my business, but my heart and inner hopeless romantic said I couldn't let it go. Every time I tried to close my eyes all I could do was re-envision what I had seen and felt and I just couldn't let something like that pass by. Love like that comes around so infrequently anymore that letting it go and allowing Dylan to keep it locked up would be unfair to him, Jade, and possibly even the world. If Dylan acted on it and he got together with Jade there was no telling who their love would impact or how it could change the lives they interacted with. Love was a lot like laughing, it was highly infectious and the love Dylan held for Jade would catch on like a plague and consume everyone in its path (in the best of ways, of course). I laughed at myself because it was moments like these that I felt I would forever be a hopeless romantic.

"What's so funny?" Jade walked past me and startled me. "Uh, nothing. Just laughing at myself. You scared me."

"Sorry. I didn't know you were having a private conversation. That's the thing with you telepaths, always inside your own heads." She tapped her index finger on her temple to emphasize her point. "Yeah, I guess." I wasn't sure how to respond to that because I had never really thought much about what others thought of me. I was always a bit of an introvert, pretending to be an extrovert. I suppose I kept up that appearance to cover up the fact that in my brain there was a constant stream of voices, thoughts, memories and moments happening and no one was allowed to know that. Jade was in the kitchen getting some coffee going and all I could do was watch her and wonder if she also shared the same feelings for Dylan. I knew he had said not to get involved, but I needed to get to know Jade better so a little prodding around couldn't hurt, right?

I folded up my blanket on the couch and Jade walked over with a cup of coffee for me and took a seat. "Thanks. So where's Dylan?" I sat down next to Jade and noticed that his bed on the floor was neatly folded up and he was no where to be seen. "He went out to get some supplies from a contact he knows. It's just us girls. I thought it would be a good time to get to know each other better." I smiled and sipped my coffee. "Definitely. I was hoping we'd have some time to get to know one another." Jade smiled and her demeanor was calm and easy going which made me feel automatically comfortable around her.

"So tell me about what happened, from the beginning, if you're okay talking about it?" She sipped her coffee casually as if we were about to discuss just another average day at work.

I smiled slightly and nodded, "Yeah, it's fine. I guess I'll start from the beginning. Um, I'm not sure how I became invisible, but it happened after my boyfriend, Aden, broke up with me suddenly." "Suddenly?" "Out of nowhere he just decided we couldn't be together anymore and it made absolutely no sense to me. I still haven't been able to figure out what happened exactly and then the next thing I knew my abilities went on the fritz and Commander Addison, from the government, was looking for me. If I hadn't been invisible he would have taken me. Which I suppose makes my invisibility a blessing in disguise. Shortly after that I ended up on the run because the Shadows were after me and I made it all the way here to New York and finally was able to stop running for a bit, but your problems always catch up to you no matter how far you run."

Jade listened intently and I had to wonder if while I spoke she was envisioning multiple outcomes to my life at the same time. She was taking it all in and pondering the short synopsis I gave her. "I'm sorry to hear about you and Aden." "Thank you." Jade was quiet and in a way that was unnerving but at the same time I could tell she wasn't the type of person to speak unless she knew she had the right words to say and she definitely thought through everything. She was a lot like Dylan in that she was more an observer than a participant in the conversation so I decided to ask her some questions.

"What about you? Anyone special in your life?" I knew I was meddling but I couldn't help myself. I needed something good to focus on for awhile in the midst of all the darkness and frustration surrounding my life. Plus, I had never gotten to experience real girl talk before. The only real friend I had had was Aden and my basis for interacting with other girls had come from books and movies.

Jade looked away for a moment and took a long, slow sip of her coffee. "There is, but it's complicated." "What makes it complicated?"

She looked at me with a sympathetic expression and I knew she wasn't going to give in that easily. "Love isn't always easy and there are often times things that try to get in the way."

I nodded, "I know that all too well. Sometimes we are our own worst enemies." "Exactly." I took a long sip of my coffee as I tried to think of a way to pry a bit deeper without it being obvious, but all the questions I could think of felt far too intrusive. I wasn't sure what the correct social protocol in a situation like this was. I had always been taught to interrogate people, not causally discuss life or matters of the heart. This was still a skill I was working on mastering.

"Tell me about Commander Addison?" Jade finally broke the silence but hearing that name slip off her tongue made me cringe. "He was the one who killed my parents soon after I was born. He's had me under his watch and care most of my life. I was raised by agents and constantly being watched and guarded like his prized possession. One day I was able to get away and he's been looking for me ever since."

"You mean the fire?" My heart froze and I felt like the world had stopped spinning and everything was in slow motion. "Excuse me?" She smiled softly and set her cup down on the table next to the couch. "I'm sorry, I know more than I should sometimes." "You know about the fire?" No one had ever talked about it before and I didn't think anyone ever would. I wasn't sure Jade even knew the real story but I had to find out. She nodded, "Dylan and I know quite a bit about you and we want to take this time to tell you what we know. I want to wait till he gets back if that's okay?" I nodded and played with the handle on my cup nervously. I was once again inside my own head and lost inside my fears, reliving a past I couldn't escape apparently. "The fire wasn't your fault." I looked up quickly at Jade and although I wasn't able to ask why I assumed my face did all the talking for me. "I know you think it was but it wasn't." "Then what happened?" My voice shook as I spoke. I had never talked to anyone about the fire before, not even Aden, and it was a weight I carried around on my soul everyday of my life.

Jade was pensive for a moment and her silence lasted far longer than I felt I could stand. "Agents Brown and Julian worked very closely with Commander Addison. We'll get into that part of your history a bit more later but he was forcing you to become something you weren't meant to be. He wanted to use you and saw the potential you had to be something useful to him and along with the agents who kept watch on you, they were performing tests and procedures to bring out abilities in you. You had no control over them and I doubt you even knew what you were capable of. If I'm right, things would happen you couldn't explain and you felt as though you had no control over your life?" I nodded and wiped a stray tear from my eye. No one had ever understood me like Jade seemed to in this very moment. Aden came close, but not like this. I felt as though Jade was a reflection of myself and I wanted her to keep talking because I had to know more, so I allowed myself to share the past that haunted me deeply.

"That night they were pushing me, I didn't know what they wanted or what they expected me to be able to do. They were yelling and screaming at me, as if I were a solider in training, and I just couldn't do anything they wanted. My emotions were taking over and I was feeling overwhelmed and angry, wishing I could make them stop. Then without warning a fire sparked in the room we were in. It was like this wall of flames formed between us. I tried to put it out, I tried to save them, I swear. I opened the window behind me to let in air so the smoke wouldn't become a problem. The door to the room was locked and the fire spread so quickly they couldn't see to unlock the door, they were stuck. I headed for the window and yelled for them. They ran after me but a gust of air came in through the window and the flames rose higher and they didn't make it in time. I don't know what happened for sure to them because I was too afraid to look behind me. As much as I despised them I didn't want them to get hurt. I took off running that night and I never looked back. I swore I killed them and it's a guilt I can't shake or get rid of. The guilt just lingers like a bad dream." Jade handed me a kleenex and I wiped my eyes trying to compose myself again. I had never told anyone that story before, not even Aden. He knew bits and pieces but not everything because I couldn't bare the thought of what he'd think of me. I felt like a murderer but I wasn't even sure I started that fire.

"You didn't do anything on purpose and it wasn't your fault." "How do you know that? How did the fire start then?" Jade looked reluctant to answer me but I was pleading to her with my eyes hoping desperately she would give me answers that I've searched for since that night. "You have many abilities and are by far not limited to just being a telepath. Pyro-kinesis is one of them. That night Agents Brown and Julian set the fire because they believed you could put it out with your mind. So although you could have set it, they set the fire intentionally, and the outcome of their decision wasn't your fault because you had no idea what they wanted you to do. Honestly, I don't think they understood that while you have many abilities, you still have limitation and pyro-kinesis only allows you to start fires, not put them out." I exhaled slowly trying to believe the story she was telling me. "Could I have put it out?" She nodded slowly, "Yes, but it wasn't something you knew how to do at the time and why they believed you would just instinctively know to do it is beyond me." I leaned back on the couch unsure what I believed about that story. "How do you know this to be true?" Jade touched my leg softly, "We know a lot about you Ember and I promise we won't keep the truth from you any longer."

Waiting for Dylan to return was driving me insane. I must have clicked through every channel on the satellite feed at least 50 times before he walked through the door. For the first time in my entire life I had two people who could tell me everything I've ever wanted to know. A part of me was terrified and the other part was thrilled. I didn't know what they would tell me or if I'd even like it but at least I would finally know the truth and they weren't keeping secrets from me anymore. Now I could hopefully understand why the Opposition and Resistance wanted to use me as a weapon. Thinking about Jade and Dylan's potential love match completely exited my brain and all I could think about was discovering who I was and hopefully more about my parents. Dylan said hello as he walked in carrying a box of parts. He took them into the spare bedroom and was in there awhile talking with Jade before they both stepped out into the main room. I turned to face them and felt like I was going to explode if they left me waiting in suspense any longer.

Dylan took a seat in the chair that was directly across from the couch and Jade resumed her spot on the couch next to me. "I hear Jade has loose lips when she's around you?"

I looked at her and then back to Dylan, "I'm glad she does. I want to know the truth."

Dylan smirked and folded his arms across his chest, "What is the magic word?" I crinkled my nose up at him because sometimes he really pushed my buttons, "Please!" Dylan thought for a second and shook his head, "Wrong magic word. Well that was easy."

He stood up pretending to leave and Jade laughed and pulled him back to the sitting area. "He's kidding." She said with a small laugh as Dylan smiled and nodded, "Just lightening the mood."

I stuck my tongue out at him and looked to Jade. "Please tell me before I explode all over your couch." Jade smiled and then looked to Dylan and he nodded and his face became serious and I knew it was time to hear the truth.

"I'm not honestly sure where to start, there is so much to tell you. Forgive me if it seems out of order or doesn't make sense. You can ask me and Jade questions and we'll do our best to help make sense of it all." I nodded and sat on the edge of the couch ready for him to start. "Our parents, yours, mine, Jade's and even Aden's were all original founders of The Guild. They were friends a long time ago and they started The Guild with the hopes that it would keep order and protect everyone. They planned to up hold the laws and create a system that would allow input from Benders and Lost to maintain balance and avoid civil unrest. During this time it was not looked highly upon that Benders and Lost formed relationships because it's been a long standing rule that we are to remain in separate worlds. My parents were the only ones who were of both worlds, so to speak, and while the others didn't mind and saw it as an opportunity to bring peace and understanding, others didn't see it that way. The four founding families remained strong and developed quite the following with Benders and Lost alike. Opposition began to form and they fought against it, because they believed in what they stood for and they saw the future much differently than it has turned out to be. Many Benders wanted my parents out of The Guild. Those who felt this way began to form their own alliances, which you know now as the Opposition. One night my parents both went missing. I was just a little boy at this point and I wasn't even aware they were gone. I barely remember them. Anyways, everyone set out to find them and discovered they had been captured by the government. Ember, your parents, went after them. To the rest of The Guild members it seemed like a suicide mission but they believed it was worth the risk. Jade and Aden's parents stayed behind to maintain order and structure to ensure that there would be people to oversee The Guild. No one thought they would come back alive. When your parents finally got to mine they had already been killed. Your parents were captured and during this time discovered they were pregnant with you. Your very existence is what prolonged their lives and gave them as much of a chance for freedom as was possible. The government wanted you to be born under their control so they allowed your parents to live at their facility, as prisoners, of course. Commander Addison was in charge and oversaw the wellness of your mother. You were born in the facility, as you know. When you were born Commander Addison attempted to make a deal. He agreed to set your parents free in exchange for you. Your parents refused to give you up to the government because you were their child and they didn't want that life for you. As an infant you showed signs of abilities that had never been active or seen in other infants before. The government was determined to have you and gave your parents one last chance to choose. They said no and the government took their lives. The government collected intel on my parents and yours and they set out to destroy The Guild and bring in all the Benders they could to study them and learn how to create a super human. Jade and Aden's parents were the last remaining Guild founders and the members wanted them to go into hiding to protect what they had started. They refused at first and held a strong front for everyone. Tension grew between Aden and Jade's parents because they began to feel different forms of action should be taken. Aden's parents wanted to seek revenge on the government for what they had done to our families. Jade's parents believed going public in that way would only make things worse and that they needed a more solid, safer plan. Neither side could agree and the Opposition and Resistance were born. A house divided. Aden's parents became consumed with anger and a vengeful spirit and their actions were hasty and unwarranted by The Guild. Sides were chosen and the issues grew out of control like wild fire. The lack of organization and structure that began to unravel within The Guild caused some close calls with the government. Jade's parents went into hiding and Aden's parents moved out to Washington to get closer to the source. They believed they could hide in plain sight and that they would find a way to even the score. Their anger and pain turned to hatred and turned their hearts black. They were never the same people they had once been. They became consumed by power and their need for control. They believed in their hearts that what they were doing was the right thing and I'm sure they still do to this day. Yet evil done in the name of good is still and always will be evil. They've always known who you are Ember, everyone has."

I was lost in this story but I had to stop Dylan there, "Wait, what do you mean everyone has?" Jade turned away from Dylan and to me, "Dylan, Aden, you and I are Guild Legacies. Meaning we are technically supposed to rise up and rule The Guild. That alone makes all of us known simply through our birthrights. You, in particular, were known for that but also before your parents died they managed to get to a letter to my parents revealing that they had a child. They wrote about the abilities they had witnessed in you as an infant. Your mother wrote about dreams she had repeatedly that you were special and that you have a purpose far greater than what your abilities could do. That you would change the world and together the four of us would awaken the world and set it on fire." "So we're like pre-destined to be friends?" Dylan and Jade laughed together softly, "Kind of." Jade said smiling. "Does Aden know any of this?" They both shook their heads, "We don't suspect he does. We've managed to keep track of both of you and he's never given us any indication he knows about any of this." Dylan said assuredly.

This was a lot more far-fetched of a story than I had expected to hear and I wasn't sure I was believing it, but a part of me felt more and more complete as this story came to life before me and loose ends began to match up and make sense. Was it possible that this fantasy type retelling of my life was true? This was the kind of plot twist you'd find in a book or movie, not real life. Maybe it was true though that everything really did happen for a reason and nothing was by chance or coincidence. Was it possible that our destinies all along had been intertwined? If this were true, it made sense why Aden and I had such a strong connection to each other right from the moment we met and why I was still fighting to bring him back. "Okay, continue, please!" Dylan nodded and exhaled slowly remembering where he left off.

"Now you know the basics of our history and our families. I know it's a rough, quick and dirty version of it all and in time we can fill in on more details but I'm assuming you want me to get to the part about you and Aden?" I nodded quickly and eagerly. He smiled softly and nodded choosing his words carefully. "From what we know, Aden found you on his own, which isn't surprising as somewhere along the lines we've all managed to find each other on our own free will. Some would call it fate, others destiny, but nothing has been forced. There is an undefinable force that attracts us all together. I'm sure you've felt it now yourself and know it as well as we do. When you and Aden met I'm sure you both believed it was simply attraction and nothing more but as you know now it was a lot more than just that. We've been monitoring you and Aden from a distance simply because we didn't want to intervene in what was meant to happen on its own. I apologize for what may seem like stalking, but we did it to keep you both safe. We've been aware of the impending war and as Legacies we do have a say in what happens. The Bender/Lost world is looking to us for answers and intervention but we've tried to remain out of it as long as possible in the hopes that we could remain safe and find each other first before making any decisions. Allowing you and Aden to remain safe and not apart of this world was our intentions because sometimes we're better off not knowing everything. You both were very happy and we were aware that Aden's parents knew who you were and we didn't believe they would allow any harm to come to either one of you. If they had we would have intervened right away. I know I sound like I'm repeating myself, but I don't want you to think in anyway that we just left you on your own or were some creepy voyeurs watching your life." Dylan sipped his drink and regained his thoughts and moved forward, "Getting back to you and Aden...He didn't choose to leave you Ember, his parents chose for him. I'm not sure that he's aware of why they made that decision and why it was so important to them that he break up with you, but he's conditioned to do as they say and I think he's even afraid to stand up to them, but they were the ones who told him he had to let you go, at least thats what we were able to make of the situation. Jade and I were hoping that he would be strong enough to realize the error in his parent's decision and fight for what you both had, but he didn't. We saw two outcomes in how all of this could go and he made his decision." I held my hand up to stop Dylan and looked between him and Jade, "Two outcomes? So since he chose one of those, what do you see happening next?" They both glanced at each other and Jade laughed to herself, "We're not crystal balls Ember. Time will decide what happens next." I rolled my eyes and sat back on the couch, "Alright, continue with your story."

Dylan smirked and set his cup to the side, "Just relax Little Bender. Continuing on...while Jade and I don't know the final outcome to this story, we do know that things were written before our time about the four of us. Jade, would you like to take it from here?" She smiled politely at Dylan and then faced me again.

"Our parents wrote journals long before any of them met. They too were destined to meet and form The Guild. It was apart of their purpose and destinies. Thankfully they recorded most of that journey and we've been able to scout out the missing journals and piece the complete story together. Our parents collectively all had an array of abilities and they all functioned differently. Some were pre-cogs who did manage to see possible outcomes for the future, others simply had abilities to see beyond this world, like your mother for example. Arya, had this gift to dream the foreseeable future. The journals she kept were primarily dream journals. As a young girl she would have these extravagant dreams that she thought were simply just the by product of an overactive imagination. Over time and as she got older, she discovered they were far more than that. These dreams actually came true and it was up to her to decide how to use the information. Long before she met your father or any of our parents, she dreamt of all of this happening and sensed deep inside the importance that her actions would hold. She lived her life very carefully knowing that each decision she made could effect the future. She had seen your father in dreams before and she saw you as well. You were so real to her even though you were a far off dream in her life at the time. She fought for you because she loved you long before she knew you. She felt the same about your father, Ash. They realized their love and relationship would have a deep impact on the world and those they encountered and they took it very seriously. They faced their share of trials but their love could endure anything. In the journals of Arya and the other parents we discovered they all had seen the same visions in one way or another at different times. When they met it was a massive confirmation for them that they were right on the path and they were destined to be in each others lives. Our futures were spoken of and seen before we existed and so far according to what they wrote we are where they saw us being."

Jade could obviously see the confusion on my face and stopped to give me a moment to question her, "Where are your parents?" Jade shrugged, "I'm not sure exactly. They have managed to remain hidden for years now. The last time I saw them I was 10 years old. At that point in time things were getting out of hand and The Guild members feared for the lives of my parents and Aden's parents. His parents refused to hide and I suppose they believed they could remain safe by living the way they do, my parents on the other hand hid and have continued to since then. I'm not sure that I'll ever see them again or if they are even still alive." "You can't just use your ability to see them or find out if they're okay?" She shook her head, "Wherever they are, assuming they are still alive, they are protected and it blocks me from seeing them at all. It's as if they don't exist." "I'm not trying to sound bad here but why would they leave you behind?" "They put me up for adoption with a Static family. They wanted me to have a chance at a real life and feared if I came with them I could be in danger too. For years I thought my parents abandoned me. I lived with feelings of rejection that ran so deep I got myself into a lot of unfortunate situations. I just wanted to be loved and know I was important to someone. That there would be someone in my life that would stay. As I got older my abilities began to develop and my Static family thought I was strange and slowly began to distance themselves from me. Eventually I turned 16 and set out on my own. I felt lost but I was happy knowing the future lied in my hands now. I had spent years dreaming and seeing all of you guys but I had no idea who you were or why I was seeing you. Then one day I met Dylan." Jade glanced over at Dylan giving him a look that spoke clearly of her love and adoration for him.

There was much more to this story then I thought I could ever understand or comprehend in a lifetime let alone a few hours. Dylan leaned forward and looked at me for a moment as if there was something written on my face. "What?" I asked him in a semi annoyed but worried way. "Nothing. I can see it all over your face that you're kind of freaking out. This is a lot to process and take in right now." I nodded and leaned back on the couch to take a break. "I'm guessing we haven't even touched on everything yet, have we?" Jade and Dylan shared a glance and Jade shook her head. "We've had years to understand all of this and comprehend it. You've had not even a full day. We don't want to overwhelm you, but we want you to be informed so that you can be well prepared for everything that is going on." I nodded and rubbed my head that was forming a massive headache. "I'm going to need some time to process everything before you tell me anymore, but I think I get the gist of it." I got up and headed out to the balcony for some air and time to think. I couldn't help it but I looked up at the sky and thought of Aden. It was the first moment I had had in awhile where I actually wanted to think about him. I wanted him there with me more than anything and I couldn't help but wonder what he was doing and if he was missing me as much as I was missing him? I mean after all we are supposed to be connected right, which had to mean he felt the distance between us, no matter how he tried to deny it.

Suddenly, I was hit with this new found energy and eagerness that I hadn't known before. I walked back inside with passion and purpose and found Jade and Dylan right where I had left them. They both looked up at me with what appeared to be surprise. "I appreciate you both telling me the truth and I know there is a lot more I need to hear and wrap my head around. In the meantime though I want to know what we are truly capable of? What makes us so extraordinary and Legacies? What limitations do we have and how far can we go?"

Jade and Dylan both looked at each other with uncertain expressions. For people who could see the future it either wasn't looking good or they hadn't seen this one coming. "And what exactly did you have in mind?" Jade asked cautiously.

"As a child I was pushed to discover what I could do but I've never actually honed many of those abilities or explored them further. I wanted to forget them. Maybe we need to take this time to explore what is hidden within us and see what we're actually capable of." Dylan looked at Jade first and then back to me, "We will, in due time. For now give yourself some time to process everything we've just told you, deal?" I nodded in agreement, for now.

CHAPTER SEVEN

Days had passed since I finally began to discover my history that was more apart of my future than my past. I had spent the days looking through some of my mom's journals and processing what she had written and what it truly means. I was finally beginning to make sense of it and accept it. I suppose seeing the journals and reading through them myself made it all seem a bit more real. Having something tangible that used to be my mom's gave me a sense of family. It made me feel as though she were still with me and that I could finally get to know her like I had always dreamed of doing. I was finding it hard to believe that my mom would have written all these thoughts down if there wasn't some shred of truth to them, she surely didn't seem crazy. Even seeing it with my own eyes still didn't take away the fact that believing in everything the original Guild members did required a great deal of blind faith that I wasn't sure I was capable of. I wanted to believe everything and I wanted it to be true, but there was that deeply hurt part of me that saw the situations as they were presently and struggled to believe these beautiful ideas and dreams. It was hard to believe that life could ever work out that perfectly. I mean in books it always did, but in real life it didn't. One of the agents I used to live with liked to remind me, "Life isn't like the movies. Nothing ever happens like it does on the screen." I always got angry when she'd say that because I felt like it was her own bitterness of how her life had turned out that made her share that with me and I didn't want to turn out like her. Yet here I was feeling hopeless and turning bitter on the inside too.

I got up off the couch and looked over at Jade and Dylan who were eating some breakfast in the kitchen. "Alright, I'm ready to believe now." They both looked up at me and somehow I got the feeling this wasn't a surprise to them. I mean they could see the future, was anything ever a surprise to them?

"Wow, you finally decided to join the living huh? Welcome back." Dylan said with his usual cocky, arrogant tone. I laughed slightly and joined them at the table.

"Yes, I had a late night again and I've been a bit consumed in the journals. Good news is, I have spent the time thinking and going over everything and I have come to my own conclusions."

"Which would be?" Jade asked raising her eyebrows.

"Which are that I don't know if I can believe in all of this completely because it still seems so unbelievable, but I want to believe. It was important to my parents and so much has happened in my life that these stories confirm, there has to be some truth in it right? I also believe we have to take a stand, like our parents. We have a responsibility to carry on where our parents left off." Dylan and Jade glanced at each other giving me the impression maybe they hadn't seen this coming…just maybe. I smiled, "It's time we take charge and stop running or hiding."

"How do you propose we do that little Bender?" Dylan asked cautiously.

I exhaled and poured myself a cup of tea. I thought about it for a moment, "We continue training and learning our strengths and weaknesses. Then we formulate a plan of action." Jade and Dylan continued to exchange their silent glances as if they were having a private conversation. "You do remember I could just butt in at any time and read your minds right?" They both laughed and Jade rolled her eyes, "We remember. We just know that this is a delicate situation and we have to be careful how we handle things. We can't just run in guns blazing and save the world. We have to think diplomatically as Legacies." I nodded and smiled, "Let's begin training then, shall we?" I said standing up excitedly. Jade and Dylan looked very unsure, but I was certain this is what I wanted to do.

Over the past couple of days Dylan and Jade had been helping me train and they were training along side me. We were discovering the main abilities we knew we had and how we could make them stronger. I had never really been keen on using my abilities much and they had become rather rusty. The training time was helping me regain confidence in them and learn what I could and couldn't do. Jade and Dylan were having fun as well getting to test out their skills and finally put their years of research

151

to use. Today was going to be an exciting day though, we were going to push the limits and see what our limitations were. I stretched my neck and shoulders knowing I needed to be relaxed and in good form to do this. Lately I was pushing myself more than normal and it sometimes caused me migraines. That was the unfortunate part of being a telepath that I had discovered years ago; the headaches. The mind was an incredibly powerful machine but even machines had limitations and sometimes they needed a rest. Dylan pulled out his laptop that held all his research and he got set up to help me go deeper. Jade sat next to him on the couch and I took a seat in the chair across from them. I watched Dylan click around on his laptop that sat in front of me on the glass coffee table. I was eager to get going and couldn't wait to see what would happen. Dylan looked at me and smiled, "Okay so we're going to see how deep you can actually go inside Jade's mind. Meaning that you should have the capabilities to block emotions, other Benders and possibly shield others around you. We aren't fully sure what you might encounter but if you're willing we are willing to help you go there." I smiled and nodded, "Oh I'm ready."

At this point I was willing to go to any extreme necessary in order to discover what made me a possible weapon. Knowledge is powerful and the more you know the more power you have. Right now we were at a massive disadvantage. Thanks to Jade and Dylan we knew more than anyone would suspect but what we didn't know was what we indeed were capable of. None of us had ever thought to push our limits before, because we never needed to. Right now we were soldiers training for a war and we had to be as well prepared as possible. I closed my eyes and took some deep breath. I knew I needed to be focused and relaxed in order to open my mind to not only read Jade but also to activate the abilities within to block her out of my head as well. What Jade and Dylan had said earlier to me was true, telepaths are always inside their own heads but apparently so are pre-cogs. Between the three of us we did very little talking at times and a lot of thinking and seeing. Truthfully it was a bit comical to see us sitting around the dinner table lost inside ourselves as we mindlessly ate pizza. Being with Jade and Dylan was exactly what I had longed for in friends my whole life, the kind of people you could just be yourself around and not have to worry about awkward silences.

Jade sat next to me in the living room chair. I glanced over at her and she smiled. "Do your worst." I burst into surprised laughter. "I might fry your brain, be careful what you ask for." She laughed with me and Dylan looked honestly concerned and troubled. "That's not funny. If things get out of hand or you don't know what's going on Ember, pull out immediately." Jade smiled at Dylan in a loving and tender way that seemed to make him melt, "I trust her, it will be fine." Dylan gave her an uncertain nod and then sat on the couch to be the observer. He would be able to keep watch and break the connection if anything did go wrong. "Remember Ember, I'm being nice here and letting you use me for this experiment but whatever you see stays between you and me." I nodded and smiled. Earlier in the week she had let me read her on a basic level and I saw how much she loved Dylan, just like I had seen in him before too. I also saw a side of Jade that was vulnerable, lonely, sad and hurt that she never showed. We promised to keep it all between us and somehow our little training sessions were making it possible for us to grow closer, even if we didn't talk about anything. We just knew each other and that was enough.

Jade nodded giving me the go to see what I could do. We were all a bit nervous about this training experiment because going deeper into someone else's mind would be a bit more predictable but going inside a pre-cogs mind was definitely unpredictable. They saw so many variables and the world was constantly spinning around inside their minds that it was impossible to know what lies deep beyond their conscious mind. I was willing to find out but hopefully I was strong enough to navigate through it. I lost myself looking into Jade's eyes and before I knew it I was speeding through her mind. I couldn't grasp onto anything solid and the sensation of vertigo began to fill my head making me want to pass out, as I fell deeper and deeper down the rabbit hole, with no end in sight. It was like Alice falling through the rabbit hole for the first time and she didn't know what awaited her on the other end. I was pushing myself further and further to try and slow myself down so that I could be in control. That was the main point of this exercise after all. I needed to be able to control my ability and not just let things happen around me. I could see faces of people, memories, feelings translated into visions and dark patches that I assumed should be avoided. I finally caught a glimpse of a face I knew and that was Aden's. If I could just focus on him then maybe I could pull myself towards that and slow down long enough to figure out what to do next. Aden's face I knew well enough that I could draw it with my eyes closed. I knew every line, feature, and crease he had and it always made me feel warm on the inside to think of him so this was the perfect way to gain control. Locking my vision onto Aden's face I was able to pull in closer to the vision that he was specifically apart of. The more focused I got the slower everything began to move and I was feeling more and more in control.

Aden was in his bedroom at home on his computer. Exactly where I would expect to find him normally. It was hard to tell what he was doing on the computer but he seemed focused and lost in the moment. I was standing in the room now and I moved towards the end of his bed and just watched him. Why was this moment inside Jade's mind and what was I missing? There had to be something important about it, right? I took a seat on the edge of Aden's bed and suddenly I could feel the bed sheets and the soft, comforting feel of his duvet. As I ran my fingers across the bedding I knew all too well and took in the familiar feel, I felt Aden's hand touch mine. I jumped and looked at him but the moment I did I instantly knew this wasn't a vision.

"Em, is that really you?" "Aden?" He slid the laptop off his lap and onto the bed and moved closer to me. He touched my face and gave me chills with the smooth touch of his skin against mine. "How are you here right now?" I shrugged, "I don't know. You can see me?" "Of course I can." I was so caught up in looking at him and taking in his features that I forgot I could actually talk to him for the first time in months. Here was my moment and I had no idea what I wanted to say. "I miss you." The lamest words I could possibly come up with and yet they were the truth and in all honesty said everything I had been feeling. "I know." I sat up a bit and moved away from his hand feeling very surprised and confused by his response. That wasn't what I was hoping for or expecting. "You know?" "The breakup wasn't easy for either of us and I'm sure it's been very hard for you but I'm happy to see you're doing well." His tone was different then I remember it being when we used to talk. He spoke robotically and there was no feeling or empathy behind anything he said. "Are you okay?" I looked him over and nothing seemed out of place to me but his eyes said everything I needed to know. "I'm great Em. Since we stopped talking I've been doing really well." He smiled and although the words sounded believable his eyes told me a much different story. Was he even aware how much his eyes were betraying him right now? How had his words, motions and behaviors become so robotic and cold? Hate wasn't a feeling I knew well although it had risen up inside of me from time to time over my life with certain individuals but never with Aden, yet I found myself in this moment hating the person he had become. Looking at him and deep into his eyes I could see a man that had given up. Laid down his weapons and given up all fight for the future, for destiny, for even the hope of something more than the bleak existence he currently found himself lost in. Aden had laid down and let go of it all and he was locked behind a wall that no one could break down...not even me.

As a last ditch effort I touched Aden's chest with my hand and laid it right above his heart. It was always the way we communicated when words failed us. It allowed us to make a connection that was impossible to make with anyone else. He closed his eyes and I could feel his body relax and everything inside of him becoming less guarded. Although I had promised to never read him before, times were different now. I closed my eyes and began navigating my way through his mind scape. He didn't push me out which I found to be a pleasant surprise and invitation to find him somewhere inside there. When I finally found him he was once again sitting in a dark corner, knees up to his chest, looking lost, alone, and frightened. This wasn't the man I knew at all and the sight terrified me. I walked slowly towards where he sat and when he didn't freak out I took a seat next to him. I pulled my knees up to my chest and glanced over at him. "Hi Aden." He glanced over at me with eyes that screamed of sadness and loss, "Hi Em." "What are you doing here?" "Hiding. I have no where else to go." "Hiding from what?" He closed his eyes and looked away. I didn't want to push him so I waited. "Everyone." Aden looked at me again and there were tears welling up inside his eyes, "Em, I know what I did was horrible and I can't tell you how awful I feel about breaking your heart." I didn't dare speak and interrupt his thoughts, I just nodded to have him continue. "I had to do it and I was scared and I know I'm a coward and not the man you thought I was or needed. I'm sorry, but I had to do this." "Why did you have to do it?" "My family." Aden looked quickly away as if someone was coming and he jumped to his feet. "You need to go and you need to forget me." "Wait, Aden, no!" I jumped up and went after him but I was violently yanked out of Aden's mind and then Jade's mind.

I found myself on the floor laying down on my back shaking. It felt like I was having a seizure but once I got my bearings again I recognized it as a panic attack. "Dylan, what happened?" Jade asked frantically.

His voice was calm, unlike Jade's and he reached out and wrapped his arms around me and a blanket. "Ember, you have to calm down. Please breathe!" I looked at him and heard him clear as day, but it felt like I was in a dream more than a reality I could hold onto. I realized I was caught between two worlds and I couldn't find my way back to reality anymore. Dylan held my face firmly between his hands and he was saying words I couldn't hear or make out and it felt as though he were trying to use an unknown ability of sorts on me but I couldn't find a foundation to grab hold of to remain where he was. I wanted to go back to where Aden was and yet I knew I had to find my way back to the present and as I tried to focus on calming down and on Jade and Dylan I convulsed and grabbed my head. A pain shot through my skull as if it was literally being ripped in half. I grabbed my head and screamed in pain. The panic inside became worse. I couldn't breathe and I surely couldn't focus on anything but the pain I felt. I couldn't tell if Jade and Dylan were even in the room with me anymore, everything was going black. Even the vision of Aden was fading quickly and the thought quickly passed through my mind that I could be dying. The pain was incredibly intense and as far as I knew this is what death might be like in some cases and the thought of it all going away was sadistically pleasant in that moment but I wasn't one to quit. I felt a cool breeze by the side of my head and I tried to find it and figure out what it was. I suddenly could see Dylan inside my mind as if he were there breaking through every ounce of pain and confusion. "Ember, you have to focus on me and listen to me okay? I can get you through this." I put every minuscule ounce of focus I had left to Dylan and he walked towards me slowly with his hands stretched out to me, as if I were a stray cat about to run away. He touched my head gently and whispered "Sleep." The pain vanished and then everything went black.

********** 3 Days Later **********

The sun was setting slowly and all I could find the strength to do was watch it slowly fall out of view behind the buildings blocking out the horizon. Jade and Dylan were seated at the small table near the kitchen having an early dinner. I knew they were there and I was fully aware of their presence but since the incident a few days ago I hadn't been able to rejoin the real world again. I found myself unable to speak, unable to process anything and more importantly I was terrified of what had happened and whether it would happen again. Jade Googled trauma and I was exhibiting all the symptoms of severe trauma but having a name and diagnosis didn't make it any easier or resolve the issue. "Ember, you sure you aren't hungry?" I heard Dylan invite me over to eat for the fifth time and there was apart of me that wanted to respond and join them and another apart of me that couldn't even find the strength to look at them. My eyes were fixed on the setting sun. There was no logical answer for what had happened when I entered Jade's mind and then met up with Aden. I hadn't even been able to explain to Jade and Dylan what I had experienced. In some ways I wanted to keep the experience to myself because I didn't want them to tell me I was crazy or making it up. I knew for a fact I had been with Aden, even if I didn't understand how it was fully possible.

Dylan cleared off the table and Jade pulled out her cellphone to make a call. She had a funny habit of pacing when she was thinking or talking on the phone and I had to wonder if it was a nervous habit she didn't know she had or the fact that she was always on the move and didn't like to remain still for very long. "Yeah, she won't speak, eat, or move. She's completely comatose and we can't take her to the doctor. What do we do?" Great, they were talking about me and I knew I should care who was on the other end but I didn't. Dylan took a seat on the couch and listened in to the conversation. I assumed neither of them had seen this happening out of all the variables that could have occurred because they both looked truly shocked and caught off guard by the experience. I knew Dylan couldn't see me but he was looking in my direction anyways. He had his usual sunglasses on and he was deep in thought and was looking at me as if he were trying to read me, trying to find a way inside my mind, but from his tight lips and strong jaw I knew he wasn't succeeding. Aden, and more recently Jade, had always told me that I spent far too much time lost inside my own mind. My mind was now a prison that I couldn't seem to escape from and at the same time the safest, most familiar place to be.

Thoughts of Aden trickled in and out of my mind as I tried to make sense of the meeting I had had with him. Sometimes it's better to hold onto someone at arms length rather than attempt to pull them close and potentially lose them. I could tell that was Dylan's plan with Jade and it made me wonder if that was also Aden's plan. Keep me at a safe distance away so that he could protect me. I loved to imagine that his motives were his brave and courageous heart shining through. Was I just fooling myself though into believing that he was somehow the virtuous man I wanted him to be? After all he did leave me on my own without any clear explanation or reason and he hasn't since come looking for me or shown any despair over my disappearance. I always believed it was simply my insecurities that made me question if he was the man I believed him to be, that my insecurities were what made me doubt he could ever truly love me, Now I wondered if, maybe, those weren't insecurities after all but the truth peeking through.

Jade hung up the phone and took a seat next to Dylan on the couch. She was looking at me for a moment before she turned her attention to him. "I have someone we can meet who might be able to help Ember." Jade spoke hesitantly, as if she knew Dylan would oppose.

"Who?" Dylan asked already display disagreement in his tone.

Jade's expression turned from hopeful to hesitant. Dylan returned her look with disappoint and disgust. "I will not work with any of them." "Just give her a chance, she's not like that." Jade pleaded with him.

Dylan turned his head away from Jade and I could see the intense pain that caused her but she remained strong and continued to keep on a brave face. "We have to do whatever we can to get Ember back." Dylan was silent and refused to look at Jade for what felt like eons. For Jade it mostly likely felt like an eternity. "Fine, but I make the call whether we work together or not." Jade nodded and stood up with Dylan. He stopped right in front of me, like a parent who was about to tell their child goodbye and to behave. "You think she'll be alright alone?" Jade slowly slid on her coat and nodded, "I think so. Where would she go?"

Dylan shrugged, "She might wake up and need us. I don't want her to be alone." "We won't be long." They left and the apartment went silent, which I actually appreciated. My mind is always such a noisy place that was consumed by my thoughts and the thoughts of everyone around me. Sometimes I wished I could just turn it off or at least ask people to keep their thoughts to themselves. I've gotten better at blocking them out but sometimes they still found their way in. As I sat there motionless and lost inside a void I couldn't seem to break from I suddenly began to hear a faint whisper of a voice. The voice was difficult to decipher and not one I could easily make out. Being caught in limbo made it harder for me to use my abilities and I was struggling to hone in on this voice that was clearly calling out to me...and by name. "*Ember?*" I could feel my frustration levels rise as I tried to focus for the first time in what felt like forever on this voice. "*Whose there?*" I reached out telepathically and got no reply. Suddenly the voice seemed to disappear as quickly as it had appeared. Then without warning the voice thundered through the silence, "*WAKE UP!*" Everything came rushing back into me at once and I fell hard onto the floor, as reality began to take a forceful hold once again.

CHAPTER EIGHT

The apartment was empty and I knew Jade
and Dylan had left to try and seek help for me, so
they couldn't possibly be the ones calling out to me
this time. It took a moment for my muscles to warm
up and my legs to move underneath me easily. I
walked slowly around the apartment as I allowed
my senses to flood back into my being and
wondered whether or not I should leave and seek
out the voice that woke me up or wait for Jade and
Dylan to return. A blinking light caught my eye that

was coming from behind a door that was cracked open slightly. I moved towards it and pushed the door open slowly and noticed the room was filled with Dylan's monitoring equipment. Dylan had never really let me see what he was working on and I always did feel as though he was hiding something from me. I felt wrong walking in uninvited but things were getting stranger by the moment and I had to know everything before I could plan my next move.

The room had multiple laptops pushed up next to each other and papers covered the top of the table. Lights blinked on a off on small devices and machines I had never seen before. One laptop had a file folder on top of it packed carelessly with papers. The laptop was slightly ajar leaving a faint light that felt as though it was calling me towards it. I moved slowly and cautiously towards the computer because somehow I knew that any move I made Dylan would track. As part of the training exercises Dylan, Jade, and I were working on we discovered that Benders track each others presence for a short time after we've left a place. It was as though we left an invisible trail only other Benders could pick up on. I lightly opened up the folder and saw Aden's name on some of the papers. Now I had to know what Dylan was up to. I flipped carefully through them and saw printouts of Aden's social media pages. Nothing jumped out at me as odd or worthy of investigation but I now knew that Dylan had been tracking both Aden and I for a long time, this wasn't out of the ordinary. I sat down and opened up the laptop all the way and saw one of Aden's social media pages still opened. I scanned it quickly with my eyes and they stopped suddenly on a picture of Aden and another girl. She was beautiful and they looked happy huddled up next to each other. My heart sank as it had the night he left me and I couldn't seem to tear myself away from the photo. I flipped through his photos and saw picture after picture of him and this girl who claimed to love him and seemed taken by him as I once was. I couldn't help but feel even more non-existent, as if I never had really mattered before at all. Was I just some game to him? I began to read through some of their messages to each other and tears welled up in my eyes. Aden told her the same things he had once told me and suddenly this truth, this reality I had lived my life believing was now all lies. He spoke to her of being the most beautiful girl he had ever seen and the love of his life. His comments rang of words that he had waited his whole life to find her and now knew what true love was. In that moment I could feel my heart and soul dying a million deaths and I began to determine that I must be masochistic because I couldn't seem to turn away from the computer. I kept probing further and further through Aden's social life; a life I didn't exist in, let alone, remain as a memory in.

I finally slammed the laptop shut and watched Aden's file fly across the floor. I didn't care if Dylan knew I had been in here or not. I was beyond caring about anything anymore. After all I didn't matter at all anymore did I? No one could see me, no one even came looking for me and Aden quickly replaced me as if I was a worn out pair of socks. Seeing how Dylan behaved made me realize that as much as I wanted to believe that Dylan and Jade, even Sam and Liz, were helping me because they truly cared, I realized now that I was just another pawn in their game to win a war or confirm some prophecy I wanted nothing to do with. I stood up and found myself raging inside with hurt that was now turning to anger. I had to do something and what I wanted to do was self-destruct, because after all why did it matter what I did anymore with my life? The good and righteous way of living, as if I was some heroine was clearly just a grandiose lie designed to win me over to one side or the other. A lie I chose to believe so I could feel comforted in a world that didn't accept me and never really would. A world that I clearly would never truly belong in.

All I could do was run out of Dylan's room, grab my coat and bag and leave. I didn't have a plan exactly except that I was going to go after the voice, after my telepathic guide, and see where it led me. I slammed the front door shut and kept running down to the quiet, dark, damp New York street. You would think in a city this busy, it would be loud and crazy and yet the area was quiet as if I were the only person alive. I took a deep breath of cold, damp air and closed my eyes trying to reach out to the voice. At first I heard nothing but my own angry thoughts zipping through my mind. I shook my head hoping to clear it, like an old etch-a-sketch, and then closed my eyes again channeling on what I remember the voice had sounded like. If I was as powerful as everyone said I was, then I had to be able to track her. *"Where are you?"* The sound echoed in my mind and at first there was no reply and then I heard a faint voice, *"Follow me."* I looked all around me as if I would be able to see who was there, but I couldn't see anyone. I focused again, "Follow you where?" I didn't hear anything but I began to get an image in my mind, which wasn't new but I hadn't expected to see the location so clearly, it was as if I had already been there before. There was a building hidden behind a door on an alleyway. The odd part of what I saw wasn't that I saw it, but that in the midst of seeing it I suddenly knew exactly where it was, which felt impossible given I didn't really know New York all that well. I didn't question it for long, I just took off running to make sure I would get enough distance from the apartment that Dylan and Jade wouldn't be able to track me, at least not easily. Everything about what I was doing they would have disapproved of instantly and right now distance was what I needed to clear my head, hopefully. As I continued running, all I could think about was how I wanted to finally take control of my life and be the one to decide my own destiny.

Suddenly my telepathic abilities became more of a tracking beacon than just simple telepathy and I couldn't help but get the small tingle inside me that maybe I could finally use my abilities for good. Maybe I could hone this skill and track people that were missing or help the police solve crimes. I laughed out loud to myself, "Yeah right." Truth was, or maybe it was my cynicism, I would never be able to do those things because I couldn't exist in this world, not now and not ever. I kept rounding street corners and found myself in a part of town that didn't seem safe, which normally I would be worried about, but not tonight...tonight I wanted danger. Tonight I would leave my old self behind for whatever awaited me and find a new life, a new Ember, and maybe the chance to exist; anywhere. As I let my thoughts and the adrenaline of a new found life take over me I suddenly halted to realize I was right in front of the doorway from my vision. I looked around to make sure I hadn't passed by someone awaiting my arrival, but it was empty. I tried the door and it was locked, but as my hand fell away I heard a piece of metal slide open towards the top. It was intimidating and comical at the same time that whoever was behind this door acted as though they were apart of an old mob movie.

"What do you want?" The voice was scratchy and unfriendly.

"I'm meeting someone here?" The guy behind the small slit looked at me more carefully before he spoke, "Oh, we've been waiting for you. Come in." We??

I entered hesitantly and flinched a little when the metal door slammed shut behind me. "Welcome Ember…We were hoping you would join us." I couldn't see who was talking to me, but his voice was smooth and easy to listen to. He appeared tall and lean from what I could make out of his shadow.

"Join you?" I was more confused then ever and despite being reckless tonight, I wasn't dumb. The man appeared slowly out of the Shadows wearing a black on black three piece tailored suit, dark hair tied behind him in a low pony tail, and designer dress shoes.

"I apologize for the abrupt welcome, my name is Romie, and welcome to the Opposition." He said it with a smile and I knew he meant me no harm but there was something much darker and sinister about this group of Bender's than the ones I had encountered previously. Behind Romie stood two other men who appeared to be keeping his guard and gave the impression they wouldn't hesitate to hurt anyone who challenged him.

"Hi, Romie. I'm honestly not sure what I'm doing here. I've had a really crappy night and I followed a voice that was calling me here, which probably makes me sound insane." Once the words fell out of my mouth, they sounded crazy but before I could dwell on that for too long a woman walked out of the Shadows and waved, "It was me. Hi Ember, I'm Mel."

I waved slightly recognizing the voice instantly. "Why did you call me here?"

She smiled and moved closer to me carefully. I felt like they were treating me like a child that might run at any second, but I was stronger than that and a lot less afraid then they appeared to take me for. "We wanted to talk with you, make you an offer."

"An offer for what?" I asked cautiously looking around at all the people now present in the room.

"We know about you and Aden, and what you discovered tonight about his new life. I know how heartbreaking that can be and I wouldn't wish that on anyone-" I interrupted her, "Wait how do you know any of this?"

"When you were lost inside your mind we were keeping tabs on you and trying to find a way to get you out. Your friends Jade and Dylan sought out my help and I managed to get to you before they could return. I was inside your mind still as you found out about Aden's new girlfriend and I could feel and hear everything." I couldn't help but cross my arms and want to crawl as deep inside of myself as I could go. I felt so violated with my personal thoughts being on blast for the world to hear, but hearing about them again made me remember why I came and that I was interested in solutions.

"So what do you have to offer me?" I asked trying to feel as though I wasn't outnumbered and still in control.

Romie and Mel smiled, "You kept yelling inside your mind that you wanted the feelings to go away, I can make them go away."

My eyes narrowed in on her because the offer was so tempting, but also incredibly unbelievable. "How?"

Romie moved next to Mel, "She's a very powerful empath and she knows how to get inside your heart and take away those feelings that are destroying you and keeping you from your destiny."

"And what do I have to give in return?" I should have been questioning how they seemed to know so much about me and what exactly Dylan and Jade had told them. Except the pain inside my soul was far too great to bear and the simple thought of it going away forever overtook logic tonight.

Romie began walking slowly around the large gathering room and I knew the price for something like this would be huge. "Join us." He said it as if he were casually asking me to dinner.

"Join you how?" Now I was beginning to feel apprehensive as this offer felt far too good to be true.

"Join the Opposition and lead with me." Again, Romie maintained his casual, conversational tone, as if this weren't a massive decision to make.

"W-wait, what?" That didn't make any sense to me. I wasn't a leader and I definitely didn't agree with the Opposition.

"You are more powerful than you know and here you will find a place you belong. Haven't you even wondered for a second how all of us can see you?" I held my hand out in front of me letting that thought enter my mind, "How can you see me?"

He smiled and stopped in front of me, "Because we care about you, and to us, you matter greatly. That is why we want to help you and why we can see you. You just needed someone to believe in you." I had no point of reference, as of yet, as to whether my invisibility really was simply based off of a need to be cared about or whether it was something more than that.

Before I could say anything Mel took my hand in hers and looked me in the eyes and suddenly I fell to the ground as the agony and pain of losing Aden came flooding back in, and the images of him with another girl flooded my mind. I remembered why I had wanted this all to go away and how much I couldn't handle it anymore. Those feelings began to turn back into anger as I let my mind focus on the fact I wasn't worth looking for, I wasn't worth waiting for, and to Aden, I would always be a memory of the bad moments in his life. He acted as though he hated me and he was merely the victim. Despite that he was the one who had committed the crime in the first place. To Aden I was the cause of his grief and heartache, and even though that was all in his mind, I couldn't change that.

"I'll join you. Take it away." I knew that I was speaking out of pure desperation, like a drug addict who needs their next fix, and despair but this kind of pain ran so much deeper than any physical pain ever could. These were the kind of scars that would leave you damaged for life. In that moment I realized that Aden hadn't just broken up with me;

he broke me. Romie smiled what could only be described as a triumphant but sinister smile. As Mel put her hands on my shoulders and led me away I began to have a sinking feeling I might be in over my head.

Mel led me down a long hallway with lights that barely provided much visibility and it was clear we were moving further and further underground. In the back of my mind I knew I should be asking a million and one questions and seriously considering the implications of my decision but the emotional side of me, the empath side that felt out of control couldn't help but want to be set free. I didn't want the pain anymore and I surely didn't see why it would matter if it went away. I mean after all I didn't exist to Aden anymore, so why should I walk around holding onto feelings for someone who felt nothing for me? The more I thought about Aden and what was happening, the more I knew with certainty that I was doing the right thing.

We walked into a room that was anything but inviting. The room was made of cold cement and had one of those fake, temporary office building ceilings that could be changed in an instant. Low wattage lights gave the room a little bit of warmth and a small table with two chairs in the center made it feel somewhat occupied. Mel led me to the table and we sat down. "Cozy." I said sarcastically and she smiled as she adjusted her chair and sat down. "I do apologize for the lack of better appearance in this room. This room is designed to be plain so it won't distract the mind." I nodded in reply as I felt my hands form into tight fists at the thought of someone rustling around my mind. She held her hands out, palms up, on the table and looked into my eyes. "Are you ready?" I stared blankly at her hands for what felt like too long of a pause and I looked into her eyes and placed my hands hesitantly into hers, "Yeah, let's begin." I was well beyond nervous as she looked into my eyes and I allowed her complete access to my heart and mind. She was strong and didn't seem to have any trouble getting into my mind or navigating to the core of the pain.

In an instant the room disappeared and we were standing together on an intricately designed, European style bridge surrounded by fog. I looked through the fog and noticed a silhouette coming towards us. "Aden?" He appeared in front of us looking indifferent and stoic as if he had lost everything inside that made him who he was.

"He can't hear you." Mel said as she looked at me.

"Where are we?" I asked taking a closer look around.

"The in between…the spaces between where you hold him inside your heart and he connects to you from. You have to severe the ties Ember."

"What?" I felt panic sweep over me at the thought of having to cut the ties myself. I wanted a quick fix and something I didn't have to control, but also a choice I didn't have to be responsible for in case I regretted it later. Sure, I was angry now but would I always feel this way? I didn't want to be the one making the final decision. I looked straight ahead at Aden and felt tears form in my eyes. They weren't tears of sadness but rather tears of anger and pain that cut like knives in my soul. It was the kind of pain you knew you'd never truly get over because he wasn't the kind of person you could ever forget. I wanted to yell at him and tell him that I hated him but that wouldn't be true. I wanted to push him and shove him until he came to his senses and would wake up to realize this wasn't right. Looking into his eyes I no longer saw home but an empty void of space that I couldn't recognize anymore. I looked back at Mel and I tried to keep my voice strong and together but when I spoke it was broken and quiet, "How do I do this?" She shrugged with a look of deep pain on her face, "Only you know what will break the ties." I could tell looking at her she was feeling everything I felt and I felt bad that anyone else would share this pain even for a second, but soon it would all be over.

Slowly I approached Aden and he didn't move except to train his eyes on me. He was robotic and less than human and nothing like I remember him being. It's incredible how you can think so highly of a person that it clouds your better judgement in realizing the type of person they really are and then they shatter that reality and you discover they aren't all that wonderful. Looking into Aden's empty eyes I knew suddenly what I had to do and I moved as close to him as I could. His eyes remained trained on mine as I placed my hand over his heart, whispered "Goodbye," and closed my eyes to lean in for a kiss. Before I could find myself lost in the sweetness of the moment, a moment I didn't want to end, I found myself on the ground screaming and writhing in pain. It felt like my very soul was being ripped out of my body and the pain I felt right now was worse than the pain of losing Aden.

Mel ran to my side and held me in her arms, "Shh…it will be over soon." My hands clenched into tight fists as I tried to fight the pain and as the pain slowly started to fade Aden faded with it. He was a ghost now and as he faded into oblivion within my mind and heart I began to feel the pain fade with him. He was the last thing I saw before I blacked out and embraced the darkness.

CHAPTER NINE

It took awhile for my eyes to adjust and to
realize where I was again. A bedside lamp helped to
illuminate the room and give me perspective on
where I might be. I sat up slowly feeling weak and
exhausted and touched the plush bed covers I found
underneath me. The room was cozy and almost

beautiful, minus the cement surrounding it. A large four post dark wooden bed surrounded me with a white sheer draping canopy to hide the cement ceiling above. Two wooden bed side tables on either side of me with a modern crystal lamp placed on top. A small vase of fake flowers added color and softness to the room. The bedding was like sitting on a cloud and engulfed the bed in stark, crisp white sheets. I attempted to stand up and the room began to spin and my legs wobbled underneath me. I was too weak to fully stand on my own and found myself sitting back on the bed against the comforting embrace of the pillows. The bedroom door opened and Romie walked in with confidence and ease. "How are you liking your accommodations?" He asked moving further into the room.

"They're nice. Thank you." I wasn't really in the mood for being social, so I tried to keep the conversation at a minimum.

He smiled as he sunk into a chair across from me, "You're going to love it here." He sound truly excited.

I raised my eyebrows, "You plan on me staying?"

He nodded, "Of course. Where else would you go?" I thought about that for a moment and thoughts of Jade and Dylan ran through my mind but I could feel the indifference towards them and even towards Romie. "Yeah I'll stay for now."

"Wonderful. I'll make sure you have everything you desire." Romie was definitely holding up to his end of the deal.

I smirked, "And what might that be?"

He stood up and walked towards me taking my hands in his, "To see the world burn." I couldn't help but smile and nod, "Maybe." He winked as he gently let go of my hands, "Together we'll take over this city. You'll see. Now get some rest, you're going to need your strength. We'll talk in the morning." Romie elegantly stood up and headed out, leaving me alone. I nodded and crawled back onto the bed and under the covers. For the first time in my life all I could think about was what I wanted, and Romie was right, that was to see the world burn.

There was a soft knock on the door about 15 minutes after Romie left. "Come in." I sat up slightly remaining under the warm embrace of my safe bed. The door slowly opened and revealed a tray of food and drinks, but it wasn't the delicious smell of food that caught my eye. I smiled as he carefully walked in with his head down and taking extra care to act invisible. My empathy may have been gone but somewhere inside I felt a ping of pain remembering what it felt like to actually be invisible.

"What's your name?" I called out as I watched him flinch ever so slightly with his back towards me as he prepared the food on a small table in the corner of the room. "What are you mute or something?" I knew my tone was harsh and abrasive but I wasn't me anymore and I wasn't about to waste time playing games either. He straightened up his black t-shirt as if it were dirty and turned to face me. I was taken aback by his dirty blonde hair that hung just slightly and messily in his eyes and how his blue eyes stood out strongly against the crisp blackness of his shirt.

"I'm Toby." He had an accent that sounded British, and his voice sent chills down my body drawing me in. "I'm Ember." He smirked and turned back to the table retrieving the tray and heading for the door. "Wait." He stopped by the door and looked at me as if he were expecting me to give him some type of command or order. "Can't you stay?" The words slipped out of my mouth before I had a moment to reason why I had said them and I watched him give me a perplexed look as he carefully thought of his response.

"Is there something else I can get you?" I couldn't decipher if his accent was Australian or English yet but his voice was like a calm breeze flowing over me and I didn't want it to stop; not yet anyways. I laughed slightly, "You act like you're my servant or something." He nodded his head slightly and said, "I am at your service."

"Seriously?" I asked appalled and intrigued at the same time. "Yes, anything you require I will get for you." "Is that like your job or something? I didn't know Benders worked as servants." His face was speaking the words he refused to say and I tried to dive into his mind but there was a block. I could tell his situation was complicated but I wasn't going to let go it that easily. "Have a lovely night, Miss Ember." A flash of sadness entered his tone, but left too quickly for me to determine if I had really heard it at all. He left before I could say another word and yet as much as I wanted to keep the conversation going I was more disappointed to see him leave. There was something about Toby that drew me in and I wanted to know more. I wasn't looking for love at this point in my life but a gorgeous companion like Toby wouldn't hurt.

In the passing days I regained my strength and found myself moving about the underground dwelling as if I owned the place. The people I now lived with I came to know as merely my army and in time each of them would serve their purpose but for now I would lay low during the day making occasional public appearances and formulate plans with Romie at night. Romie spent time helping me to refocus my thoughts and to see things more clearly. He helped me to recognize my true position and destiny and that while I had spent years hiding and keeping my abilities at bay I didn't have to be that person anymore.

On most days I kept to myself and remained in my room, but Romie informed me that if I wanted people to follow me they had to feel as though they knew me. I didn't want to befriend any of them but I had to at least make it appear that I was accessible and apart of their world. Today I found myself eating lunch with a group of girls around my age but we had nothing in common.

"Oh my gosh, you are so pretty." I looked up from my plate at Christine, the youngest of the group, and smirked and looked away.

"Seriously Ember, you really gotta own your looks girl." I raised my eyebrows with a sigh to look at Monique, who was next to Christine. Across from Monique was the third girl, Katelyn, and it amazed me how they all dressed alike, talked alike and acted alike. I knew they were expecting a response from me and I didn't really care if they got one or not, but I knew they wouldn't stop talking to me unless I acknowledged them. This reminded me of high school all over again and the mundane conversations that girls had frequently, both publicly and mentally.

"Doesn't it ever bother you not having your own identity?" I asked the question and took a sip of my water.

The girls looked back and forth at one another rather confused, "What do you mean?" Katelyn asked softly.

"Well look at the three of you, all dressed the same, you practically could be triplets." My voice was snarky, tinged with a bit of annoyance and I could see the slight hurt in the girls eyes but they bounced back quicker than a teeny bopper at a One Direction concert.

"Oh my gosh, you're so right. I have the perfect idea. Come on girls." They all jumped up following Monique, who seemed to be the leader for the moment. I went to take another bite of my food but was quickly pulled away from the table by Christine. "Crap." I said under my breath as they dragged me along with them to what appeared to be a hair salon. The salon was built into the side of the cement hallway making it look more like a dive you'd get a tattoo at, rather than a place to receive a top notch beauty treatment.

I stood there with my arms crossed, eyebrows raised, "Why am I here with you?"

"Oh come on, lighten up. We're just getting our hair done." Monique said heading inside.

"Great, have fun." I turned to walk away when suddenly the idea of getting my hair changed up a bit intrigued me. I turned around and walked into the salon as the girls quickly followed behind me.

A bright colored hair dresser approached us and I couldn't keep my eyes off her fire red pixie hair. "What will it be ladies?"

I smiled, "It's time for a change." She returned the smile and escorted me to the back, "I'm Heidi, and I can give you whatever you want Ember." I sat down in the salon chair and leaned back as the cape was placed over me. Looking in the mirror I saw the girl I used to be as I touched my long brown hair and let it flow through my fingers. "I want bright colored highlights in my hair. The color of fire."

Heidi smiled widely and nodded, "Oh that I can do." She left to get the colors and I stared my own reflection down not even recognizing the girl in front of me anymore. The old Ember was gone and she would never be coming back again. I should have been sad at the loss of who I once was but instead I smiled coldly and closed my eyes as Heidi began to part my hair.

I didn't dare look into the mirror while Heidi worked on my hair because I wanted to see only the final product. So I kept my eyes closed and allowed myself to get lost in the heat of the blow dryer and the smell of the bleach that was slowly leaving my hair with every warm breeze that swept over it. "All finished. What do you think?" I opened my eyes and in the mirror before me was the new Ember. Waves of bright red and orange ran like waterfalls through my brown hair. I touched them adoringly and nodded as I looked at Heidi, "Perfect. They are absolutely perfect." She smiled kindly at me and removed the apron, "This is on the house." I winked and smiled back. I knew Romie would hold true to his word that I could have anything I wanted and this was only a small beginning. The girls I had come with began calling out to me but all I could do was roll my eyes and leave them behind in the salon. The truth was I didn't care to make friends and relationships at this point in my life were only going to be a distraction and I couldn't have that.

As I headed back towards my room Toby caught my eye. He was in the corner of the hall with two other guys and he was laughing. It was the kind of laugh that was contagious and made his eyes sparkle. I stood there for a moment just watching him because he was being his true self in that moment, and even though I couldn't read his mind I could see this warm glow emanating from him that drew me in, like a moth to a flame. The person I saw before me was carefree and relaxed and anything but the timid servant demeanor he normally had when he made his visits to me during the day and night. I shook the thoughts about Toby out of my head and walked past him slowly enough to try and overhear what was so funny but also so that I could see if he noticed the new and improved me. From the corner of my eye I saw him quickly glance my way and hold his gaze a little longer than one would normally do if they were just looking and I couldn't help but feel triumphant.

Everyone around here watched me come and go because they were fascinated by the stories that circulated around as to who I was but they now knew me as a co-leader in the war they were planning and they wanted to see what I was capable of. I was used to their looks and admiration in some cases, but with Toby I knew when he looked at me, he truly was interested in just Ember, the girl, nothing more.

A few hours later, as expected, there was a soft knock on my door and Toby entered in carrying a tray with my dinner. I liked the predictability of Toby's daily visits and I always made sure to be there when he stopped by. I sat at the small table in the room and watched him closely as he placed the tray gently on the table and organized the contents for me. "Good evening, Toby." He didn't make eye contact with me, as always, and simply nodded to acknowledge me but left it at that. His lack of, hello, or reply was like a slap in the face. I sighed signalizing that I was highly annoyed, "If your job is to give me what I want then I want you to talk to me." I was a bit thrown off by the arrogant and entitled tone to my voice but Toby didn't even flinch. He simply tightened his jaw and swallowed hard, clearly weighing whether to oblige or not. "Enjoy your evening." His voice was soft and calculated and he left gracefully but quickly. His lack of interest or willingness to abide by what I was requesting upset me greatly.

I shoved aside the meal and stormed out of the room to find Romie. He was mingling with people in the common area and I huffed my way right up to him so he had no choice but to acknowledge me.

He looked up from the chair he was sitting in with a look of amusement that only angered me more. "What has you so upset sweet Ember?" He raised his brows as I centered myself and spoke as calmly as I could.

"I want Toby to talk with me. If he's going to *serve* me then I at least want him to do as I ask." Romie let out a laugh so strong it shook his whole body as the others around him joined in. "Darling, he's not to be spoken to or with for that matter. Why would you ever want to speak with someone so below you?"

I could feel the center of my forehead crease, "Below me?" He nodded and gained his composure again, "Yes, below you. Toby isn't one of us and he's lucky he's here at all."

"Well what is he then?" I was short with my tone as I didn't want to engage in his usual banter and wanted him to get straight to the point.

He shrugged tiring of this conversation, "We're not exactly sure yet. He's either a Static or Lost, either way not worth your time or interest." Romie waved his hand dismissively.

"And he chose to join you?" I asked feeling suddenly defensive. Romie's laugh once again filled up the room. "Oh Ember, sweet, young Ember, there is much for you to learn I see. Of course he didn't choose this, it was chosen for him. He simply is promised our protection in return for his services." Romie explained quickly and simply.

"He's a slave?" I asked now completely outraged.

Romie clicked his tongue against his cheek, "That's such an ugly word, besides slavery was abolished years ago. We prefer to think of it as more of an agreement. We keep them safe and provide what they need and in return they serve us. No harm in that, right?" Romie asked shrugging the whole conversation off. I wasn't sure exactly what was forming inside me but it felt like a storm that was fighting to break through but I didn't know where it was coming from or why it even arose when I didn't feel anything for anyone but myself anymore. I flicked my wrist at Romie, dismissing myself from the conversation, and left as he resumed his conversation unfazed by my response.

I didn't feel in control of myself at the moment, I felt as if something else were taking over and I was trying to fight it but I couldn't seem to make it stop. My feet kept moving in a direction I didn't want to go and I found myself outside an open area full of cots and people. I looked around at the people living there, watching them go about their lives. Their lives here were anything but the ones Benders working for the Opposition lived. We lived a life of luxury and never wanting for anything but they had so little. Their cots were barely holding together, blankets that looked hard as sand paper and no personal space and barely any belongings whatsoever. The area looked more like an emergency evacuation center than a place for people to live. I walked further in looking for Toby and the cavernous space that was filled with echoes of conversation, only seconds before, went completely silent. Knowing what I now know about their situation it makes sense why they either respond in fear or silence because they've been trained to do so. I walked through the room looking at people who refused to make eye contact with me as I searched for Toby. I found myself walking slowly through the large room looking at all the families and children. A pair of twin girls caught my eye that were playing with ragged dolls on the floor next to a cot. Growing up under the watch of the government wasn't easy but even I had had it better than these children.

I heard the sound of a male clearing his throat and I looked up to see a rather displeased Toby in front of me. He looked in my general direction but didn't quite make eye contact, "Ember." He did his customary nod of the head to acknowledge me and I remained silent forcing him to look up at me.

"Can we talk?" I asked quietly, trying to keep the conversation somewhat private. I wasn't sure what I wanted to talk about but the words came out before I could stop them. My mouth had a rather annoying habit of betraying me. He shook his head, no, and I sighed. "Cut the crap Toby, my rules, not theirs." I heard a slight gasp in the room as I said those words but Toby remained unmoved. "As you wish." He followed me out of the room and while everyone's heads remained down as we passed by I could feel their eyes staring at us as we walked away.

I led Toby down multiple hallways to an underground river that I found a few days earlier. It was the only quiet place I could find where no one else ever seemed to go. I took a seat and invited Toby to join me. He was hesitant and his body was tense and rigid, but he did comply. He didn't say a word as we sat there silently both challenging each other to break the silence first. I honestly had no idea why I had sought him out or wanted him there with me so I decided to wing the conversation.

"I know what you are." The words came out of my mouth sounding more like a thin threat than an opening to a friendly conversation. I saw his head quickly turn to face me and I met his glance confirming what I already knew to be true.

"You're not a Static are you?" His mouth clenched closed tightly and his hands balled up into fists. While I still couldn't get past the block on his mind I could read his body language and he was deciding whether to give into my little game and forfeit the rules or remain the slave he was conditioned to be.

He looked back at the river and finally answered quietly, "I'm not much of anything."

"Please save it for someone who cares. I'm not here to feel bad for you, I'm here for answers." I spoke harshly and Toby turned to face me with what I could only interrupt as rage, "Then why the hell am I here with you?"

I sighed to express my irritation, "Because you do something to me and I want to know what ability you have and why you're pretending to be something you're not?"

He laughed with such indignation that it almost felt like a slap to the face. "I'm the one whose pretending? Have you even looked in the mirror lately?"

I was taken aback by his comment and before I could compose my thoughts he continued with his speech clearly not worrying about the risks of talking with me anymore. "We all know your story, everyone has been talking about you. Poor little Ember, who got her heartbroken and was too selfish to accept it and move on like normal people do. Too selfish to see the destruction and pain around her because she was consumed by wanting back a man who clearly never wanted her in the first place. You were sent here to save this world and you turned your back on it and for what? And you know what's the real kicker Ember? Everyone here claims they took your empathy that you somehow are incapable of relating to other's feelings or sensing their feelings anymore but that's a lie isn't it? You still feel and you still feel everything we feel but you're trying so hard to convince yourself of this grandiose lie because you so desperately want it to be true. Do you want the truth? No matter how hard you try to change it a lie will always be a lie." Toby stood up and ran his hands through his dirty golden locks of hair and slammed his fist back down to his side as he turned with his back to me added one last point, "Oh and just so you know not everyone needs an ability to make you feel something." Then he walked away.

I was left alone to watch the water quietly ripple by as I was filled with a self righteous anger I couldn't seem to calm. Maybe Toby was right, all I could think of was myself but then again wasn't that the point of leaving behind feelings for others? Wasn't that why I came here in the first place? I shouldn't care what he or anyone else thinks of me but somehow his words stung deeply and I wanted to run after him and force him to respect me and treat me better but I didn't. I just sat there motionless, searching for a reflection in the water but there was no reflection in this dark hallway. It felt rather symbolic of what my life had become; void and empty. All roads seemed to lead back to simply disappearing from the world. Maybe I would cease to exist again but the real question was if that happened for what reason would I allow it to happen?

*　　*　　*　　*

Weeks had passed since I had lost my empathy and I honestly didn't miss it. There was something wonderful about waking up everyday and not feeling pain or anything for that matter. I was adjusting to living underground with the Opposition and beginning to understand their side of the story more clearly. Romie and I spent a lot of time talking about their vision and plan for the future. He was extremely passionate about his cause and seeing it through. It's amazing how there really are two sides to every story and how each side honestly believes they are doing what is right. Normally, I would have been the one to judge on a moral scale what was right or wrong but the Opposition had me as a dedicated member now because the only thing that ran through my veins was indifference for a world I didn't care about anymore. This world had done nothing for me but bring me heartbreak and pain and why should I care to save them now? Clearly Benders were the higher species and while my parents had forced us to remain hidden those rules no longer needed to apply. My parents lost their lives and for what? As an heir to The Guild I wanted to make sure Benders got the chance to live their lives as they had always been entitled to. Statics fought in wars all the time in the name of freedom and peace so what difference would it make if Benders did the same? Benders had often times been held captive and forced into battle to aide the Statics so why couldn't the rules be reversed? We weren't doing any good for anyone sacrificing our own lives so that Statics could live in what...Peace? They weren't living in peace, they were destroying themselves a little more everyday. The Statics were out for blood and power and it was time they realized they weren't the most powerful thing on this earth. I was tried of living a life on the run and being forced to deny who I truly am. If we were allowed to go public we could use our abilities for good and make the world a better place, or at least that was the overall propaganda the Opposition preached.

Leaving one of many preliminary meetings regarding the upcoming Guild meeting I found Toby hanging outside the conference room. I caught his eye and he gave a slight nod of his head as he walked towards the hallway with the river. "Have a great night." I said as I slowly and casually walked in the same direction as Toby but keeping a safe distance. Making sure I wasn't followed I slipped down the last hall and found Toby standing by the river waiting for me. He turned to look at me with a grim face that made my stomach turn.

"Are you really going forward with this?" His voice was harsh and demanding and his hands were clenched into fists.

"With what?" I was utterly confused by his accusation and his sudden defensive body language.

"The war." His words were short and concise and filled with anger.

I nodded confidently, "Yes, it's what is best for us."

"Us? Meaning you and the other Benders correct?" With every word he spoke his anger rose with it and there was apart of me that still was completely in the dark about why he was as mad as he was.

I nodded. "What's this about Toby? Last time we spoke you weren't afraid to voice your opinions I assume now is no different."

His lips formed a hard straight line and he nodded, "This war is wrong Ember and I don't know what they've told you but they want power and destruction. The people here are only looking out for themselves and what they can gain and I don't believe that's who you are."

I laughed out of pure amusement, "And how do you know so much about who I am or who I'm not? You said you know my story but let's be honest that *story* isn't who I am anymore." Now my words were getting defensive and antagonizing.

His face softened gently as he pulled his hands out from the pockets of his jeans and kept his eyes on mine, "I was kind of hoping it was who you still were."

"Why? That version of me was weak and insufferable." I didn't like people challenging me by thinking they knew who I was meant to be. I thought I had left that behind when I joined the Opposition.

He shrugged, "Well from what I know that version of you was kind, compassionate, loving and brave. You may only see the heartbreak and Aden when you look at that version of yourself but the way you loved him, the way you fought for your love is far greater than just a sad story. Men would kill for that kind of love."

"Please enlighten me and tell me what makes it so wonderful?" I was speaking in such a deeply sarcastic tone at this point that I wasn't sure if I would even pay a thought to anything he had to say from here on out. Toby had no right to judge me or act as if he knew me. Our brief encounters didn't make us friends and if he was basing everything he knew about me off rumors then he would find himself surely disappointed by the truth.

He slowly moved closer to me and I could feel a warmth emanating from him that held me captive and made me never want to leave his side. "The world needs that version of you now. We need you to fight for us, we need you to love us enough to not give up on us." He was so close to me now that I could feel his warm breath on my skin as he spoke and when he took my hands into his I felt a pulse of electricity surge between us.

"What are you?" I asked quietly ignoring his previous statement.

He smirked softly, "I'm Lost."

The words came involuntarily and softly as I replied, "Aren't we all?"

Something about him made me lose my defenses and it was a feeling I hadn't felt since I was last with Aden. I was so free and confused when I was around Toby and I couldn't understand why. I suppose that was the great caveat of Benders…you never really knew when it was just a side effect of their abilities you were experiencing or something real. Toby continued to hold my hands and his eyes continued to hold my gaze as I waited for him to make the next move.

"Sometimes Ember, we have to look beyond ourselves and beyond our brokenness to discover the true destiny that we were meant for. Your life up until this point was no mistake and the convictions you've held as wrong and as misled as they feel were anything but. I know how terrifying it can be to hold onto a belief that seems ludicrous because everything around you says it's wrong and just a dream. But this Ember, this, right here, right now is real. Every choice you've made has led you to this point, are you really going to let it just end like this?" He continued to hold my hands tightly in his and his eyes remained locked on mine holding my gaze tightly.

"What do you want from me? All I am is a supposed weapon, a ticking time bomb, nothing good can come from me. And what makes everyone think I am some type of hero or savior to the world? I'm just one person and there isn't anything different about me that entitles me or destines me for this role. I find it really hard to believe that everyone wants me to lead some revolution when I can't even sort myself out." The words escaped my lips as a soft whisper, so soft I wasn't sure he even heard me.

Toby sighed quietly and touched my cheek with his fingers so softly it sent involuntary chills down my body. I leaned in to his hand desperate to feel something more than just chills.

"What do you feel?" He whispered the words to me as he moved his face closer to mine, again keeping his eyes locked on mine.

"Numb." I closed my eyes to break his gaze from mine as the words left my mouth in a sad, quiet whisper. I opened my eyes and looked away from him but allowed him to keep holding my hands and face. "I feel nothing. I thought when they took my empathy it would make me stop feeling for others, mainly Aden. Except when they did that its like I stopped feeling everything. I've sat in my room at night forcing myself to try and cry because that's all I want to do and not one single tear will fall. I beat tirelessly at the punching bag in the training area until my knuckles bleed longing to feel anything, even if it is just physical pain. And here I am, with you, and all I want is to feel what I know you could make me feel and I feel nothing." I could feel my heart racing and the feeling behind my eyes that told me I should be sobbing but again the tears wouldn't come. My body may still respond physically but my heart and soul were lost. Despite the numbness there was apart of me that longed to get close to Toby. It was unfathomable that I could feel this way about anyone other than Aden, but yet it was happening and I wanted it to happen. I barely knew Toby, but I couldn't deny, there was an intense pull between us. The kind of pull that you read about in great love stories where two people are meant to be. All my life I had believed we were destined for just one person, but now I wasn't so sure. Or could it be that I had gotten it all wrong and Aden wasn't actually the one I was meant for?

Could I be looking into the eyes of the one my heart had called out to my whole life?

I closed my eyes again because I was hoping maybe tears would find their way to my eyes but before I could try and force the moisture to come I felt warmth on my lips. My lips parted as Toby's crushed into mine. He pulled back for a second and I opened my eyes to see we weren't in the tunnel anymore, we were now standing in the middle of a gorgeous, ancient, green, garden that belonged to a castle. It was the kind of castle I imagined being in Scotland and before I could ask him how we got there, he pulled me tightly against himself and kissed me again. I gasped as I took in the warmth of his body and the way it collided with mine. And then it happened, small tears found their way to my eyes. They didn't come because I was sad or upset, they came because for the first time in a long time I felt something…peace.

Toby pulled away and suddenly we were snapped back to reality, but he still kept his hands around my waist. He was just about to speak when the moment was shattered by someone shouting his name. "I have to go." He held my hands for a moment longer before reluctantly turning and running back down the hall, "I'm coming." Toby lingered briefly at the end of the hall and I knew he didn't want this moment to end as much as I didn't want it to end. The reality we both faced was that living here neither one of us could stay in a moment like this forever. I may not have been able to feel much for anyone else but in my own selfish heart I felt disappoint watching him leave. But as much as I wanted to demand him to stay, I knew I had to let him go.

CHAPTER TEN

I woke up to one of Romie's assistants, Mikey, barging into my room informing me that an unexpected meeting of The Guild was to be held immediately and my attendance was not voluntary. After agreeing to get dressed and attend he left to awaken whomever was next on his list. As I moved towards my closet I noticed a note on the table I usually ate at. I picked it up and unfolded it carefully noticing a short handwritten note inside.

Ember,
What you are is love and love is the strongest weapon of all.

-Toby

I couldn't help but smile at his short note because something about it reached the depths of my heart in a way I didn't think was possible anymore. Toby was climbing inside the deepest part of my soul and that had me excited and confused all at the same time. In my confusion on what all of it meant or didn't mean with Toby, I did know one thing for sure, I wanted to keep getting closer to him. I folded the note up and placed it inside the bedside table drawer where no one else could find it. As I finished getting dressed and headed towards the common area to leave with everyone else, I couldn't help but wonder what Toby's motives really were? It didn't make sense for him to trust me so blindly and it surely didn't make sense for him to believe in me when he knew nothing about me. There had to be something bigger at stake to risk it all for the possibility of love.

Walking outside into the crisp, cool air helped to clear my head that was filled with thoughts of Toby and allowed me a moment to see it was just before sunrise. The dark sky was showing signs of light fighting its way to break through and hadn't yet been allowed to change into a bright array of colors officially ushering in a new day. The Guild had apparently demanded a cease fire as the current arising issue at hand effected all Benders causing us to all convene for a meeting to discuss the issue further. I waited outside for the rest of The Guild members to join me and was surprised to see Romie joining us this time. Usually he let others represent the Opposition in these meetings as he felt they were irrelevant. "Joining us today are you?" I asked as he stood next to me awaiting Mikey to get the car. He smirked at me, "Unfortunately, I was not given much of a choice this time." Other members chatted quietly as we awaited transport to arrive and no one seemed to have a clue as to why we were all being suddenly summoned to this meeting. Not being familiar with how The Guild worked exactly I was fascinated to attend for the first, official, time and learn more.

Once transport arrived for us we immediately rushed down to the meeting that was being held about ten blocks away. When we arrived to the all too familiar dark hallway and then open arena filled with Benders, it was buzzing with activity despite the early wake up call. As I walked in side by side with Romie and the rest of the Opposition leaders I caught eyes with Sam and Liz. Their mouths gaped at the sight of me; the physical sight of me, and I assumed the fact I was with the Opposition as well. Romie placed his hand gently in the small of my back and led me towards the long table in the center of the room. As I took my seat next to Romie I found myself reliving the last and only time I had been in this place and discovered that to everyone in this room I was merely a pawn in their game called war and left before I could be taken advantage of. While I was well aware that the

Opposition still wanted to use my abilities to meet their own needs they at least had the honor and respect to be open about it and not try to hide it from me. I respected them for their honesty and wasn't upset that they wanted to use me because I made the choice, on my own, to allow it to happen. Sam and Liz were trying to bait me and trick me into letting the Resistance use me and that I wasn't okay with. I made my best attempt to not make eye contact with Sam or Liz, but when I did they wore masks of betrayal and hurt on their faces and I couldn't help but wonder if Dylan and Jade would look the same if I were to see them. My thoughts were interrupted as Drake, the moderator, joined us at the head of the table.

The meeting was quickly called to order and despite the sheer volume of people packed into the damp, dark warehouse like space it was silent. "Welcome and thank you for joining us here this morning. An issue has been brought to the attention of The Guild after some time of conducting surveillance and investigation." The moderator spoke slowly as if he were choosing his words and tone carefully. "We have reason to now believe that the Static government are the ones behind the missing Benders. They've been capturing our people to use them against us." The room erupted into hushed whispers and voices of outrage. Despite being exhausted from waking up so early I could tell the information we truly needed was either being withheld or just not shared at this moment so while the room sorted through their shock I reached into the moderator's mind to see what he knew. As I ventured deep inside, thankful he hadn't thought to set up a block, I discovered a visual of a location I sadly knew all too well. I sorted through countless documents and surveillance photos of the base in Washington where I grew up. The minute I saw the name James Addison float across numerous pieces of paper I had all I needed and I pulled out of the moderator's mind. I hadn't planned on speaking during this meeting but I couldn't help it, I had to speak up.

As the words began to escape me it caused everyone to immediately fall silent, "And what are we going to do about it?"

"And who exactly are you?" Drake spoke in a rather flustered tone.

I stood up staring Drake, in the face, "Ember, daughter of Arya and Ash, Guild Legacy." The room hushed and Sam and Liz exchanged looks between each other that didn't hide their fear of what I had become.

The moderator broke the silence, "Welcome Ember. It's an honor to have you here. We've waited a long time for the legacies to join us." I nodded as I sat down and leaned back in my chair.

I didn't hold the same sort of pomp and circumstance as everyone else for this show they seemed so dead set on maintaining. "The man you're looking for James Addison, yeah well, he's a horrid man and I am in full support of whatever you'd like to do to him." The moderator looked stunned that I had grabbed that information before he could reveal it and the rest of The Guild looked confused. "Don't be so shocked that I read your mind and jumped the gun. When our people are missing we don't have time to waste with formalities. Not to mention I know James Addison personally so I'm kind of your best asset right now."

I glanced over at Romie who wore a smirk that screamed of his proud feelings towards having me on his team as the rest of The Guild just sat there unsure what to say or do. Ryan began to stand up to object but the moderator held out a hand to silence any further comments and looked at me as if I were the only person in the room.

"You are very much like your parents." I waited a moment to see if that was all he would say or if there was more to his comment and the rest of the room was obviously waiting as well because it was quiet enough that I swore I heard someone's stomach grumble. "We know of your relations with Mr. Addison, Ember, and we would like to speak with you more about that at a later, more appropriate time. Right now we must remain calm and work together." The moderator was careful to maintain his calm and poise when he spoke and I couldn't tell if what he said was actually just for me or everyone? The truth of the matter was we were divided. We now had to ask ourselves if we were going to join together, once again, as we once had when my parents were alive, to save our people, or if we would continue to put our own personal opinions first out of pure selfish ambition?

"So tell us what exactly are they doing with the other Benders?" Rilo said with haste and irritation. The room once again came alive with noise and voices shouting out in concern. The moderator again held out his hand and the room was silenced. Maybe it was my past that caused me to be so weary of people with that much power and authority but after this meeting was over I definitely wanted to investigate a bit more about who this moderator was and why everyone respected him so much.

"From the intel we have gained, the government has been capturing Benders for years, which we have been aware of for quite some time. We've always been hunted and misunderstood but the new information we have discovered is that they've been finding ways to test us and modify what we can do to use it against us and in hopes of aiding the Statics." I laughed quietly at them because that couldn't be more true. I was one of their "experiments" and I knew all about the testing they were attempting to do. Then again, that was quite a few years ago and since then they could have come up with even more ways to push our kind to the breaking point and I was never fully privy to exactly what they wanted from us. All I knew was they planned to weaponize us and try to become us.

Sam raised his hand from across the table and was granted permission to speak, "We've always known that the government has been trying to study us but I think we'd all like to know what makes now any different than before? Why has it become such a critical matter?" Everyone around the table nodded in agreement and looked to Drake for answers.

"Through our surveillance teams it has been discovered that what the media has deemed worldwide natural disaster is actually the work of Benders. There is nothing natural about it." The room fell silent again as everyone sat motionless. I had to admit it made perfect sense and I wasn't sure why I hadn't connected the dots sooner. The Shadows that hunted me were somehow connected to the missing Benders and the destruction they left in their wake could only be explained as a natural disaster because to the unassuming Static world that was all they knew it to be. No one spoke as everyone took a moment to let the information settle in and I took the silence as an opportunity to question this information further, "So the missing Benders are the Shadows then, right?" All eyes were turned on me as if I had just spoke gibberish. Drake looked at me as he exhaled slowly, clearly not appreciating my lack of respect for his position, "Do you care to elaborate on that, Ember?" He raised his eyebrows as he spoke like a teacher who doesn't appreciate when the students deviate from the plan.

I stood up and looked around the room, "Some of you may or may not know my story that brought me here. For quite awhile I was physically invisible and not a soul could see me. There didn't appear to be a logical explanation for this occurrence and I've still yet to completely figure it out. When you cease to exist from the living I suppose it throws you into a heightened state of awareness. What ultimately set me running were Shadows that began hunting me. Have you ever found yourself consumed by a grief that you can't explain? Found yourself suddenly thinking dark and depressing thoughts when you have no reason to? That's how they get us. Commander Addison had found me and shown up to my apartment, accompanied by the Shadows. I don't know what else to call them other than Shadows because that's all they appear to be and they creep up on you out of nowhere. The found me when I used my abilities." I shuddered thinking about the encounters I had with them in the past and my eagerness to destroy them.

"Up until now I hadn't put two and two together, but I believe the Shadows are somehow the missing Benders that Commander Addison is using to seek the rest of us out with. I encountered them awhile back when I first met Sam and Liz. You can ask themselves, they couldn't see them when they attacked us but the destruction they caused was definitely visible." I managed to finish my speech about what I knew and hoped it was enough to infuriate The Guild into taking down Commander Addison once and for all.

Drake and the rest of the Benders looked at Sam and Liz, "Is that true?" Drake asked suspiciously.

Sam nodded with Liz, "Yes, it's true. Ember sensed them before they arrived and once they did the ground began to shake as if we were experiencing an earthquake." Drake scribbled down a few notes and then turned back to me.

"Ember, you believe the reason you can see them is due to you previously being invisible?" I nodded in response to Drake.

"Yes. It was the first I had ever seen of them. I'm confident that they've followed me here. Commander Addison was never pleased with my disappearance from his care, and he's been on a personal quest ever since to bring me back. I'm not saying these Shadows are only after me, but they've definitely been seeking me out with a vengeance. They are powerful and they will not stop until they get what they want." Murmurs were heard around the table as everyone looked to one another for understanding and answers.

Drake held out his hand and once again the room went silent, "This has been an ongoing issues for years. We've known that Benders are taken and go missing frequently which caused us to begin our surveillance in the first place. Now the threat is growing and effecting not only us but Statics and Lost alike. We are divided in our beliefs as Benders, but I hold true that we can all still agree we exist to protect this world and our people. The natural disasters, as they've been deemed, put all of us at physical risk but also risk of exposure in a negative light. If Statics discover in any way that Benders are behind these horrendous events we will have no hope of ever entertaining the thought of living publicly or remaining hidden again. These are our people and we must handle the situation accordingly. We will meet again in five days to discuss options to end this once and for all. You are dismissed."

Everyone stood up to leave and Romie once again placed his hand on my back keeping me with the group. As we left I found myself deep in thought over what had been discussed at the meeting and also the reality that I was no longer unaligned in the eyes of The Guild. My appearance with the Opposition aligned me officially and I hoped it was the right side to be on.

CHAPTER ELEVEN

Since returning from the most recent Guild meeting, leaders of the Opposition had been busy trying to think of resolutions for the current problem that would also tie into their original desire for full exposure of all Benders. The conversations were endless and exhausting. The amount of time the Opposition spent trying to mastermind this grand plan was relentless and during most of the meetings I found myself lost in my own thoughts on the issues. There wasn't long until The Guild was due to meet again and time was running out for the

Opposition. They needed to be prepared to present their case to The Guild in such a manner that even the Resistance would approve without being aware of the full terms and conditions. Romie asked me to be present for the next Guild meeting and I agreed. After all I was a rightful heir, wasn't I? We were in a defense meeting organizing our strategy and plans for the upcoming meeting when the halls outside were suddenly filled with yelling and the sounds of feet running through the halls. The room became instantly silent as everyone froze, but Romie and I jumped to our feet ready for action. During my stay with the Opposition I had become less of a girlie girl and more of a solider ready for combat. "Stay Em, I'll look into this." "No, I'm going with you." He sighed and nodded, "Fine, let's go." We moved carefully out into the hallway and Romie grabbed a guy that was running by and pushed him against the wall. "What's going on?" The guy was breathless and in attack mode, "Legacies just forcefully entered the compound." "What?" Romie's eyes lit with a fiery rage and seemed to mimic the same fears as the rest of the Opposition, that the Legacies were here to attack them. I ran my hand through my hair as a force of habit when I was annoyed or frustrated. "Oh calm down, I'll handle them. Have them meet them in my room." Romie, and the guy he held against the wall, both looked at me as if I were crazy, but I just ignored them.

Despite the chaos that was running past me I casually walked to my room knowing it would be Dylan and Jade that had found their way to me. There wasn't anything more I could say to them or offer them now. They like everyone else were just people I used to know and while they had served their purpose they were no longer needed in my life and I couldn't imagine what they'd think of me now because I surely wasn't who I used to be.

I was sitting on the love seat in my room awaiting their arrival. The door to my room opened and Jade and Dylan were escorted in like prisoners. They weren't very cooperative prisoners either. "The less you struggle the easier they'll be on you." I said watching them as they were pushed into the room and the door shut loudly behind them.

"Ember!" Jade ran to me arms wide open and I held out my hand to stop her. I didn't want to give her false hope that things could be as they once were.

"That's not necessary. Please be seated." I motioned for them to take a seat in the two chairs that were positioned in front of me. Dylan walked over tight lipped and looking angry, arms crossed over his chest. Jade looked crushed but took a seat as instructed and remained silent.

"What brings you both here today?" I asked kicking my feet up on the coffee table in front of me. "Surely it wasn't to see my new hair." I said with a snarky laugh.

"Damn it Ember." Dylan finally spoke and slammed his fist down onto the chair arm. "What?" I asked defiantly.

"You got your wish didn't you? You let them take your empathy." I could hear the disapproval and disdain in his voice. I remembered the conversations we had had where he begged me not to change who I was. Yet it wasn't his decision to make. He wasn't the one who had to live this nightmare over and over again.

"Yes, I did and I'm better off for it." I said with deep resolve in my voice.

"Are you? Are you really? From where I'm sitting you seem to be a cold hearted bitch." Dylan's words lashed out like a cobra looking to kill, but I remained unmoved.

"DYLAN!" Jade yelled at him but he just stood up and angrily paced the room, but I wasn't phased by his response. "It's fine Jade. He can say what he wants, it doesn't bother me."

Dylan walked over to me getting in my face, "See…see that is exactly what I'm talking about. Don't you feel anything? Isn't there any part of you that evokes any type of emotion?"

"Of course I feel things. Just not the things you want me to." Dylan flinched slightly at that comment and I knew I had hit a nerve, but I kept my eyes locked on his. Sure Dylan and I had had a connection before, but ultimately it was just a distraction from the love he denied in his heart for Jade. Jade touched Dylan's hand gently and pulled him back to the chair where he sat down with so much frustration and pain that I wondered if he'd break the chair.

Jade was silent for a moment as she gathered her thoughts and steadied herself enough to speak. "We came Em, because Aden is in trouble. Aden and his family were captured by Commander Addison and we need you to help us get him back. I know he's probably the last person on this earth you want to think about right now but you know as well as I do you are the only one who can save him. We can't go in there without you."

I scoffed at her proposition, "Why would I save him? He's done nothing but hurt me. He destroyed me."

"No, you destroyed yourself." Dylan said angrily and Jade quickly placed a hand in front of him stopping him from continuing.

"I know he did and he doesn't deserve your help or anyone's help for that matter but you remember what they did to you and your parents in there, do you want that life for anyone else?" She made a solid point and no, I didn't want that kind of life for anyone else but saving Aden was such a small issue compared to the war we were about to enter and the issue of the missing Benders, it didn't really seem worth the energy.

"Look, I just can't help you right now. I'm busy trying to save all of us and sometimes you have to look at the greater good. Aden has made his choices, just like we all have, and we all have to face the consequences of those choices." Dylan was just about to say something when there was a soft knock at the door that immediately grabbed everyone's attention. "Come in." I knew Toby was on the other side of the door and even though the situation was tense currently I couldn't wait to see him. He was like a burning sun illuminating my days that felt as dark as night. Toby walked in hesitantly, obviously sensing the tension in the room and set down a tray filled with cups of tea and small pastries. "Thank you, Toby." He looked at me and smiled softly as he exited the room. I watched him leave and for a moment forgot that Jade and Dylan were in the room until Jade broke the silence,

"What about Aden, Em?" I shook my head chasing away the thoughts that Toby's presence always brought with them and looked at her, "What about him?"

Jade shrugged showing a bit of frustration, "I thought this whole quest of yours was about reuniting with Aden but when that guy walked in the room I caught a glimpse of a very different possible future. I've never seen that possible future before." I couldn't help but smile slightly as I let my mind drift to the thought of a future without Aden and with Toby instead. "Well the quest began that way but I don't want Aden anymore and he doesn't want me. Sometimes you have to learn to accept what is and stop chasing fantasies." I looked at Dylan and Jade, and while I still held true to my promise to never invade their thoughts I could predict the question that they both wanted to ask but were holding back, "And for the record there is nothing going on between Toby and I."

Dylan scoffed sarcastically, "But you'd like there to be something." I shrugged, "It's complicated." I said letting his gaze follow my eyes to Jade and then back to him, "as you know."

Although his mind was off limits to me, I could read the rage on Dylan's face and through his body language and it appeared to be swallowing him whole. Before another word could be spoken he stood up and moved with a speed I hadn't experienced before and left the room slamming the door behind him, but Jade remained behind. I really had nothing more to say to either of them at this point, because as we all knew, my mind was made up. I knew that Jade and Dylan meant well and that their intentions came from the deepest places in their hearts but it wasn't enough for me. I couldn't honestly say that I was happy where I was with the Opposition, but then again happiness is a fleeting feeling and that wasn't something I had to worry about anymore. I was indifferent to everything and everyone...well almost everyone. Thoughts of Toby floated through my mind for a brief second sending goosebumps over my skin. As quick as the thoughts came they left as I noticed Jade was still before me wanting more out of this conversation then she was getting.

Jade's expression was pained and carried traces of anger and frustration that didn't seem completely directed at me. "I know you think I made the wrong decision in giving up my feelings, but I didn't. Don't tell me you haven't considered it yourself?"

Jade was almost motionless as if she were paralyzed by an unseen force. "We've never really had much time to talk before, Ember. There is very little you actually know about me. I know it may seem as though you know me well and for all intents and purposes you do. Yet you have no idea the internal battle I have fought through and what it has done to me on the inside. If you will listen I will share my story, because you're right, we're not all that different. The Legacies are so interconnected that sometimes it scares me how much alike we all are." I adjusted myself in my chair and nodded. I wanted to hear her story. There was a presence in how she spoke that let me know hearing her story was important, at least to her. After all Jade and Dylan had done for me the least I could do was listen to her story for a little while and indulge her. My emotions may be gone but I still had great instincts and the ability to read people didn't stop at just minds, I was good with body language too, and I knew this was a story worth listening to. "Please, tell me."

There was a moment of silence as if Jade couldn't decide where to start or how to even form the words she was looking for. She fidgeted nervously and uncomfortably in her chair and looked around the room as if the answers were magically written on the walls somewhere. "I'm in love with Dylan." I smiled and laughed softly, "I know."

"No you don't. I love him in a way that is painful. A way that requires me to question my sanity every single day." I was intrigued by her comments because although the feeling was now a faint, distant memory, I had known that feeling once as well. I used to feel the same way about Aden.

"When Dylan and I met we were still fairly young and it changed me and my life forever. There was a time we were inseparable. We spent every moment together and sometimes it was just to talk about nothing or to watch the clouds float by in the sky. Other times we'd be engaged in deep conversations about our lives, our hopes, dreams and the future. I could feel the instant attraction.

The way he made me feel scared me to be honest with you. I had never felt anything this strong before in my entire life and every part of it freaked me out because I was falling fast for him and while I believed he was also feeling the same way, I had no way of knowing for sure. My dreams and visions matched up to everything that was happening and the more time I spent thinking about Dylan or spent with him the deeper the connection became. It began to feel like two halves being sewn together and I couldn't imagine how it would feel if suddenly we were ripped apart." Jade stopped for a moment and I could see the fear rising up in her eyes as she began to relive these painful memories. She gained control and composure and continued with her story.

"My fear of what could happen pulled me away from him. I wanted to love him and him to love me and I wanted everything I had dreamed of and seen to be true. Yet how can you hold onto something like that when it seems too good to be true? After all, aren't dreams just dreams? The moments we spend imagining the futures we want? That's what I began to tell myself. I began to doubt everything I was and everything I knew to be true. I was a girl who lived by blind faith, even though I could see everything before it happened. Normally faith is believing in an outcome you have no logical reason to believe will occur but my visions always change and while I can see possibilities I have no idea which will actually happen. The future is just as unclear for me as it is for you and I have to trust that I will follow the right path and make the right decisions. There was something about Dylan and the way I felt for him that made me question everything about myself. I knew allowing myself to fall for him would be the biggest leap of faith I had ever taken because for the first time in my life I wasn't control of my future, he would be. Ember, I fell so hard for him and my world spun off its axis and knowing how painful it would be if he rejected me, I bailed out before he could."

I held up my hand slightly to interrupt her story. "What do you mean you bailed out before he could?" Jade took a sip of water and looked at me with eyes that screamed of a lost, broken and scared little girl. It was as if I could see her emotions from this time and relive it with her. Or was I just seeing my former self reflected in her eyes? "Dylan never said he loved me and I never told him either. It was just a feeling we shared that made me believe he did. I really believed he did love me, even without proof, but my own doubts and fears got the best of me and I left. I distanced myself from him and looking back I think it really hurt him. He's never been the same since then." Her words got softer towards the end and she looked down at her fists which were now balled up together tightly. I could tell she blamed herself for what had happened to Dylan.

She cleared her throat and exhaled slowly before starting up again, "He moved in with Sam and Liz and locked himself up in his bedroom with his gadgets. It wasn't until you came along that he actually came out of there and began to live again. Dylan just shut down and the person he had been suddenly didn't exist anymore. I felt guilty because I've always believed that I did it to him. I've lived this whole time wondering if maybe he really did love me like I loved him and when I pulled away if that ripped out his heart like I was afraid he'd do to mine? I tried to lie to myself and tell myself I didn't love him and that I didn't really see the future with him that I had seen. I had seen us having children, a daughter and later a son. I saw us being happy together and sharing in a love that would be more powerful than any love this world had ever known between humans. There are not enough lies in this world that could make me forget the truth of what I felt and had seen. More importantly there wasn't anything that earth shattering that could make me forget what I knew deep in my heart to be true. Friends told me I was crazy and that this was just some fantastic story I had made up for myself. Very few people ever believed me and I learned to keep it to myself. Dylan and I would occasionally run into each other and when we did he was polite but distant. Every time he was like that towards me it broke my heart all over again. Seeing him again and being around him always reminded me of why I fell in love with him and reminded me of what was meant to be between us, but now never would be."

Jade's story truly did remind me of how I used to feel for Aden and the dreams and convictions I held deep inside for our future together. Listening to her story was like going through an out of body experience. I was taken back to those memories and occasionally would feel a ping of pain from what had been, but for the most part I couldn't relate anymore and was able to only just listen.

"So if you know all this to be true and feel the way you do, why not confront him? Why not be with him?" I couldn't seem to understand how she could simply just pretend her feelings didn't matter.

Jade smiled in a way that made me realize she had her reasons and she was still fighting the truth. "I don't know that he really loves me or ever did. We're from two different classes, Lost and Bender and I think sometimes he doesn't feel I'm worth the risk. Being together is a risk because of who we are and where we come from, but to me, he's always been worth that risk. The problem I have is that everything I've seen and felt in the past, does not match up to reality as it is now. Dylan shows absolutely no sign of loving me in any way other than a brother loves a sister. It's like the 3 of us are one big family and that's all we'll ever be."

"How do you know Dylan feels that way if you haven't asked him?" It was difficult for me because I knew exactly how Dylan felt about Jade because I had seen it when I read him. I saw how he looked at her when she wasn't looking and I could feel the pain inside he felt being close to her and not being able to truly be with her. I promised Dylan I wouldn't say anything about what I saw or what I knew and I was beginning to question whether that was a promise worth breaking or not?

Jade touched my hand and looked me in the eyes. "Do you think I'm crazy?"

I laughed at her ridiculous statement, "Of course not. How could I? We live parallel lives Jade. Everything you feel I felt before with Aden and I've questioned my sanity many times since he left me. Hell, I physically disappeared when he left me how could I not question my own sanity? I have spent months feeling as though I am losing my mind and going insane. How do you love someone who doesn't even begin to love you? How is it possible to believe you are meant to be with someone that can throw you away as if you never even mattered? Why risk your heart and soul to fight for them when they were never willing to fight for you? Logic tells me I'm crazy and doing everything wrong. That I should have gotten over him and left him behind like a bad nightmare. The thing is he won't go away and he's a ghost that has haunted my soul everyday since I met him. I've been stuck in this terrible intersection between faith and humanity. Do I trust what I know in my heart and soul but can't see or do I look at the facts and what is right in front of my eyes and trust that? My humanity tells me I am wrong and that I'm crazy." I laughed at how crazy I felt whenever I thought of how determined I was to fight for the love Aden and I shared.

"This whole world I've found myself in with The Guild, the Legacies, my parents, your parents, the whole thing is so far fetched that I wonder how any sane person could believe any of it. Yet here I am believing it enough to lead people into a war. What does that make me? Crazy or bold and brave enough to embrace a future that has not yet come to pass because I know it's worth it? I gave up my ability to feel because it was making me lose my mind. I have never loved anyone like I loved Aden. I loved him so much it hurt because it felt impossible to ever show him how much I truly loved him and impossible to ever love him enough." For a brief moment I could remember how defeating it felt to love with all your heart and soul only to feel as though it would never truly be enough.

"The hardest part of all of this wasn't just losing him in the unjust way that I did but it was continuing to believe we were meant to be when everything around me said it was over. Jade, love is the most powerful weapon in the world. I saw what it did for Aden and even myself. I saw the fire come alive inside him the deeper our love grew, but as with anything that powerful, people will always try to stop it and take it away because they can't stand the possibility of someone being more powerful then they are. We can spend the rest of our lives questioning ourselves and our mental stability but I don't think we need to."

Jade's eyebrows arched up and I could tell she was curious to my logic at the moment. "Why not?"

"Because we know the love was real for us. We can't speak for Aden and Dylan but for us it was real and that made us strong. I think we were meant to love the way we did because it was what the world needed. It was apart of who were meant to be. We were meant to show the world what true love really is; it's a sacrifice of self for those who need it most. It's standing up and fighting when it isn't your fight but you do it because you will take the bullet for the one it's really meant for. It's being the person for others that you've always needed. It's knowing deep inside that there is no greater ability on earth than to love with abandoned hearts and to love recklessly in that you do not fear what you can't control because when you look at the one you love you are willing to give it all up for them if you have to. We are strong because we were willing to fall with no guarantee or promise of a safety net to catch us. We were bold, brave and courageous to fall before we ever jumped. Our love doesn't make us weak or crazy, it's quite the opposite. It makes us world changers and it makes us powerful and those who have tried to tell us we are crazy and wrong are the ones who see the power this kind of love yields and are willing to stand in our way and do anything to stop us."

Jade sat back in her chair and I could feel the thoughts buzzing through her mind. I didn't need to read her to know what was coming next. "So if you believe love like this is meant to change the world then why did you give it up?" Suddenly I felt something snap in my mind. It was as if I had been inside her head and borrowing her empathy when I said what I had. Now that connection was severed and I was back to who I really was.

"Love makes us weak...it breaks us. Why would I ever want that again? Why take the risk? I think I learned my lesson like a child who burns their hand on the stove. It looks like a good idea at the time and then you get hurt and know not to do it again." I was set in my new found beliefs.

Jade on the other hand wore a look on her face of disgust, irritation and annoyance. Like a parent who knew they were right but their stubborn child wouldn't listen. "Love didn't make you weak

Ember, you said so yourself. You allowed yourself to give up. This was your choice and it's going to be the world and those you once loved who suffer the consequences of your choice." Anger grew in Jade's voice as she shared her feelings for what I had done.

Maybe she was right but I had to believe the world was going to be better off without me running around dreaming of a fairytale love that would never be. How was that story ever going to positively impact the world? Jade stood up and took a deep breath. "Look, maybe you don't want to save Aden or his family but I know you want to see the facility destroyed. Isn't it worth coming to give Commander Addison what he deserves?" Jade spoke more calmly now and traces of anger were slowly leaving her with every deep breath she took.

She was right there was a part of me that wanted to see that place destroyed as much as I wanted to wage this war. Plus, if we could put an end to his regime then the issue of the missing Benders would be resolved as well and the Opposition could get back to solely focusing on the war. "Alright, I'll come. When do we leave?" I was now feeling a rush of excitement at the idea of storming the gates of the facility. "Once we find a car." Jade replied.

I smiled at her, "Already got one. Let's go." I led the way out of the room, eager to get on the road.

We left the room and found Dylan leaning against the cold cement wall outside, arms crossed over his chest. He didn't move at first and I didn't look behind us to see if he would actually follow.

"Are you coming or going to spend your time sulking?" I called out to him as Jade and I walked ahead. I heard his footsteps pick up as we headed towards the staircase that led us outside.

Right before we reached the door I felt someone softly touch my arm and I looked over to see Toby. "Can we talk for a moment?" He asked quietly and cautiously. I nodded and told Jade and Dylan to wait a second as I joined Toby.

"What's up?" I asked with a softness to my voice that only Toby could bring out of me.

"Where are you going?" He asked sounding rather on edge.

I sighed, "Apparently on some stupid rescue mission, but the truth is I'm out for fire." His face was serious as he looked me in the eyes. Toby's expression changed from a man who was concerned

246

to one who felt he had to say goodbye but didn't know how to do it.

"Toby, I'll be back in a few days." I said touching his arm to reassure him.

He gently moved a stray piece of my fringe behind my ear and left his hand a little too long on my cheek before he dropped it at his side. "Can you promise me something?" His face began to soften as he held my gaze.

I shrugged, "That depends, what's the promise?"

"Promise you won't hurt anyone." I laughed out of surprise but quickly stopped when I realized he was being serious. "I can't promise you that. Why would you ask for that?"

He was cautious as always but he took my hands into his and kept his eyes locked on mine, "Just promise me you won't hurt anyone and you'll return safely." I squeezed his hands, "I can't promise I won't hurt anyone because where I'm going isn't exactly safe. But I will promise you that I won't hurt anyone without cause. Deal?"

He smiled softly and nodded, "Deal. I'll see you in a few days." I kissed him softly on the cheek before I turned to leave and waved goodbye as I joined Dylan and Jade and left. I wanted to look back one more time but I didn't, because I could feel the weight of Toby's worry deep within me and it was more than I could handle at the moment.

There wasn't a soul nearby as we walked outside and around the corner to a row of locked up, one car garages. Silence was never a welcomed friend of mine because when the chaos of thoughts (mine or others) wasn't coursing through my mind I found myself thinking of things I didn't want to think about; like Toby. Leaving him wasn't as easy as I expected it to be. I mean I was supposed to be lacking feelings and yet all I could do was feel when it came to Toby. He was like the antidote to my lack of empathy and I wasn't sure how I felt about it (no pun intended). Focusing my thoughts on something more constructive, something I could actually control, I closed my eyes and focused my ability on the lock and it snapped open. I winked at Jade and Dylan as they stood there shocked and surprised. Although, the reality was they weren't shocked by what I could do, but rather that I was condoning breaking and entering.

"Wait here, I'll bring out the car." I walked into the dark garage and got into the bumblebee yellow Camaro. I drove it slowly out into the alley way and unlocked the doors for Jade an Dylan to get in. "Let's go."

CHAPTER TWELVE

We drove along the interstate quickly and quietly. No one spoke a word as music softly played on the radio to fill in the silence. I could see Dylan in my rearview mirror as I drove and he didn't attempt to hide his feelings at all. He leaned back in the seat with his arms crossed over his chest, lips tightly locked in a single, firm line and a sadness that brought his whole face downward. All I could do was shake my head to brush it off and look at the road ahead. Jade was facing her window watching the dark world whiz by and sat so still I wondered if she were still awake. When I tried to read her, her feelings and thoughts were rather simplified in that she chose to focus on what was coming rather than what was right in front of her. I had a feeling that her revealing her heart and soul to me about Dylan wasn't easy and especially being stuck in a car with the man she loved. She was right, we weren't different at all, I was trying to focus on what was ahead to keep my mind off Toby and she was doing the same to keep her mind off Dylan.

I finally decided to break the silence. "So what do you guys see happening when we reach the facility?" Jade slowly looked at me and shrugged, "There are always multiple outcomes, so it's hard to say exactly how this will go down. Hopefully though we can get in and get out."

I could sense her thoughts now as she was beginning to open up more, "You're worried this is a suicide mission, aren't you?" Dylan sighed as his reply and Jade's look was a forced mix of empathy and patience, as she chose her words carefully. "It's definitely a possibility." I couldn't help but laugh sarcastically, because it seemed as though they were blaming me for the downfall of this mission already, "It's a possibility because of who I've become?" I asked trying to hold back my irritation at their assumption.

I heard Dylan creak on the leather seat behind me as he leaned over the center of the seats, "Of course it is Ember. I mean we're going into this trusting you'll have our backs but can we even trust you?" His words hit me like a verbal slap. I could feel my foot press down even harder on the pedal below accelerating into the 100's. "You called *me* into this mission and if you want my help I suggest you treat me with a little more respect." I heard Dylan scoffs as he threw himself back against the seat, "Right, like you deserve that." "C'mon Dylan, what is wrong with you?" I asked angrily trying to keep my eyes on the road and my mind tuned in for any obstacles ahead.

"What's wrong with me? Are you kidding me right now?" His voice was filled with an anger that oozed of shock and deep pain.

"No, I'm not. What gives you any right to judge me for getting rid of this pain inside me when you know you'd do exactly the same if you had the choice?" My words mimicked his anger as they came flying out of my mouth.

"That's where you're wrong. I wouldn't change who I am to fulfill some selfish desire. Pain reminds us we're alive, it makes us stronger and all you are is a coward Ember. And maybe I am judging you but more than anything I am pissed as hell that you would just give up." He spoke the words quickly and all on one breath.

"I didn't give up on anything but Aden. I'm still in this fight and I'm still here." My tone continued to mimic his. Dylan scoffed and shook his head, "Really? What happened to the girl who was so outraged that a hierarchy existed making people like me, who once used to be your friend, nothing. We are *nothing* to this world but disposable. You could have changed everything for everyone but instead all you can see is what you want. You don't give a damn about the rest of us or what your parents fought so hard for."

"You're just angry that I bowed out of this crazy fairy tale that you and Jade seem to think Aden and I are apart of. I'm sorry Dylan but I got real and what I'm dealing with is reality. What you and Jade think is real is just some crazy story someone thought up a long time ago that sounds extraordinary but isn't realistic at all. No one can predict the future like that, not even you. The future can always change, you said so yourself." I knew I was already walking on thin ice and Dylan was about to crack. I saw Jade look at me and I could feel her calculating a reply.

"It's not about predicting the future Ember. Yes, the future can always change and maybe this idea that the Legacies are called to be apart of each others lives is just some whim of wishful thinking, but everything else is true and real. I know it sounds far fetched and it's hard for us to wrap our heads around. People spend their lives dreaming of becoming a hero or being called to something great but no one ever expects it to happen. No one ever expects to wake up one day as if they were living inside a movie and discover what we have about ourselves. So, yes I get it, I understand but the absurdity of it all doesn't change the truth of what is real. This is real whether you like it or not and reality doesn't just go away." Her words became increasingly sharper as she spoke.

I sighed wanting to fight everything she had just said because I was still struggling to believe that I could ever be anything more than I already was, but I didn't have the energy to fight her right now. In fact, we had been driving for a couple hours and I really needed a restroom. "Can we make a bathroom break?" I asked quickly changing the subject. Jade and Dylan both nodded silently and I headed off the next exit towards the nearest gas station. A quick refuel of the car and some provisions for the rest of our drive would be welcomed, that I was sure of. Even if I could be sure of what was ahead for us.

Once at the gas station Dylan and Jade headed towards the bathroom first and left me behind to fill up the car. I looked at the pump and for a moment was tempted to see if I could alter it to give us gas for free but decided that was stealing and pulled out a credit card instead. Dylan thought I had become a cruel, cold hearted version of myself but I still had some heart within me to try and do the right thing. As the gas finished pumping Dylan and Jade returned. Jade and I agreed to grab some food and drinks quickly, after I used the restroom, and then we'd be on our way.

Jade and I walked out of the mini-mart holding bags of snacks and drinks for the remainder of the trip and saw Dylan leaning against the car. "Dylan, will you drive? I'm getting tired and and I want to be well rested for when we arrive." I asked stretching a bit before getting into the backseat. He shrugged as he took the keys from my hands, "Sure."

The only sounds that could be heard as we drove were the crinkling of food wrappers and the occasional slurp of an emptying soda cup. Apparently Dylan didn't believe in listening to music as he drove. I attempted a few times to turn it on with my mind but he always turned it off. Something about needing to concentrate harder if he was going to drive. "The thing is Ember, in case you forgot, I can't see, Im legally blind. So I have to rely on my ability to see everything ahead of me before it's there and I can't have additional distractions stopping me from doing that."

He was just as angry and cranky as he was when we had started the trip. "Alright, fine, no music." I threw my hands up in the air in mock surrender and leaned back against the seat. Jade sighed and shook her head letting us know she was highly annoyed, "Will you two stop bickering like children?" Neither Dylan or I responded but instead I laid down in the backseat, using my jacket for a pillow.

"Oh come on." I woke up to Dylan having a minor panic attack and bright red and blue lights flashing behind us. "Are we getting pulled over?" I asked as I sat up looking out the back window.

"It would appear that way." Dylan said through short, shallow breaths as he slowed down the car and began to move onto the shoulder.

"What happened?" Jade turned to face Dylan and then looked back at me,

"I don't know. We must have been going too fast. We weren't really paying attention to the speed limit." Dylan pulled over carefully to the side of the road and looked back at me, "This is so illegal. I'm not allowed to drive when I am legally blind."

I laughed at him. "Relax, like this is the most illegal thing we are going to do tonight? We're about to break into a government facility. This is child's play. Besides use your abilities to get us out of this."

"I can't control people's minds like you can." Dylan's voice was moving from panicked to angry very quickly.

"Yes, you can. You're a legacy. I've researched it a bit and we all have additional abilities." I saw Dylan glance at Jade with doubt as she nodded in agreement and support.

"We've always known there were other dormant abilities. Might as well try now to figure out what they are." Jade's voice carried a weight of uncertainty to it but she managed to still speak gently to Dylan in an effort to calm him down.

"If you can't do it, I'll back you up." I said patting Dylan on the shoulder as the officer appeared outside the window waiting for us to roll it down. This was a minor road bump in our plans and one we would undoubtedly look back on and laugh about one day.

"Do you know why I pulled you over son?" The officer spoke with a heavy mid-western accent indicating we had found ourselves smack dab in the middle of the USA.

"Uh, no sir. I'm afraid I don't." This was the first time I had ever heard Dylan speak in such a formal and proper manner. It almost didn't sound like the same person at all.

"You were going about 95mph on a highway that is clearly marked 65mph. License and registration!" The officer began writing up what was undoubtedly a ticket as Jade rummaged through the glove compartment to find the registration information. Dylan pulled out his wallet and reluctantly handed the officer his New York state ID. As I watched the officer look down at the ID I tapped into his mind providing him a manufactured image that would change Dylan's state ID into a full license. I had no way of knowing if I was actually getting through to the officer except for the fact he wasn't immediately asking Dylan to step out of the car. In the past tapping into Static minds was a piece of cake but the officer seemed to be examining the license longer than he normally should. It was as if something inside his mind was letting him know he wasn't the only one in there. Or maybe I hadn't given him the right information for the license that I should have. I held onto the connection and glanced over at Jade. She gave me a small nod indicating that she had seen the outcome of this event and we'd be okay. The officer finally handed Dylan back his ID and we all exhaled out the breaths we were holding in.

"Son, it's the middle of the night why in God's green earth are you wearing sun glasses?" The officer held his flashlight directly into Dylan's eyes and Dylan didn't flinch. He shined it on Jade and I and we remained still as he moved it around the car.

"Well sir, my future is clearly so bright I have to wear shades." Jade and I let a small laugh escape us as we tried to hold more in. Dylan might have been quoting an old 80's song, but there was a fair amount of truth in his words.

"Do you think I enjoy jokes, son?" The officer clearly wasn't in the mood for cheeky responses. I held back providing anymore help so we could see what Dylan would do next but I was ready if he needed me. Jade and I watched as Dylan touched the officer's hand that was holding onto the door frame and the officer went silent. I heard Jade gasp slightly as if she somehow knew what he was doing. I watched as the officer seemed to have been transported somewhere else, as he gazed off dreamily into the far distance. He was looking out at the empty field to our right as if he was seeing something we couldn't see.

"We've got a 10-54 and 10-57 in progress. This is Car 3 on it's way to the scene." Dylan let go of the officer as Jade and I waited to see what had just happened. "Son, you got lucky tonight. There is an emergency a county over I have to get to. Now go and if I catch you speeding in my town again you will not be this lucky. D'you hear?" Dylan nodded solemnly as the officer took off jogging to his car. We waited until he had sped away down the highway before Dylan turned to face both Jade and I. Dylan wasn't showing any sort of emotion and it was hard to get a read on what he was thinking or what had just happened. Jade and I watched him carefully waiting for him to speak but he broke out into laughter instead.

"What did you do?" Jade asked excitedly as she touched one of Dylan's hands.

"I showed him a fake event happening a county over." Dylan shrugged and held onto Jade's hand as he stroked her fingers softly with his thumb.

"That is awesome! What did he see?" I asked leaning forward towards the front seat.

Dylan gained his composure again as he kept holding onto Jade's hand as if her touch alone could keep him calm and balanced. "I showed him a group of cows that were out of control and running cars off the road. Consider it a bad case of cows gone mad." Jade, Dylan and I all burst into laughter as we were high off the adrenaline from the moment. Finally Dylan was becoming more open to what he could do. He may be Lost but that didn't mean he wasn't powerful. He reluctantly removed his hand from Jade's and shifted into drive and pulled back onto the highway to complete the rest of our journey to Washington.

CHAPTER THIRTEEN

When we finally reached the government facility, we decided it was safer to park as far away from the facility as possible. Everything about the area reminded me of my childhood. As crazy as it sounded, I had fond memories of playing by myself in the grassy field while the soldiers engaged in combat training around me. I used to pretend they were a ballet company putting on a private show for me as they moved in formation. I also had horrible nightmares of what awaited us inside the facility. As we sat in the car attempted to devise a plan on how to get inside without drawing too much attention to ourselves, I found myself growing more and more impatient with the moment I had been anticipating right around the corner.

Everything within me wanted to run right in with a reckless spirit that I couldn't tame. I didn't feel this way because I was eager to see Aden, in fact I wasn't all that eager to see him at all, but I was eager to see this facility burn to the ground and to confront the nightmares that have haunted my sleep for years. I was in this for fire and I couldn't wait to sit back and watch the flames grow higher into the dark night sky. Jade and Dylan seemed less eager to run in guns blazing and I couldn't blame them. They were still the good guys, the ones who believed good could come out of this situation and saw the glass as half full for us. I had long abandoned those fantasies and in all honesty I didn't even know what hope felt like anymore. Hope was an ideal now, not a way of life, as it once was for me. For a moment as we were parking the Camaro in the darkness away from the base, I allowed myself to wonder if I could remember what hope felt like, to remember a time when I could dream of a future that actually made me want something more than what I could tangibly hold onto.

Dylan's voice interrupted my thoughts and I was thankful for the break because these types of fanciful distractions weren't something I needed right now. "So we're going to need to make sure we have this planned perfectly before we go in. We all come out alive, *right,* Ember?" Dylan looked over his shoulder at me from the front seat with eyebrows raised and a look that matched his condescending tone and I couldn't help but roll my eyes at him.

"Yes, we all come out alive. I know the plan." I waved my hand dismissively at them like Romie had done to me many times before. Jade turned around as she joined Dylan in giving me a very parental look and before she could say a word I held up my hand and shook my head, "You look at me like I am insane and maybe I am but sometimes the insane people do the most amazing things. I'm not as loose of a canon as you both seem to be thinking I am. Yes, I did read your minds and I'm glad I did because the lack of transparency in this mission is going to get us all killed."

When I had read their minds before we arrived at the base I had seen an array of possible outcomes for this mission. The only common thread in all of them was they saw me dying. The vision wasn't clear it would happen tonight or even at the facility but it was clear that every foreseeable future excluded me. Jade frowned at my attitude and I couldn't help but cross my arms and lean further against the backseat most likely appearing un-phased by the whole scene that was about to unfold but I was worried about everyone. I may not have the ability to feel empathy anymore but lately there was a part of me that had a massive war raging inside that no one knew about. That war began when I met Toby and ever since I've been fighting against the feelings that have begun to rise up again. You can only deny who you are for so long before one side wins over the other or you succeed in forgetting yourself completely. I was working hard to achieve the latter of those two options, not because I wanted it per se but because it felt easy and after everything I had gone through recently, I wanted an easy life more than I than I knew was possible. I was willing to surrender my longing for the easy life temporarily because I wanted to fight first more than anything and the excitement and adrenaline ripped through my veins like a drug and I was feeling like an addict who couldn't get enough.

Jade sighed and put her head in her hands and Dylan looked back out the front window. I began recapping the plan in the same manner the sergeants I had grow up used to do. "So let's go over the plan again. We don't need weapons because we are the weapons and the very sight of us will send everyone inside into a panic. They know what we can do, they've been studying us so let's make sure we hold back for as long as we can because that will confuse them and we need that to buy us some time. I know the layout of the facility so I'll guide us through telepathically. I'll be giving you an image of what is ahead constantly so stay tuned in; don't check out. If you need to say something, just give me the clue telepathically. I can stay connected to both of you and listen in at the same time. Any questions?" I saw Jade and Dylan look at me with what appeared to be surprise and concern. My time with the Opposition had turned me into the warrior Commander Addison had always dreamed I would become. This wasn't a side that either Dylan or Jade has gotten to experience before. To them I was just a girlie girl trying to win back the love of my life and now I was anything but that. I was in battle mode and I was going to let all my adrenaline and frustration propel me to storm the gates and take this place down.

I felt a hand on my shoulder and looked to see Dylan there. His lips were a straight line as he stared at me and I knew he could see me more clearly than anyone with working eyes could. I turned to face him and put my hands on his shoulders. "It's going to be okay Dylan. We're going to be just fine." I saw his lips pull into a tight line showing his concern and he exhaled. "I believe you but I also know that we are going into a place that you want to see burn. Don't let your personal emotions get the best of you Em." I knew it was another element I would have to try and fight, I had promised Toby that I wouldn't harm anyone without cause, but right now all I could think about was getting in there and accomplishing the mission.

We walked through the front doors and to my surprise there was one guard at the front desk and he was sound asleep. He looked more like a rent-a-cop than an actual military police officer and the drool sliding slowly out of his mouth didn't help with the intimidation factor at all. I looked back at Dylan and Jade and shrugged as we continued moving in further. We had known getting past the front desk would be the easiest part of breaking in. I couldn't help but wonder why it had been immensely easier than expected. My instincts were telling me this had to be a trap, they had to know we would come, but it was too late to turn back now. We crept down through a hallway keeping close to the walls. The only sounds we could hear was that of our breathing and the sounds of our shoes hitting the government standard formica flooring.

I held up a hand and stopped Dylan and Jade. We all exchanged a glance of confusion, "*I thought you said this place would be swarming with guards?*" Dylan spoke telepathically to me as he managed to maintain his usually cocky and condescending tone.

"*They should have stopped us, or tried to stop us from the beginning. I don't know what's going on. We have to keep moving forward.*" I responded to Dylan and sent out a telepathic signal to see if I could locate any one else close by but I was met with silence. "*This could be a trap.*" Jade joined the conversation and I nodded in agreement, "*It could indeed be a trap but there is only one way to find our for sure. Let's keep moving.*"

A few more empty hallways and I began to hear thoughts of men nearby. We were still on the first floor of the facility but too far in to turn back now. I gave a quick nod to Dylan and Jade to let them know they needed to be ready. We walked around the corner of the hallway and there were three men in camouflage watching television and eating a late night snack. The three of us made an abrupt stop as all three of the men turned to look at us. Instantly they went into defense mode and drew their guns. Seeing a gun pointed straight at me wasn't a first and I was pleasantly surprised to see that Dylan and Jade weren't phased by it either.

"On the ground. NOW!" One of the men yelled at us as he inched closer with his gun aimed directly at us. I held up my hands in surrender and saw Dylan and Jade do the same. We looked harmless enough, right? Right above the men I noticed a row of lights and immediately knew my first plan of action.

"*Watch this.*" I telepathically cued Jade and Dylan into my plan. As I focused on the light above it began to flicker. At first the men stayed trained on their targets but as the lights began to flicker more erratically and crackle they all looked up momentarily. Just as quickly as they had looked up the lights went out leaving only the small television on behind them to provide any light for the room. I showed Dylan and Jade the route we needed to take and waited for them to devise a plan of how to get around the soldiers. Jade began to get an image in her head of the men being thrown in jail. I smirked at the made up image and began to broadcast it to the men. Their chaotic fury of trying to find us in the dark ceased as they focused on the imaginary future they all wanted to avoid. I held the image in their minds causing them to freeze in place as we crept quietly around them and moved through the door into another hallway.

"Shouldn't we disarm the cameras since you're apparently great with taking out electronics?" Dylan commented as he pointed to the security cameras that were in every corner.

"I don't think I can take out the whole system and stay connected to both of you, Dylan you're the tech whiz why don't you figure something out?" Dylan sighed and looked back to Jade for reassurance. I don't think I could ever truly get over how sweet their bond to each other was, I just wished they would admit to each other and themselves how they really felt. *"Ember, I don't have the mind warp abilities you do."* Dylan responded in a tone that conveyed his frustration and personal disappointment in himself.

"So? You have other abilities. Don't think about it so much and just do it." I was sounding more and more like the agents who raised me and I felt slightly guilty about all the years I hated them when in fact I could see they were in some odd way trying to help me. Dylan walked over to the nearest camera and if he stood on his tip toes he could reach it. He examined the camera silently as Jade and I kept a lookout for guards. He touched it with his hand and closed his eyes but nothing seemed to happen.

He looked back at Jade and I and said, *"This is ridiculous. I have no idea what I'm doing. I'm pulling inspiration from books and movies. A little help?"*

I shrugged unsure what help I could give him. I wasn't fully sure how far his abilities went and what advice I could offer that would make this go any quicker. Jade walked over to his side and touched him softly, *"Just think about all the tech you work with and how it works. Find a way to get inside it and re-route the signal."* Dylan nodded and looked back at the camera.

He didn't move or respond right away and I could see in his thoughts that he knew far too well how the camera system worked and just what to do to turn it off. He closed his eyes and again touched the camera. I watched the red recording light fade on and off and when it didn't come on again I knew he had succeded. Jade hugged Dylan as he rejoined our group and I smiled his way. He waved us ahead, clearly wanting to get this mission over with.

Once the camera system was disabled the facility went into high alert. There wasn't a better way to announce our presence then to disarm their system. Instantly the onslaught of guards we had been expecting came our way. We were shutting down lights and using telekinesis to move guns out of their hands. A few guards were injured in the process, but I hadn't broken my promise to Toby, yet. As we continued to move through the facility we found we were catching the guards off guard at every turn.

It had been years since I had been back but some things you just couldn't forget like the way the fluorescent lights stung your eyes after prolong exposure to them and how every part of the facility felt more like an insane asylum than a government testing area. The walls at one time had been painted an off white color and from time and wear they were now a dingy brown. The linoleum floor was easy to clean and take care of which made it

272

practical but it had signs of wear as well. Then there was the smell, the smell of industrialized cleaners that hit you right in the back of the throat. There weren't any windows looking outside and the only windows you could find led into dark, undisclosed offices. We had taken the lower three levels and had finally arrived at the underground holding cells. This was going to be our biggest challenge because it was the most heavily guarded and it wasn't going to take long for more guards to join us once they got their bearings back from our earlier visit. When we arrived at the cells it was quiet. Too quiet. I glanced back at Dylan and Jade, *"This doesn't seem right. Do you guys see anything?"* Dylan shook his head, no, but Jade was gazing into the distance and I knew she was seeing something. We waited for her to come back to us and she looked horrified.

"We can't go in there." She spoke out loud to us and grabbed Dylan's arm as if she intended to pull him back to safety on her own.

"Why? We've gotten this far we can't turn back now." I whispered to her wanting to know what to expect.

"I don't know how it happens but we end up captured and it's not pleasant." Dylan put his hand over Jade's and patted it trying to calm her.

"Then we make it a point not to get captured." Dylan spoke with such certainty that I had to wonder if he was seeing a different version of our future. It felt as though we had the upper hand knowing what to expect and made me feel confident that wouldn't be our future.

I nodded in agreement and we moved slowly through the doors into the holding cells. It was possible that the guards had all moved to the upper levels once they realized the others we no longer communicating. We crept quietly and slowly around the corners making sure that the security cameras were still off before they could capture us on film. The halls were filled with clear glass cells allowing one to study the detainees. Most of the cells were empty which was much different than when I lived here. As a child I would come down to the cells with Commander Addison frequently to see what Benders could do and in most cases witness the torture they had to endure if they refused to comply. I shuddered at the memory of it all and refocused back onto the mission at hand.

We walked carefully together down the row of cells looking for Aden and his parents. When we reached the end of the hallway trapped by a wall, we looked back down the row of cells. "*They aren't here.*" I still spoke telepathically to Jade and Dylan to keep with our original plan. I began running through the possible places in my head they might be and showed Dylan and Jade an alternate route back upstairs where we could head next.

We took off quickly heading back out the way we came when suddenly I froze in my tracks at the sound of my name. "Em. Don't!"

Dylan and Jade hit my back as they came to a halt. We stood there close together looking straight ahead at Aden. He was at the end of the hall with a gun pointed to his head. Looking at him standing in front of me for the first time in months should have made my heart explode in an array of emotions and sentiments but truthfully all I could think about was how to get Jade, Dylan and I out of here.

I held up my hands in the air and walked forward slowly. "Alright, shows over. Its me that you want. So let these guys go and I'll happily go converse with Commander Addison." My tone was snarky but somehow I felt it was warranted, after all this used to be my home.

The guard scoffed, "Sure, like that would ever be an option. I'm sure you remember how things work around here Ember."

I telepathically spoke to Jade and Dylan again, *"Remember, we are the weapons. Do whatever we have to do to get out of here. Now."* I began focusing my thoughts on the guard that was holding Aden hostage and trying to make a connection with him to re-route his thoughts somewhere else. I couldn't seem to break through. I kept trying and still nothing. I could feel my heart racing the harder I tried as I realized they were somehow blocking us. I looked back at Dylan and Jade who wore the same worried expression on their faces as I did on mine. This was not part of the plan. *"There is only one guard, we can take him."* I said trying to remain confident in our escape.

"He has a gun." Dylan pointed out. *"If he doesn't shoot Aden first, he'll try for one of us."*

"It's a risk we have to..." My train of thoughts were cut off as the doors holding what I thought were detainees opened up to reveal more guards running towards us. It had been a trap and we walked right into it. *"NOW!"* We took off running towards the guards and I held up my hand to focus my energy toward the lights. The lights blew out and in their place emergency lights came on. I tried to move the guns aimed at us away but I was being met by massive resistance.

We were running straight ahead towards the guards and a piercing pain began running through my head rendering me paralyzed. I dropped to the floor grabbing my head and watched as Jade and Dylan fell with me. I couldn't block it and I couldn't make it stop. It felt as though my brain was being ripped apart from the inside out and it wouldn't stop throbbing. Whatever this was it was holding onto the nerves inside my brain and causing immense pain to radiate its way through my head and now my body. I was beginning to black out from the excruciating pain and as I tried to hold onto consciousness I saw a guard nearby with his eyes closed. Was it even possible our people were working for them now? Dylan and then Jade went limp and the last thing I saw was Aden being taken away.

Light. Darkness. Light. Darkness. It seemed to be a continual pattern for me now and I wasn't sure or at least aware exactly how long it had been going on for. I couldn't seem to focus on anything or keep my vision steady enough to make sense of where I was. My head was foggy and I was fighting to gain control of it. The last time I could remember feeling this way was right before I had left the facility. I willed my right hand to move towards my left arm and as I suspected there were needles. I was being drugged. The only way I had ever gotten out of this before, during training exercises, was to focus on something tangible. It was a skill I learned in combat training called grounding. People often used it during anxiety attacks. It allows me to focus on something concrete in little amounts until I am able to clear my head. It was not easy to do but I knew that it could be done and I had to start quickly if I had any hope of finding Dylan, Jade and Aden. I started with what I could feel. I could feel my skin, cold and dry. I could feel upholstery under my finger tips and under my elbow. I forced my arm to move towards my other arm as I felt tape and tubes covering my veins in my arms.

I then moved onto what I could hear. I could faintly hear the tape crinkle under my the weak touch of my fingertips. I could hear faint beeping sounds that I took to believe were machines nearby administering the drugs. I could hear my arm scratch across the surface of the upholstery and I could hear my breath escape my mouth slowly and evenly. My vision was growing steadier as I continued working on grounding myself. I tried to focus in on where the machine sounds were coming from. The sounds were weak but as I focused in I swore I could hear multiple beeps close by. I tried to ignore the frustration that was rising up inside of me to make sure it didn't interfere with my progress but if there were multiple beeps then maybe it wasn't just me who was being drugged. Maybe my friends were here with me, just like Jade had predicted in her vision. I opened my eyes and tried to focus on the last sense and that was what I could see.

At first try all I could see was light shining in my eyes. It forced me to blink and pushed me to surrender back to the darkness but I tried moving my eyes away from the light. Moving my eyes felt about as easy as moving two semis with my pinky finger. I wanted to move my head away from the light to see where I was and who might be with me but it was feeling close to impossible. I closed my eyes to block out the light and tried to focus on what muscles and motor skills I needed to make my head move just a fraction of an inch and maybe I could see beyond this light. There was a huge difference between trying to will yourself to move and actually being able to do it. Although somewhere in the process of focusing all my attention on moving my head I managed to drown out just enough of the drugs to move my head to the right. I opened my eyes slowly, as they were still far too heavy to open with ease and saw the outline of somebody seated next to me. The light mixed with the drugs was still preventing me from focusing clearly but I was once again trying to will my eyes to focus beyond the fog that clouded them from seeing clearly. I had to know if it was one of my friends seated next to me. I closed my eyes again and tried to focus on the rhythmic, distant beeping and once I had that in my head and could keep the rhythm with my finger I knew I was gaining back some control. I took a shallow breath and then forced my eyes open again. I still had my head turned to the right this time allowing me to see clearer and I could see Aden. Instantly it felt as if someone had placed my heart in a vice and it was being cranked till my heart was crushed into oblivion. *"Oh no..."* the thought swept through my head all too easily. The drugs made me vulnerable and removed my abilities. That meant the block on my heart and on my empathy would be gone too, or at least temporarily disabled. I continued to will my eyes to stay open as I tried to focus in to see if he was waking up too. I couldn't see clearly enough to make out more than his shape and it was one I would recognize anywhere. I forced my hand towards my left arm and began to rip out, one by one, the IVs. Thankfully, the only good part about the drugs was that I couldn't fully process the pain I should be feeling and that made it easy to focus on the task at hand.

Once the tubes were removed I could feel myself gaining a little more control of my faculties, but not enough. I raised my hand to block out the bright lights that were trained in front of us to see who was around keeping guard. I didn't see anyone in the immediate area which I knew bought me only minutes at best to try and wake everyone up. I slid forward in the chair working on willing my legs to hold me up as I attempted to stand. I looked to my right and saw Dylan next to me and Jade to his left. Their breath was shallow but they were still alive and hooked up to the same IVs as I was, making it a bit easier to know what to expect and how to respond. I continued to inch closer to the edge of the chair and noticed slight movement on my right. Aden!

I looked over at him and he was coming to. His eyes were blinking slowly as he tried to regain consciousness. I forced myself to stand up and leaned my hands on either side of him on the arms of the chair, "Aden? Can you hear me? Aden, please wake up!" I spoke softly in the hopes of waking him up before anyone could hear me. His eyes had stopped blinking and he wasn't moving anymore, except for his own shallow breaths. I removed the IV tubes from his arm as gently as I could and let them fall down beside him. I slowly moved over to Dylan and Jade, propping myself up on an arm of each of their chairs, "Jade! Dylan! Can you hear me? You've got to fight this and wake up. I can't get us all out." The reality that I couldn't free my friends and was completely helpless brought tears to my eyes. They stung deeply reminding me it had been a long time since I had last cried. But now was not the time for my emotions to rage out of control. I had to find a way to focus on anything but the flood of repressed feelings that were rising up unwillingly.

I touched Dylan and Jade's hands but they didn't move. I began frantically removing the IVs from their arms and letting the clear bright violet liquid drip out onto the floor. Hopefully the drugs would begin to wear off and they would wake up. "Please guys, please, find the will to wake up." Again, willing something to be true and it actually being true were too very different things. I didn't know what else to do beyond begging my friends to wake up. I was too weak to carry them and I couldn't use my abilities to get rid of the guards, or at best, fend them off by myself.

"Em?" I turned back towards Aden when I heard him whisper my name. With every second I was away from the drugs I was finding it easier and easier to move around.

"Aden, can you hear me? We have to get out of here now!" I saw Aden nod in agreement but he was too weak to move. I leaned towards him and threw his arm over my shoulder and began to pull him forward. This was definitely one of those moments when my hero complex forgot to remind me that I was about 50 or so pounds lighter than Aden and also quite a bit smaller in height. I struggled against his size but continued to drag him on forward allowing my adrenaline to save our lives to take over.

The closer we got to the door the more Aden came to. I knew once we were somewhere safe and could regain our abilities we could go back and get Jade and Dylan. "Aden, please you have to stay with me and you have to focus." I was trying to give Aden the best pep talk I could but it was hard when I was still trying to keep focused myself so that I didn't completely surrender to the emotions that were surfacing more and more. I stopped us right before we moved through the door and pushed it open slowly. I looked around and didn't see any guards giving us a chance to at least move out of this room of horrors. Once we were out of the room I could regain my bearings and figure out where to go next. We pushed through the two swinging doors that resembled something you would find in an operating room or butcher shop.

Aden was beginning to walk on his own now, although he still kept his arm tightly around me, as if he were doing the best he could to keep me safe. Aden's protection was a feeling I had long since forgotten and feeling it again now wasn't exactly what I needed to get us out of here. We found ourselves in a small holding area or foyer that had two more of the same creepy doors leading out to a brightly lit hallway. Those doors had plastic windows on them and allowed me to look out into the hallway.

I carefully peered outside, "The coast is… ADEN!" When I turned back around Aden was being ripped out of my arms and pulled back by two heavily armed guards. I stood very still trying to plan a way out of this but I couldn't think of one this time. I felt a pair of arms pull me back tightly almost dislodging my shoulder and Aden and I were held apart, once again. I felt something sharp against my neck and I froze looking at Aden as if he could tell me what to do. Pain streaked across his face so intensely that I wondered if someone had hurt him physically.

"Em!" He yelled out my name and then began fighting with what little strength he had against the men who held him at gunpoint. "Let her go!" He was lunging forward and before I could do anything or say anything the needle was inserted into my neck and I felt myself losing consciousness again. "Em! No...."

I couldn't feel anything anymore. All I knew was that I was trapped somewhere between reality and my own mind's landscape. In my mind everything was at peace. I wasn't really anywhere in particular but I felt free and I didn't have to fight anymore. I was able to just float in and out of existence as I pleased because the world inside my mind wasn't at war. Intermittently I would hear voices that shattered the peaceful existence I had created for myself, reminding me that the world I had created was simply a byproduct of defeat. "She's too powerful. We need to up the dosage on her." "I don't care what he said. If she dies all the better. They mean nothing to me." These were the voices I heard faintly outside my peaceful world but couldn't identify. What they said should have outraged me, it should have sent me into defense mode but I was in no position to fight.

I was content remaining in this moment of surrender until I saw him, "Aden?" My voice was a soft whisper and I found it impossible to believe it could have carried across the riverbank to where Aden was standing. Yet somehow he must have sensed my presence and he turned to face me. There was a sudden onset of relief across his face as he moved quickly to the edge of the riverbank.

"What are you doing here?" I asked standing up and making it to the edge of the riverbank to get as close to him as I could.

"I came to find you. Don't you remember how we always used to do that?" He smiled weakly and I couldn't help but return the soft smile.

"I don't know how to get us out of here Aden. I've failed all of you." I looked down at the steady stream of water moving beneath me.

"You haven't failed us Em. We'll find a way out. You just can't give up that easily." He spoke with a shaky confidence at best but tried to keep the moment light.

I paced around the edge of the river watching the water race down the embankment as if it could somehow whisper to me the plan I needed. I was struggling with the reality that mere hours before this I was a full fledged warrior preparing to launch a war that would inevitably effect the world and now I was thrown back into being just a girl lost in the world. I looked up at Aden to see him watching me closely. Thoughts raced through my mind of everything I had wanted to say to him since he left me but now was not the time to dive into any of that.

"Do you have any ideas Aden?" I tried to keep my focus on the water so that I wouldn't lose determination looking into Aden's eyes.

"No. These men are heavily armed and they've taken away what makes us who we are which is our main chance of survival." Now he was sounding defeated.

"They've only temporarily disabled our abilities." I was processing my thoughts out loud now because I could feel an idea rising up I just had to figure out the logistics. I began to think of how the Opposition took my empathy away only for these drugs to bring it back. Aden was right, our abilities were apart of who we are and they may be able to lie dormant but they were always going to be there. "Our abilities can never be taken from us they can only be suppressed. The question is are we stronger than the man made drugs? They think they know everything there is to know about us but what if they don't?"

Aden was listening intently and his eyebrows perked up slightly, "What are you getting at Em?"

"We're here, Aden. In this...place, wherever this is and if we're here together then that means somehow we surpassed the drugs that are blocking our abilities, unless of course this is all just a dream." I looked at Aden and smiled and held my hand out in front of me. He watched as I closed my eyes and began visualizing my hand being placed over his chest. I knew it was a long shot because if this was a dream then anything I attempted here would ultimately succeed. The only hope I had right now was that if I could gain control of my abilities here in this place than I may have a fighting chance of getting us out of here and out of the facility. When I opened my eyes I saw that Aden now had his eyes closed and his hand was placed on his chest where I had imagined mine would be. This let me know he was getting my telepathic message and I

288

had to try something bigger and less predictable. I looked behind Aden and saw a large boulder. I held up my hand and aimed it toward the boulder. If I could make it move using my telekinesis then that had to be proof we were still in control. In one realm or another. At first the boulder didn't budge at all. I sighed in frustration as Aden turned to look at what I was doing. I focused all my concentration on the boulder and began to watch it wiggle free of the ground and slowly roll toward us. As it rolled it began picking up momentum and found its way straight into the riverbank with a splash big enough Aden and I had to jump out of its way. The water kept moving around it, unfazed and unwilling to be stopped, and I knew I too could be like the water. Aden slowly looked up from the boulder to me. I smirked at his surprised expression. "Okay, this is going to be about mind games. Will over matter. It's who we are, it's what we do." I said pacing along the riverbank again.

"What are you planning, Em?" Aden's eyes narrowed in concern as he stood still watching me think and pace.

I finally stopped and faced him again. "Jade and Dylan have seen my life ending sooner rather than later. I have nothing to lose at this point. I've fought these drugs before when I was a lot younger and I think I can do it again but not just for me, for all of us."

Aden's face fell and went a few shades lighter than his normal dark skin tone. "They predicted your d-death?"

I nodded, "Yeah, they don't know that I know. We hadn't been together in awhile and they seemed a little more intense than when I had last seen them. So I broke my personal rule and read them, that's when I saw their vision."

Aden was knocked off his axis and everything looked like it was spinning out of control for him. "Visions can always change. Don't go rushing into dangerous situations just because of something they think might happen. You can't be reckless like that."

I scoffed at him trying to tell me what to do, "And what gives you the authority to tell me how to live my life? You released yourself of that quite awhile ago if memory serves me right." I stopped myself from allowing the flood of anger that was sweeping over me, to side track me from the goal at hand. Although it didn't take away the longing to want to rip into Aden. I inhaled deeply and let out the breath as slow as I could. "Look, this isn't the time for either of us to contemplate what is or isn't. I either try to save us or we all die. It's a risk that has to be taken."

"You still haven't answered how you're going to do it." I could hear the bitterness in Aden's voice as he held back his own words and emotions regarding "us."

"I'm going to try and go inside my own mind. If I can read others then I have to be able to access my own on a deeper level. Once I'm inside I can find the specific spot that the drug is effecting and reroute it so it doesn't work anymore. Once I accomplish this I can then jump into each of your minds and do the same. Then we get out of this place once and for all."

Aden ran his hand through his hair and shook his head, "No, that's a horrible idea. I've never heard of any psionic being able to use their abilities on themselves and if you do manage to accomplish this feat how are you getting back out? You're creating a door that locks behind you."

"We are wasting time Aden. Get out of my mind and let me go." I stared Aden in the eyes and it felt more like we were challenging each other to see who would break first. I wasn't sure if he was aware that he could use his abilities on me even in this mental landscape. We were in a place stuck in between reality and dreams and it was our place to meet when distance or time kept us apart. No one else could find us here because it was a place of our own making and only we had the keys. Which also meant we weren't bound by rules or limitations between each other but I don't think he realized that in this moment. I was thankful he didn't seem to have access to the slew of emotions that were wrecking havoc on my soul. Emotions I had thought were completely dead but clearly you can only try to pretend they don't exist but they will always be there. Aden looked more and more pained as he fought himself on whether to leave me or to stay. He wasn't moving and he left me no choice but to force him out.

I closed my eyes and created a block between us that broke our connection. When I opened my eyes again, he was gone. I walked away from the water and leaned against a nearby tree trying to steady myself. Everything within me felt like a chaotic blackhole that would either implode or explode and neither felt like a very good option. If I couldn't control my emotions anymore there was no way I could guarantee the survival of all of us. All I could do now was try to get inside my own mind, which I had no idea how to do, in the hopes that I could try to block the drugs and gain some control back to try and save my friends.

I felt my legs give out beneath me as I slid down the trunk of the tree behind me and onto the cold, dewy, grass covered ground beneath me. I focused on the sound of the river rushing past me and closed my eyes. Normally when I wanted inside another person's mind all I had to do was focus on them and I'd find an easy way in. Most people don't guard their thoughts as well as they guard their hearts. A person's mind could be a very easy place to access for good uses, or otherwise, but how do you access your own mind when you aren't sure what your weak spot is? My breath became more and more steady as I allowed myself to calm down and try to discover a way into my mind.

The thought of Toby arose and my first instinct was to dismiss it but then I held onto it for a moment longer because he may be the way into my mind. I could have tried getting inside my mind through thoughts of Aden but those thoughts were now compromised. Aden brought about chaos within me and even though my feelings for him were returning it wasn't what I wanted. My mind would do whatever it could to protect me from the pain that came from seeing Aden again and therefore would keep me locked out. Toby on the other hand intrigued me. When I met him I didn't have the opportunity to truly decide what I felt or didn't feel because of the block on my empathy. I was only interested in self-preservation and yet every time Toby came around it felt like he could break through the block without even trying. Toby was like an the antidote to this drug in some way and for the first time since meeting him I was ready to see where my heart would go if I truly opened up and gave my heart to him. I began thinking back to the first time he walked into my room and the first few times we spoke. I thought back to our kiss and how it caused a spark to ignite within me. If that was the last moment I ever remembered then it would be one well worth taking with me, wherever I might find myself. For a moment I had forgotten about the facility or trying to save my friends. All I could think about was that moment with Toby and how much I wanted a moment like that again.

I opened my eyes and found the riverbank was gone and I was sitting down in a dirt trench. Sounds of explosions rang out around me and dirt and debris blew past me. I looked down to see my otherwise pristine black combat gear was now covered in a light dusting of dirt. I carefully stood up to look beyond the edge of the trench and saw that a war was happening around me. There were guns and cannons and tanks completely surrounding the small hole in the ground. My trench was right in the middle of this battle. I knelt down again looking for a shield or weapon to give me a hope at safe passage but I was completely defenseless. Then it occurred to me. This was my mind. This is what had become of all the beautiful thoughts and landscapes that once inhabited here. Now it was filled with war and destruction and more importantly the inner war that I fought within myself everyday of who I would become. These were my armies and weapons of my own design. Possibly mixed with weapons that were byproducts of the drugs coursing through my veins. If I could figure out what was my own design and what was that of the drugs I could stop it. I sighed in contemplation as I knelt down in the trench and bombs flew over my head like sadistic wishing stars.

Over the course of these months spent trying to find myself again I had come to find that everyone else believed I was capable of much more than I believed I was. To me I was just a telepath who had no real control over her abilities. I was a girl who had been forced to discover other dormant abilities at the cost of others lives. And yet knowing I could do more than just read minds wasn't enough for everyone else. They still believed I was some type of super weapon. Able to summon something deep inside of me that would go off like a bomb. How all of these people, Resistance and Opposition alike, knew this about me when I had no inkling of this information myself, escaped me. Yet if it was true, then how could I summon that part of me now? I stood up in the trench and crawled out onto the level ground laying low to avoid being hit by any gun fire.

I stood up and pressed both of my hands out to the side and yelled, "STOP!" Instantly the battlefield went silent. I looked around the circle of weapons and masked fighters as they stood frozen in action. I exhaled and walked over towards a cannon. It appeared so out of place for modern weaponry that I had to question why it was here. As I ran my finger tips along the edge of the cannon that was still warm to the touch I was infused with the knowledge that Benders had been around since the beginning of time and this was the ancient part of me that held onto my past, a lineage I knew very little about. I walked over to a masked fighter next to the cannon who was holding a gun. As I reached out and touched the gun I could feel energy flowing out of it. I wrapped my hand around the barrel of the gun and gasped as I could feel the weapon becoming one with me. Was it passing it's energy onto me or was I simply becoming one with the weapon? I kept a hold of the gun and closed my eyes allowing myself to feel the energy, power and strength that came from the weapon. Instinctively I held out my other hand and felt as though I could now control every weapon that was surrounding me. I opened my eyes to see bullets and cannonballs flying in slow motion towards the center of the battle. I removed my hand from the barrel of the gun and pulled it slowly towards my other hand and watched as I could control the movement of the flying bullets and cannonballs. I led them toward the center and right as they were about to meet I managed to set them on course with their normal speed again and watched as they collided together exploding into a glorious white light, as if the Heavens had exploded, that blinded everyone on the field.

The men all looked away from the light residue that now remained, but I kept watching it and held my hand out as I moved towards it. I walked into the light and felt the power overcome me as I surrendered to it. I closed my eyes and felt everything around me shatter into a million pieces.

When I opened my eyes again I was no longer on the battlefield, I was back in the facility and saw that Aden, Jade and Dylan were slowly coming out of their drug induced haze. The IVs that held them prisoners had fallen away, dripping their destructive fluid to the ground, and everything in the room was powered off. I could still feel the effects of the drugs lingering in my system but I had succeeded in overcoming them and was confident that whatever came next would be easy to handle. Or at least i hoped the worst was behind us.

Dylan was doing his best to help Jade rise to her feet, although he was still unsteady on his own legs. Jade took her opportunity to hold on tightly to Dylan and rest her head, in the place that was perfectly made for her, right under his neck. I was struggling to gain composure and strength when I felt two hands grabbing mine. I looked up and saw a silhouette in front of me that I would recognize anywhere, it was Aden. With the room being mostly dark and still not being able to see clearly it made it hard to figure out what we should do next to get out of here alive. I took Aden's hands and let him help me to my feet. He held onto me as we stood there silently and at first it felt comfortable and forced. Then the embrace just began to feel foreign and wrong. I pushed myself away from him and caught a quick glimpse of Aden's face as it reflected his pain all too clearly.

"Are you guys okay?" I asked moving closer to Dylan and Jade. They both nodded and remained in each other's arms. "What the hell happened Ember?" Dylan looked at me expressing his fear and also concern, while still giving me his usual angry tone.

"We were drugged just like you guys saw happening. I'm sorry, I was overly confident that seeing the future ahead of time would prevent it from happening. I just didn't realize there were other fine details we'd miss." Jade moved away reluctantly from Dylan, but kept her arm looped in his. "How did we get out of this?" Jade asked casually.

"I don't know how to explain it but I was able to get us out. We can figure out the details later but right now we have to get out of here." I stumbled slightly as I began to head forever and Aden caught me. In that moment the emotions I was holding inside for him began to surface and I pushed his hands away. He gave up the right to help me or be there for me when he left me and he couldn't just resume where we left off.

"Aden, where are your parents?" As much as I didn't relish in the thought of trying to rescue them and thus postponing our escape it didn't seem right to just leave without them. He ran his hands through his hair which usually meant he was lying, but given the stress of the moment I excused it as a nervous habit, "They managed to escape when I was taken as part of the plan to trap you guys. I'll connect with them once we're out of here." I nodded and accepted his answer then "How do we get out?" Jade asked as she exhaled.

"All we can do is what we had planned in the beginning. I'll link to all of you, show you the map and we go straight for the exit." I began to form the link to their minds knowing we were racing against the clock. As the link was formed we began moving forward into the darkness towards the faint light that shone through the plastic doors ahead. For the first time since we began this mission I was truly feeling nervous, exposed and not reckless confident anymore. The drugs would take a bit longer to fully leave my system and until then I didn't know how to be strong and the warrior I knew I was meant to be. I felt like I was failing everyone by not being able to get them out of the facility safely. We pushed through the plastic doors and there weren't any guards around. Our escape must not be public yet and that was one thing we had working in our favor. As we moved through the hallway slowly I felt Aden grab my arm and walk alongside me. He whispered in my ear, "Stop feeling like you're a failure. You know you are far more than that." I looked at him in disbelief and shook my head to make him stop talking and keep moving forward. The time would come when we could talk but right now wasn't that time and his encouragement only made me feel angry and that distracted me from the mission at hand.

As we rounded the corner that would lead us to the stairway we heard movement inside. I telepathically spoke, "*Guards ahead, let's make quick work of them and move forward, don't look back.*"

Everyone nodded and we opened the stairwell door moving in with caution and prepared to attack. There was no one there. We went up the first flight of stairs and it was empty. Maybe the drugs had caused me to hallucinate hearing guards or maybe they had decided to move ahead? The further we went up the more I was beginning to feel in control again and feel more like myself. The drugs couldn't leave my system quickly enough. We went up the next flight of stairs and again no guards. We stopped and looked at each other, *"Is it another trap?"* Dylan telepathically spoke.

I shrugged reaching out to see if I could hear any thoughts ahead. Then again clearly these guards were able to block our abilities and we were once again at a disadvantage. There was much we didn't know about our abilities and how they work and that also put us at a huge disadvantage. It's amazing how you never recognize your weaknesses until you are face to face with them. At the top of the third flight of stairs we waited by the door that would lead us to the main floor.

We relied on our normal, non-Bender senses to listen for any signs of guards outside the door. The only sound we could hear was the faint buzzing of the fluorescent lights. I opened the door slowly and looked outside to make sure the coast was clear. I remained on the fore front to ensure that if anyone was going to get hurt, it would be me and not my friends. As we walked into the empty hallway I could envision the front door ahead and it felt far too good to be true that the exit would be that easily reached. We stopped and exchanged some glances between each other hoping someone had an idea of how to get out of here without getting caught in another trap. Aden looked at me with intrigue and I could tell he was reading me. Despite the predicament we found ourselves in, due to trying to save him and his family, he was interested in knowing where we stood now that we were reunited and the deeper he looked the more I felt my empathy block return. "Your emotions are really hard to read." He whispered in my ear. I smirked at him and nodded in reply. It was a triumphant moment knowing I was in control again.

   "I guess our only options are to stand in this hallway until someone comes for us or risk it and make a run for the exit." As I shared my thoughts with everyone they nodded in agreement and I could tell we all knew our only hope of freedom was a kamikaze effort to make it to the front door. Without another word or thought we all took off running. Dylan held onto Jade as he ran with his super speed leaving Aden and I in the dust. We managed to keep up not far behind them and we could see was the exit about a 100 feet away. We kept moving closer and closer to the door until all

the lights went out instantly and a metal gate was dropped over the door. We stopped dead in our tracks waiting for the onslaught of guards but it was just us. We huddled close together waiting for whatever surprise attack may be coming our way. The suspense of waiting was beginning to wreck havoc on us and I suppose that was all part of the plan.

"Ember, I've waited a long time for you to return." Commander Addison's voice echoed through the building over the PA system. I got chills hearing him call my name. "We've blocked all the exits and stairwells, there is no where for you to run."

I sighed and yelled out to Commander Addison knowing he could hear me, "Let my friends go and you can have me. I won't put up a fight." There was silence for awhile until he spoke again, "I want to meet your friends."

Guards rapidly approached and the sound of guns cocking could heard as they surrounded us. *"All we can do is go with them. Let's not fight just yet."* I spoke to my friends as we were ushered back down the hallway towards what I remembered to be Commander Addison's office.

We were escorted into Commander Addison's office and the door was shut and locked behind us. We all remained close to each other for support and waited for Addison to enter. He walked through a side door revealing his peppered hair and army regalia. He walked slowly and with a smile that made me want to throw up. "Ember, it's been far, far too long. You never visit." He spoke calmly to me, as if this were some sort of family reunion. I rolled my eyes at him as he took a seat in his desk chair and spun around to face us. The drugs had completely worn out of my system now and I was back to my warrior self and already trying to formulate a plan. The tension in the room was so thick I swore you could see it looming above us like a fog growing thicker and thicker by the second. With every second that tension grew my anger grew with it because I was face to face with the man who stole everything from me and all I wanted to do was take everything from him.

"There is no point in standing, please take a seat everyone. Ember, as you most likely remember this room utilizes technology that blocks your abilities so you are defenseless in here." He said with a slight laugh as if he had some how gained the upper hand. I tried to remain in control and not jump across his desk and strangle him. "We'll stand."

Commander Addison may have blocked us from using our abilities but I could tell by the looks on Jade, Dylan and Aden's faces that they were more afraid of what I would do than what Addison would do. All three of them were familiar with my childhood and knew the disgust I held in my heart for the man in front of us. I was standing so close to Commander Addison that I could smell the tuna fish he had eaten just hours before at dinner and it made my stomach turn. Everything about this man was rancid and revolting from his breath to his soul.

Neither one of us moved and it felt as if someone had frozen us in time permanently but eventually one of us would break. "What are you doing, Ember? You know I can destroy you."

I scoffed at his comment, "I hate to break it to you but you're a little too late for that." I pointed back at Aden who wasn't far behind me, "He already beat you to the punch. There isn't much left of me to destroy. And if I remember correctly a person without anything to lose is the most dangerous kind." Commander Addison flinched slightly as I rubbed that bit of truth in his face; words he had spoken to me often growing up. I could also feel Aden tense up behind me as I dropped that truth bomb on him as well.

Dylan and Jade stood next to each other and through my peripheral vision I could tell they were both trying to see what was about to happen and calculate their next move in time to prevent total destruction, and being in the dark made them feel like fish out of water. "Look at you little girl, growing up before my eyes. You've always talked a good game but the truth is you are nothing without your abilities so what exactly are you going to do now? Curl up into the corner and promise you'll behave? I've got you all cornered and there is no way out." His words continued to grow more sinister every time he spoke. I looked back at Aden, Jade and Dylan, wishing I could telepathically speak to them to somehow let them know it would be okay. I was completely blocked off and all I could do was hope that the traditional form of eye contact would somehow let them know that I had this under control. Judging by the looks on their faces they weren't reading me the way I had hoped they would. All they could see was the rage in my eyes.

In their eyes I was a ticking, unpredictable time bomb that they had no idea how to stop. They wanted Commander Addison to get what he deserved as much as I did, but they didn't believe in killing a man as a form of justice. "Well believe me I don't need my abilities to destroy you. I've been well trained thanks to you. What exactly do you want with us?" My words were harsh and cut through the tension like a knife as Commander Addison burst into laughter.

"What do I want with you? Your parents, under extreme torture to save your life, revealed a lot about who you really are and who your friends are as well. I want the four of you to join me and my army." I heard a laugh explode from Dylan's throat that expressed his disgust for the offer.

"There is no way we'd ever join you. I escaped from you years ago and I will never be apart of this again. You're a murderer and you have no soul. You're killing innocent people and you don't even care. We won't join you so either let us go or you'll wind up dead."

Commander Addison scoffed and took a second to look at each of us before his eyes landed on mine, "I'm the one killing innocent people? Don't you remember Ember, that this all began because of you? You were the prototype. You were the one who gave me the intel I needed to capture every Bender that I have. You were the one who gave me the insight and tools into how I could create the Shadows. You are the ultimate weapon and you are the one with blood on your hands." It had never occurred to me, even for a second that the reason the Shadows were after me and seemed to respond to me was because I had been responsible for creating them. I could feel my legs going weak but the desire to kill Commander Addison kept me standing strong.

"I will kill you." The words crept slowly and viciously out of my mouth. I was in shock from this revelation and horrified. The only thing I could do was try to put an end to it once and for all. I saw his gun laying on the corner of the desk and I was calculating a plan of how to grab it swiftly enough that he wouldn't have time to respond but he knew me far too well.

Commander Addison lunged towards me but I was fast enough to move to the side and watch him stumble. He had just barely gotten his footing as I used the desk to do a cartwheel and kick him back towards the wall. I was quick, but so was he, and in an instant his gun was pointed straight into my eyes. I was looking down the barrel for what felt like minutes contemplating my next move, but it was mere seconds before I pulled my arm up hitting down hard onto Addison's forearm making his hand release the gun. I seized control of the gun and pressed it against Addison's forehead.

"Mm...I guess combat training wasn't such a good idea for me after all." I mocked him as he remained still.

"You may have been well trained but you won't hurt me." He responded overly confident. A laugh escaped my mouth as I was truly offended by his assumption. "And what makes you so sure of that?"

"You care too much. It's always been your downfall. You're an extremely talented telepath, amongst many other abilities you've shown us, but your telempathy, your compassion stops you from being as powerful as we all know you could be." I could feel my jaw tightening reliving years before when he would tell me these same words. The last thing I wanted was to be perceived as weak and incapable of being powerful. Yet I knew becoming that powerful required surrounding to the darkness and I refused to do that.

I cocked the gun into place ready to shoot. My only concern was revenge and my moment had arrived. "Ember, stop!" My arm was quickly pulled away and I was no longer looking into the void less holes of Addison's eyes but now Aden's warm, soulful eyes. "What the hell are you doing? This doesn't concern you!" I snapped harshly at him. Going from one man who had ripped my heart out as a child to the other one who more currently had ripped my heart out wasn't really a good enough reason to stop my actions.

"This.is.not.who.you.are." He spoke the words slowly making sure to emphasize each one, as if I wouldn't hear him clearly otherwise.

"You don't know me anymore and I'm no longer your concern so take your hands off of me." Aden and I locked eyes in a standoff as I retrained my gun on Addison. Aden made very calculated moves as he slowly pulled his hand off my arm and placed it on my chest. His abilities may have been inactive but his warmth, his natural all encompassing warmth caught me off guard. I hadn't felt his touch in months and I could feel this part of me fighting to break free but it was buried deep inside my soul. If a soul could wage war inside ourselves then mine was doing just that and winning.

As I kept my eyes on Addison and the gun I had trained on him I heard Toby's voice in my head,

"Promise me you won't hurt anyone." My chest cramped up as I remembered the promise I had made him and as much as I wanted to break that promise I couldn't seem to stand the thought of disappointing Toby. I dropped the gun and grabbed at my heart. I could feel my airways closing up and it felt as if the walls were closing in around me. It took every ounce of energy left within me to grab Aden's hand and push it away from me. I knew what he was trying to do and in normal situations it would have rendered me defenseless, but I wasn't the girl he left to fall apart outside his house months before. His touch now caused an epic war within my soul that was determined to battle till the death of who I was or who I've become.

I grabbed hold of Addison's desk to steady myself and saw Addison reach for the gun again. "Ember, move!" Aden yelled and reached forward but in stubborn pursuit of maintaining control with him around I didn't move and replied, "Don't tell me what to do." My words came out like a small child engaged in a sibling rivalry.

"ENOUGH!" Dylan screamed and the room went silent. Before I could think of my next move or process what was happening I saw Addison frozen half bent over his desk, arms reaching out for the gun. I looked at Aden and he was still fumbling through his movements as to whether he should help me or stay back. Jade and Dylan were on the other side of the room and Jade was looking at Dylan in shock.

"What did you do?" She asked him quietly, "I don't know exactly. I just was seeing time stop and it did." Dylan stood still as if he were afraid his movements would cause Addison to move. "Is everyone here frozen in time?" Jade asked looking towards Addison's door. "I don't know." Dylan said shrugging.

"I can't breathe." I dropped down to the floor closing my eyes and trying to focus on calming myself down and Aden knelt down to join me. "Just breathe, Em. You're going to be okay. I'm going to help you up, okay?" His hands were halfway towards me but he stopped midway waiting for my approval. I nodded and felt his gentle touch as he helped me up.

Jade opened the door slowly and peered outside giving us the all clear. Aden maintained a gentle hold of me that I allowed myself to find comfort in, just slightly. As we moved through the facility we discovered all was silent now and the guards that were on patrol were frozen like

Addison. "This is surreal, Dylan." Jade said as she stopped for a second to wave her hand in front of a guard's face, watching as his eyes remained from and refusing to blink. Dylan smirked at her and placed his hand on the small of her back and encouraged her to keep moving forward. "Guess the Lost aren't as useless as everyone seems to think." Hearing Dylan mention the Lost instantly made me think of Toby again and a sharp pain hit my heart reminding me that I missed him greatly and that after what had happened tonight he was the antidote to my lack of empathy and heartache, and he was where I belonged.

When we reached the door to leave the gate was still down. I was in no condition to raise it and I wasn't sure who would take the lead now. Dylan's new found ability obviously made Jade want to test her own. She held out her hand as I had done earlier and the gate began to move up. I couldn't help but smile as I watched my friends suddenly coming into their own and realizing even though I was now with the Opposition, they would be just fine on their own once we returned back to New York. We ran out of the facility to the car we had parked in the darkness. I couldn't help but stop at the gate and look back with a feeling deep inside that we would regret not destroying this place. Jade touched my arm lightly, "I know it feels extremely unresolved but we did the right thing tonight." I exhaled and headed back to the car with Jade. I really hoped honoring my promise to Toby and not destroying the facility and everyone in it really was the right thing to do.

CHAPTER FOURTEEN

The drive home already felt excruciatingly long and it had only just begun. I was awkwardly placed in the backseat next to Aden, while Jade and Dylan were in the front. Dylan had chosen to drive once again now that he knew he could get away with it, and I think he secretly loved breaking the law, not to mention he was on a strange adrenaline high from freezing the facility. I was still feeling terrible from the panic attack that had taken over me earlier and all I could think about was sleeping the entire trip back home but Aden's presence was keeping me awake. No one was talking as we drove, but it was understandable given what we had just been through. What I couldn't understand was why Dylan and Jade insisted on having Aden return to New York with us, rather than leave him at home with his family. In my opinion he didn't have anything to do with what was happening in New York and he'd be better off staying out of it and out of my way. After seeing how he responded in Addison's office I knew without doubt that Aden was going to try and stand in my way and I didn't want that or need that right now. His feelings for me were still clearly present and knowing how Aden worked he would try to win we back by rushing in to save the day, but I didn't need him to save me or help me for that matter. What I needed was to restore my energy, get back to base camp, get back to work and find Toby. Finally having Aden back in my life made it clear that whatever Mel had done to me when I arrived at the Opposition's headquarters had worked because all I felt towards him was irritation.

"Are you doing okay?" Aden was quiet when he spoke but there was a nervous twinge to his voice. It was the kind of sound a person makes when they know they've done something horribly wrong but are hoping the other person will forget with the niceties.

I looked over at him and sighed, "Please don't talk to me." His face dropped in the way only Aden's ever could, like a puppy that has just been scolded.

His face fell in sadness but also frustration because in true Aden form, he hated what he couldn't understand and my anger towards him he couldn't seem to grasp. "Why does it have to be like this, Em?"

"Because you ripped my heart out and left me completely alone. You can't just walk back into people's lives whenever it feels right for you. I waited for you Aden, but you never came and so I moved on. Nothing is the same as it was and you missed your chance; it's too late now." As I leaned my head back onto the seat I caught eyes quickly with Jade in the rearview mirror. Her eyes were sad and pained expressing her disappoint with how everything was turning out with the four of us. She had every right to feel that way too because the truth was, it was heartbreaking. Heartbreaking that love could cease to exist so easily and quickly and that something this beautiful could turn so dark.

I closed my eyes to shut it all out and just pray that we got back to New York quickly and I could attribute this whole experience to just a bad, very, bad dream of a life I no longer was apart of.

Time passed by quietly and the only sounds that were heard was a soft bit of pop music playing from the radio. Jade had turned it on to drown out the silence and it helped me relax and gave me something to focus on, which I appreciated. I was stuck in that place where you are halfway between sleep and yet still very aware of the world around you. When Jade, Dylan and Aden began speaking I was all too aware of the conversation, but too far gone to actually participate. I did the only thing I knew I could do, I pretended to be fully asleep and yet eavesdrop at the same time. Dylan and Jade started up a quiet conversation in the front seat that clearly was meant to exclude Aden and I.

"Do you think what Addison said about Ember being responsible for the Shadows was true?" Jade asked softly to Dylan.

"I don't know. It makes sense in a lot of ways. She obviously didn't know about any of it, even though he's making it seem like she did. Despite who she's become I still trust her and I don't think she'd ever willingly sign up for anything that would hurt people." I could hear Dylan's fingers sliding anxiously around the leather steering wheel. They both fell silent again for awhile until Jade broke the silence and decided to include Aden.

"Aden, are you doing alright? Do you need anything?" Jade always had a very nurturing tone to her voice and it had a way of calming your senses.

"I'm good, thank you. I really appreciate all you guys have done for my family and I. How do you guys know, Ember?"

"Well we'd like to believe we've always been connected but we met recently in New York under interesting circumstances." Jade laughed quietly to herself as if she were reliving the moment we met all over again.

"Interesting circumstances? I don't understand." Aden's tone was caught somewhere in between a jealous ex-boyfriend and a small child who was about to grow up too fast once he discovered the truth about this world.

"Ember met Dylan first and he introduced her to me. When we both met Ember she wasn't visible like she is now, which made the situation very interesting. We made it through though." Jade was very matter of fact about it all but at the same time seemed to be taking it easy on Aden for the moment by not dropping too much information on him at once.

"She was invisible? Is that even possible? I mean I know psionics can do some pretty crazy things but how does a person just stop being visible?" Now Aden's voice was filled with excitement and he wasn't holding back.

"Benders. They call themselves Benders." Dylan finally joined the conversation, "And it's very possible to become invisible when you don't feel like you matter much to the world." There was a harshness to Dylan's voice that came rather unexpectedly. It was the kind of harshness that came out as protective and tinged with a bit of hostility.

"What are Benders?" Aden always liked to focus on what he could process at the time and ignore feelings or the truth of how much he may have hurt someone, and it came as no surprise that he would do that now.

"Benders are what you, Jade and Ember are. You call them psionics but the correct term is Bender. It means that you can bend the laws of physics." Dylan was remaining short with Aden. His replies came out sounding like he could care less if Aden was informed about this world or not and I secretly was hoping he would decide to drop Aden off on the side of the road in the middle of nowhere.

"If we're Benders, then what are you, Dylan?" Aden was now beginning to match Dylan's tone with one of his own. Except Aden's tone didn't come out protective or strong, it came out as if he were challenging Dylan.

"I'm Lost. It means I'm half Static, an average human with no abilities, and half Bender." Dylan left it alone at that and it was clear Aden was formulating a reply but Dylan decided to speak first, "Look Aden, there is a lot you clearly don't know and that's fine. We can teach you everything you need to know in time just like we did with Ember, but there are more pressing matters at the moment you need to focus on. If you're going to stick with us then get yourself in check and man up. You left Ember, fine, it happens and it sucks. But the effect of your decision is far greater than just a broken heart. She isn't herself anymore because she went to great lengths to forget about you. Lengths so great that she is about to wage war and that war can't happen. So you better start helping us figure out a solution to get Ember back before she's gone forever." His tone was a mixture of anger, sadness and defeat as he reflected on what had happened.

The car was silent once again, eerily silent and I felt Aden fidget in his seat for a moment before he reached out and gently moved a piece of hair away from my face. "What do you mean get her back? She's here with us now." Aden dropped the in control, challenging tone and traded it for a much softer one that had previously been reserved for talking with me.

"Ember gave up her empathy. Somehow a fairly powerful empath found a way to tap into that part of her and block it out. We don't know how to get it back but without it she's only looking out for herself. Getting her to come save you and your family was near impossible." Jade helped break up the tension between Dylan and Aden by joining the conversation again.

"She hurt that much that she'd give it all up like that? I was wondering why she changed her appearance and didn't act the same as she used to be." Aden's voice was small and for the first time since our reunion he sounded as though he were finally beginning to understand how deeply he had hurt me.

I heard Jade move in her seat to face Aden, "Do you know what it looks like when a soul is broken?"

Aden must have shaken his head no because Jade continued to speak. "It's like loving the stars. They are so perfect in every way but in reality they are just reflections of a light that died a long time before we got to see it. No matter how much you love the stars they can never love you in return. They shine for a time and then fade away only to never be forgotten. Their beauty and wonderstruck feeling lingers in your soul for eternity. And yet no matter how much you love the stars they'll always be this distant reminder of what you can't have, but by that point it's too late because they've become such a deep part of you and you're wrecked forever by that kind of love." I could hear Jade's voice carry from a different direction monetarily and I assumed she was glancing at Dylan.

When she continued again, her voice was aimed back at Aden. "They are ghosts, Shadows of another life and they haunt your soul until it breaks and there is nothing left. From what Ember has shared with Dylan and I about the love you two shared it was pretty powerful. It sounds like the kind of love that would change you either for the better or worse. In this case it changed you both for the worst. I don't think it was the love that did that but rather the fear of losing something so great that made it turn out so badly. We really love and care for Ember and it broke our hearts when she left us for the Opposition. We aren't going to give up on her, though, just like she didn't give up on you."

I heard Aden sigh and he began nervously tapping his fingers on the door handle. "What kind of war is she about to get into?" He sounded indifferent when he spoke as if suddenly he too could feel nothing anymore.

"The Opposition is a group of Benders who believe that we should live out in the open. That it's not fair for us to have to hide all the time and they want to over rule the Statics. Dylan and I don't really associate with either side of The Guild, but I suppose if we had to choose we'd be on the side of the Resistance, and that also is a group of Benders trying to stop the war from happening. We can't live in peace with the Statics. They hunt us, as you've now experienced and going public with what we can do would only make us greater targets than we already are. Either way, the Opposition will stop at nothing to achieve their place of power and dominance in this world, even if that means seeing the world burn." Jade spoke like a true rebel set out to stop something she'd never be a match for.

"When will this war take place?" I could feel Aden touch my hand gently and stroke my fingers, one at a time. I had no doubt this was becoming more than he could handle and that he was beginning to see me for who I really was now and not who he had left me to be.

"We don't know what they have planned or what their timeline is exactly. The Guild still meets regularly to try and compromise on the situation but now that they have Ember on their side they have the ultimate weapon." There was a lot of sadness in Jade's voice that sounded like someone who knew they were defeated before they even got a chance to try.

"Who is The Guild and why is Ember the ultimate weapon? I mean, Em, wouldn't hurt a fly. How do they expect her to lead them into war?" Aden laughed slightly as if everything he were hearing was a truly great fabricated story.

"The Guild guides Benders. Your parents helped create The Guild in fact. All of our parents founded The Guild. And I don't know what it's going to take to convince you that the girl sleeping there next to you isn't the girl you once knew. This

Ember gave up a long time ago and refuses to fight the good fight anymore, because she no longer realizes the value of love. Love has become a weakness to her and she got rid of it."

Before Jade could speak again Dylan piped up, "Look there's a Denny's up ahead. Let's stop for some food and a bathroom break and you can spend some time with your sweet, loving, wouldn't hurt a fly Ember. See what you think." The car swerved off the highway as Dylan parked the car. I decided now was as good of any time to wake up seeing as he slammed on the brakes rather hard.

"Geez, are you trying to kill us?" I asked sitting up in the backseat and rubbing my head where it had hit the door handle.

"Aw, it's nice to see you too sleeping beauty." Dylan maintained his sarcastic and disappointed tone as he got out of the car and the rest of us followed. We walked up to the entrance and Aden gently grabbed my arm and slowed me down letting Jade and Dylan go ahead.

"Can we sit together? Just you and me." Aden asked as sweetly as anyone could and all I could do was laugh at him.

"Are you kidding me? No, you can't sit with me." I saw the crushed look in his face and then the flash of determination that went through his eyes.

"Don't laugh at me. I'm serious. We're sitting together." He spoke to me as if he owned me but I was too tired to fight. I rolled my eyes and sighed, "Whatever."

We walked inside and he requested a seat for two. It had been a long time since we had been out anywhere together that it felt extremely familiar but on the other hand it felt like a chore and something to get through. I immediately picked up the greasy, laminated menu that was placed on the table and used it as a buffer between Aden and I. My naive hope was that I could get through this meal quickly and without having to talk to Aden. Couldn't we remain like ships in the night and just keep passing each other by? As I set my menu down and caught eyes with Aden I realized that wasn't going to be a possibility in his mind. "Alright, so get on with it." His lips quirked up at the side into not quite a smile but also slightly a smirk.

"On with what?" He set his menu down and placed his hands on the table in front of him. It felt more like an interview now than two people casually chatting.

"Get on with why you wanted to eat together." I was maintaining my strong and blasé attitude but the truth was, sitting there, in front of him made me nervous.

Aden waited until we had ordered our food to begin talking. "I wanted to catch up, see how you've been? It seems like a lot has changed since I last saw you." He must have been nervous too because he kept messing with the sugar packets that were next to him.

I nodded, "Yeah, a lot has changed." I sighed and tapped my fingers on the formica table. I didn't have patience for this game of pretending things were okay, when they weren't and when they probably never would be again. "You can't honestly expect me to sit here and fill you in on the details of my life as if we're two friends who just haven't seen each other in a long time. We're so far beyond that."

I noticed a slight twinge of either pain or anger on Aden's face but he was quick to fix it and remain neutral. "Are we far beyond that?"

"Yes, you made your choices Aden and you walked away. These are the cards you dealt and you can't just walk back into my life as if nothing ever happened." Our food arrived and I found myself thankful for the excuse to not talk much while we ate.

Aden took a sip of his soda and then began assembling his burger. Watching him do that felt like it was just yesterday and we were on a normal date. At the same time thinking of those past memories only ignited an anger inside of me even more and made me focus on the food in front of me to forget the old memories.

"Em, I know that I messed up and I made a huge mistake. I heard a lot from Jade and Dylan on he car ride here about how things have been going for you and I want to be your friend again and not your enemy." His words were honest and real but all I could do was read between the lines and know that there had to be more to it than that.

"I don't know what they told you, but trust me, I'm fine. I have a future ahead of me and one that is going to change the world." I couldn't help but smile as I thought about life back in New York with the Opposition and how soon everything would change for all Benders.

"How are you going to change the world?" Aden's face was serious and concerned which clued me in to the reality that he was fishing for information about the war Jade and Dylan warned him about that I was apparently leading.

"Benders deserve equal rights in this world. We've spent our lives hiding and running away from people who want to use us or destroy us. That's all about to change. I don't expect you to understand, just like Dylan and Jade don't, but I believe in this." I took a bite of food and watched as Aden processed what I was saying.

"They said you were going to start a war." His eyes locked on mine again and I could tell he was trying to use his abilities to reach me and all I could do was smirk.

"First of all, stop trying. I have learned how to block most everyone's abilities. Secondly, yes, we are planning a war but it's the only option we have right now." I looked down as a piece of french fry fell off my plate and onto my lap. I couldn't help but take in my military grade black pants and black boots that I now wore.

Aden wanted to speak but I looked up and stopped him, "I was raised a warrior Aden. You saw a glimpse of my past life tonight back at the base. I wasn't given the chance to entertain dreams of being a princess or ballerina. Sure, I wanted to be something like that and while I attended school I

331

was envious of the other girls who got to be those things, or at the very least dream of being those things. My days and nights were spent training whether in combat or abilities. I was trained and raised to be a super solider of sorts. It's the world I knew and even though I was like a bird in a cage longing to see where the sky could take me, I didn't have much else to go on. When I met you, it was like being set free for the first time in my life. I was able to be whatever I wanted to be. Being with you allowed me to be a girlie girl and to wear dresses and makeup. I had a reason every morning I woke up to do my hair and feel pretty." I couldn't help but smile for a brief second remembering how fun it was to get dressed up sometimes and do my hair and feel like a delicate girl rather than a solider.

"My life before you was hard and I did things I am not proud of. And I'm not looking for sympathy, but I want you to understand that who I've become isn't something new or radically different than what I've always been. It's just you're finally seeing me as I am and not as you wanted me to be." I finally removed the fry off my lap and tossed it onto the table next to my plate.

Aden was silent for awhile as he sipped his drink and took in my words. I was all too familiar

332

with his silence. He was either trying to calm himself down before he spoke or was simply processing what I had told him. Those two emotions were hard to determine between when it came to him.

"For someone who supposedly gave up their empathy you sure seem to have an awful lot of feelings?" His tone came across in a highly annoying and accusing manner and he wasn't doing much to hide the challenging look on his face either.

I smirked and took a slow sip of my soda, "I'm still capable of feeling things, I just simply gave up my ability to feel anything for you."

My words were like a harsh slap to his face and then straight to his heart. I couldn't understand why it mattered whether I felt anything for him or not anymore. He was the one who chose to leave me and he was the one who chose not to come after me. Did he really expect that I would have spent all this time waiting for him? It was an impossible notion to me that he would be that egotistical and think that highly of himself to expect something like that of me.

The restaurant was maintaining it's usual busy hum of extraneous conversations and dishes being clinked together as they were moved here and there but I found myself able to block all the sound out as if time were standing still and I focused in on Aden in an attempt to make him see reality now as I saw it and to feel the void he left within me. The connection caught Aden off guard as he placed both hands on the edge of the table trying to maintain control. My time within the Opposition had made me stronger and I could use my abilities in ways he could only ever imagine. His eyes were forced to lock on mine and I held his gaze in silence as I let him feel the numbness that surged through me.

I allowed him access to the last memory I had of my former self right before I gave up hope for him and I and surrendered my empathy and heart to darkness. I took him through the pain and terrifying process of having Mel block my empathy. I pulled him out of my mind and kept him looking at me as I spoke softly so only he could hear.

"Aden, I loved you in a way I never thought was possible to love another human being. I've spent months holding onto hope that we could be together again and that the love you claimed to have for me was as real as you said it was. I believed you with the most deepest held convictions of my heart. I fought for you because the only thing that made sense to me was that someone had done something

to you causing you to act the way you did. And
maybe they did because when we'd connect it was
dark and lonely inside your mind; like a war torn
world that may never recover from the devastation.
I don't know what caused that kind of destruction
but I became the collateral damage to your inner
war and in order to survive I had to do whatever it
took to break free from you. There may be some
alternate universe out there somewhere where we
ended up together and we were happy. I like to
imagine that to be true but this is reality and there is
a cause and effect for everything we decide to do. A
tiny ripple in the system can bring it all down. I
don't think I'm what everyone claims I am. Heck, I
don't know if the four of us are really all that
important to the entire system like everyone seems
to believe we are. What I do know is you were my
world for a time and it came crashing in around me
and suddenly everything I thought I knew was
wrong. Everything I believed had been a lie. I'm
trying to rebuild the world for what it really is and
stop living a lie. Love wasn't strong enough to
weather the hard times together. Love was the
biggest fairy tale of all and I bought into it because
of you and just like a child who grows up to
discover that life is anything but a fairytale." I kept

my eyes locked on Aden's and found myself growing angry at him and myself for letting it all get this far.

"My love wasn't good enough, but I can help our people come out of the Shadows and live freely and that's what I'm going to do. Your one decision to let me go was the ripple in our timeline that will change the history of our world forever. You can join us and fight this war to set Bender's free or you can be our enemy. Either choice you make it's too late to go back to what we had before."

The connection between us was released and the sounds around us returned reminding us that life will go on with or without us. We have only the choice of what role we will play while we are here. And my choice had been made. There was nothing Aden could do now to stop the chain reaction of what had already begun. I watched as he sat back against the vinyl booth and exhaled deeply. His eyes were glassy as if tears would fall any second now. I looked away to see where Jade and Dylan had gone to in hopes they were ready to leave.

Before I had time to stop him Aden was over on my side of the booth and sliding in next to me. "What are you...?" I couldn't even finish my sentence before he had me blocked inside the booth and without hesitation he placed his hand over my heart firmly and looked me straight in the eyes. I held his gaze daring him to try whatever he had in mind.

"If you're so sure of everything you believe now then you shouldn't have any trouble dropping your guard and letting me in." He kept his hand firmly in place over my heart, as he always used to do when he wanted to connect with me in the deepest of ways and his eyes locked on mine with such precision and determination I couldn't look away.

I sighed out of frustration because while the feelings for him may have been taken away the memories of our time together were like ghosts that haunted me in moments like these. Somehow my memories failed me in allowing me a glimpse into how he used to make me feel when he'd place his hand over my heart like this and stare into my eyes. I was angry that my mind was now my own personal traitor. I was determined for him not to succeed because I refused to let him have any power over me anymore. I closed my eyes for a moment and steadied myself and when I opened them again I looked right into his eyes and said, "Go ahead."

Never before had I seen a fire in Aden's eyes like I did tonight. He was determined to reach me and I still couldn't understand why. The question kept running through my mind of what had changed since I last saw him that made him now want to make the effort to be with me. Aden always had a bit of a hero complex and the thought ran through my mind that maybe he simply wanted to try and be the hero of this story and I was nothing more to him than a damsel in distress. Either way I let my block down and allowed him to read me and connect with me like we had done many times before.

Suddenly I looked around and we weren't inside Denny's anymore. Aden had a strong hold of my hand and I could feel the invisible tether that held us together in this moment and it made me feel what I could only describe as anxious. "Where are we?" I asked looking around and not quite recognizing the location.

"We are in the Capitol State Forest, otherwise known as the Black Hills." Aden said pulling me forward gently.

It was hard to see much of anything since it appeared to be the middle of the night and except for the light of the moon and stars above everything was cloaked in darkness. As we walked forward I saw Aden's car ahead. It's bright, silver exterior was like a beacon of light in the otherwise all encompassing darkness that was around us. We didn't go all the way to the car but stopped a few feet away. "Why are we stopping?" I kept waiting for something to happen but all was still in the forest.

Aden took a moment to gather his thoughts and I kept my eyes focused on the car expecting something to happen, even though it never did. "This is where I went after we broke up."

I narrowed my eyes and looked at Aden trying to make sense of what he wanted me to see. "And?"

He kept his hand in mine but turned to face me. For the first time since we broke up I could see the compassion and pain inside his eyes. He wasn't holding back anymore and there was something about the way he looked at me that made me feel vulnerable too. "Em, I came here to disappear. I couldn't live with myself knowing what I had done to you." Aden looked ahead at the car and swallowed hard and then turned to look at me as he took both my hands into his. "You have to forgive me. I didn't know the depth of what I was doing." His face was washed in agony and regret and I still didn't understand what this was all about.

"I don't understand why you brought me here. You broke my heart, we've moved on, all is forgiven. So why run away to the hills?" I allowed him to hold my hands even though his familiar warmth was causing inner conflict within me. I could feel myself wanting to fight against the block on my heart I held for him and the part that apparently wasn't dormant for his affections either.

"No, you aren't understanding." He sighed and ran his hand through his hair and finally I was beginning to understand that what he was trying to tell me was bigger than just a quick apology. He gained some of his composure back and held my hands again. "Ember, my parents have always known who you are. They knew your parents a long time ago. When I approached you at school, the day we first met, I knew who you were. I don't mean in the sense that I knew you as my classmate, I mean I knew you in the sense that I was told to become friends with you. My parents urged me to befriend you and gain your trust. They didn't exactly tell me why but I also didn't have much of a choice. I figured it wouldn't hurt being your friend. You didn't seem to have any at the time and I thought it could work in both our favor." Aden took a moment to sigh in anguish before continuing and I could feel my heart seizing up and racing inside my chest as if it were pleading him to stop. I didn't want to hear anymore but I knew I had to know the truth. "I admit I tried the conventional ways to get your attention and when they failed I used my abilities on you. I made you feel things that would encourage you to befriend me and I'm not proud of it but I didn't feel like I had any other options. When I told my parents you weren't coming around I was encouraged to form a friendship at any cost. Em, you have to believe me that I didn't do this with any ill intentions, I honestly believed it was harmless."

"You manipulated me into becoming your friend?" My words came out shaky as I forcefully pulled my hands out of his and kept them close to me. Somehow he was able to break past the block on my empathy and emotions because I could feel the inner battle winning in favor of the old Ember and I could feel the pain rising up within me with a fury like no other.

"Listen to me, please. I'm not done. Yes, I, "encouraged" your friendship with me but once I got to know you I really was glad we were friends. You're an incredible girl and knowing you were like me in so many ways drew me in. I was falling in love with you shortly after we met. That wasn't forced or fake, that was 100% real. Except that I was fighting those feelings because my parents were pressuring me to date you. Everything within me knew something was wrong with the way they kept trying to pressure me to get closer to you. For awhile the lines just blurred together and I couldn't tell whether my feelings were my own or just the by product of wanting to please them. Regardless, the more time I spent with you, the more I realized these feelings were indeed my own. I couldn't imagine spending a second without you. Choosing to be with you was the best decision I had ever made and I don't regret it for a second. It may have started as my parent's idea but it definitely was all mine when I finally asked you out on a date and later told you I loved you. I know you think I lied and yes, I did in some ways, but when I told you I loved you, I meant it wholeheartedly, Ember. Once we were together my parents seemed content and they weren't pressuring me anymore. They acted like normal parents again and life felt right finally."

Aden took a moment to catch his breath and he involuntarily reached out to touch my arm but I backed away. He cringed and quickly dropped his arm at his side. "I don't even know how to tell you this because I don't know if you'll ever stopping hating me for it but here it goes. The night we broke up, as unbelievable as this sounds, I did it to protect you. I had overheard my parents talking on a conference call the day before. They thought I was out with you and I had come home apparently too early. They were speaking with a man, I didn't know, about you. I listened in to the end of the conversation and was horrified by what my parents were planning. They were going to turn you in to the government, Em. They were going to give you back."

Aden stopped for a brief moment to wipe a stray tear before continuing. "I rushed in the minute they hung up the call and demanded answers. I never got them that night. My parents attempted to re-route my thoughts on the matter and in some ways I guess they succeeded. The next morning I woke up with this deep, gut wrenching feeling that I had to say goodbye to you. I couldn't remember fully what had happened to make me come to that conclusion but I knew with so much resolve in my heart it was the only way things could be. I thought I was protecting you and doing right by you. I swore I would never hurt you but what choice did I have? Either I would hurt you and give you a chance at a free life or be selfish and stay with you and watch you get taken. You'd be hurt either way but at least this way I knew you'd have a chance at life." He stopped for a brief pause and I couldn't help but wonder if he expected me to thank him or deem him my hero for what he had done.

"My parents and I getting captured wasn't by accident and didn't happen at random. It was a staged event. Somehow my parents know way more than I ever knew was possible and they knew your friends and others were tracking them. They worked with Commander Addison in the hopes that once you heard we were captured you'd return and in exchange for our cooperation he could keep you. You're like some sort of trophy prize to him. It's sick really. While we were at the base I discovered that my parents have been working with Commander Addison in studying our people and discovering ways to transfer our abilities to regular humans. They said they were doing their civic duty and helping their country by making people stronger and more able to fight outside enemies. They really believed what they were doing was the right thing. But evil done in the name of good is still evil, right? You want me to choose a side in this supposed war you want to wage, but Em, I'm a prisoner of this war. I can't choose a side because I'm already compromised. So yeah, I brought you here because much like you becoming invisible to the world, I wanted to do the same. I tried to disappear from my parents and tried to connect with you and find you. Sometimes I thought I was getting through but I could never really decipher between daydreams and what was real anymore."

All that Aden had said left me speechless and once again I felt like my world was spinning out of control and about to fly off it's axis. Looking at Aden I felt a dark anger rising inside of me. An anger that was trying to consume me. There was something else though, something resisting that anger from taking over every part of me and that was the small, but strong part of me that wanted to believe what Aden was saying was true. I just couldn't seem to find it within me to believe anything anymore. When I was with the Opposition everything seemed to be black and white. It was us against them, the Resistance, and The Guild as a whole was against the government that kept trying to hurt us. Now knowing that Aden's parents, who help found The Guild, were working against us too, added a whole new dimension to everything. And Aden was right, he was compromised. He had this innate desire to please his parents and longed for their approval so how could he be trusted anymore? My hands were balled into fists so tightly they were turning white. Everything within me felt unleashed and uncontrollable. I couldn't stop the feelings from breaking through anymore and I couldn't seem to focus on any one thought, as a million were flying around inside my mind. I was desperately grasping for some foundational truth to rest on but nothing and yet everything was making sense now. I closed my eyes to try and contain the chaos that was growing inside me and it was the loud and terrified screams that snapped me back to reality. I gasped as I opened my eyes and saw Denny's in complete darkness and small pieces of glass on the table in front of me. I had done it again. I had blown out the lights with my abilities once again proving that my ability to feel was a danger to everyone.

"Are you okay? What happened?" Aden was hovering over me and I pushed him away.

"I'm fine. We need to leave." Once Aden had given me room to move I slid out of the booth, dropping a few dollars for the meal and went to find Dylan and Jade. As we moved carefully through the dark restaurant I could hear waiters and waitresses urging patrons to remain calm and assuring them it was a random power outage.

Dylan and Jade found us towards the front entry way. "What the hell happened?" Dylan asked as we all instinctually headed out the door.

"I blew out the lights." I said flatly as the car was unlocked and we got inside quietly.

"Cool party trick." Jade said trying to break the tension in the car. I knew she and Dylan both had to have seen this moment with Aden coming. I was assuming since no one got hurt they were okay with it happening in the hopes that it would awaken my empathy again and soften me up. At the moment though apart of me was definitely awakened and was eager to return to New York. I didn't know yet what I would do but in my current state anything was possible and I assumed it wouldn't be good.

CHAPTER FIFTEEN

Being underground made it hard to keep track of the day and night. When I sat up in bed I saw Jade and Dylan snuggled up together on the couch and Aden was on the floor next to my bed. I hadn't seen anyone yet except for Romie's henchman, Mikey, who had said my "friends" could stay one night. How generous. Who I had been eagerly waiting to see was Toby but he hadn't made an appearance yet. I decided to not waste anymore time and to go see Toby myself. I quietly slipped off the non-Aden side of my bed and headed for the door.

The place was quiet and no one was up moving about as usual which led me to believe it was late at night still or early morning. I headed to the area where Toby lived feeling more and more anxiously excited to see him with each step I took. When I arrived everyone was sleeping in their respective cots. I wasn't sure where Toby's was and I couldn't risk getting him in trouble, which meant I had to try and find him some other way. I stood on the outskirts and closed my eyes trying to reach Toby telepathically. I came up empty. The stupid block put on their minds was really getting annoying. All I could do now was find Toby the old fashioned way which sent a surge of excitement through every inch of my being. I was becoming so used to using my abilities and relying on them for everything these days that having a brief moment of being "normal" sounded incredible. I began tip toeing through the cots as quietly as I could; I still hadn't discovered any hidden abilities to silence my movements. A few people stirred in their cots causing me to freeze in my tracks. Being here was against the rules and I knew that despite my favor with Romie this could get both Toby and I in major trouble. As I tiptoed through the cots and looked at the sleeping faces surrounding me I couldn't understand why everyone treated these people like slaves and the lowest class possible. It wasn't their fault they were born into a world that saw them as a threat and most of them weren't threats at all. The fear Bender's carried around with them everyday caused them to force the Lost into living this shadow of a life and it wasn't fair. They deserved a chance at a happy and prosperous life just as much as anyone else did. I was getting so caught up in my thoughts that I almost tripped over Toby's cot. When I lost my cadence and stumbled slightly he immediately woke up and on guard, bringing with him two other guys who were sandwiched in next to his cot. "Toby, what the hell man?" One of the guy's voice was groggy and disjointed as if he may or may not be fully aware he was awake yet. The other guy on Toby's right however surprised me when he held up his hand and produced a soft white light and it hit me right in the eyes.

"How did you do that?" I tried to keep my voice to a whisper but in my excitement it came out more like a loud gasp.

He snickered back at me, "Really Bendie, you're going to ask me how?" Toby stood up and hit him lightly in the shoulder and began to pull me out of the makeshift camp. As we moved further and further away from the guys, attempting not to wake anyone else, I heard one of them whisper to Toby, "She's going to get you killed man." The light went out plunging their world back into the Shadows and Toby and I were outside now.

"What are you doing?" He was whispering and still holding onto my hand as we moved as far away from the camp as possible.

"I wanted to see you." We moved into the tunnel, that was now more our secret meeting place than anything else it might possibly be used for.

"You can't just barge in there like that. There are rules Ember, and you're breaking like a million of them." His face was tight and tinged with an anxious edge that made him look older than he actually was.

I moved away from him and ran my hand through my hair in frustration, speaking sarcastically to him, "Glad to see you too, Ember." I faced the wall staring at it's blank canvas and then knelt down right there and sat on the backs of my heels. "What would be so bad about me getting caught there with you?" I didn't hear Toby moving towards me but I felt his warmth as he took a seat next to me, "Death. That's what would happen if we were caught together." My head whipped around to look Toby in the eyes as I couldn't believe what I was hearing. "Why would they kill you?"

His features turned suddenly soft and tender as he looked at me empathetically, "This is our world Em. Lost and Benders can't be together." He touched my cheek softly as if taking one last moment with the very thing he couldn't have.

I shook my head, "No, Lost and Benders have always been together. Sure, it wasn't well accepted but it didn't mean death. You must have it wrong."

Toby inhaled and then exhaled slowly, "The world was different once and I guess when we're in times of pending war the rules have to be different. I don't agree with it and I truly believe in my heart you don't either. That's why I've always known you would set this world free."

Everything he was saying finally was beginning to make sense, even in the smallest of ways. All I could think about was the fact that my presence with him could lead to his death and the conversation with Commander Addison began running through my mind again. Death followed me like a shadow and I would consume everything in my reach. The block on my empathy had lost a lot of its strength and while I still tried to maintain it, emotions were breaking through. Tears began to well up in my eyes as I turned away from Toby, "What is happening to me?" The words fell out of my mouth in a sloppy pathetic whisper.

His arms wrapped around me and I could feel his breath by my ear as he whispered, "It's okay to feel." I turned to face him and our noses were touching and our eyes locked on each other. I remained there for a moment just taking in his every feature before I pulled back just enough to breathe freely. I didn't know what to say or what to think. Truthfully, I could feel again, but not in the way I was familiar with. Maybe these things just take time to find their way back to us or maybe I was just deathly afraid of what would happen if I allowed myself to feel again and love someone knowing it could lead to their death.

My time with Jade, Dylan, and Aden, and more recently my moments spent with Toby, had ignited in me a spark that was turning steadily into a flame. I was beginning to find it harder and harder to maintain my general disinterest in life beyond my own concerns and was feeling the ever present pull of the world around me. Toby lifted me up slowly and as I kept my eyes locked on him a few tears fell down my cheeks betraying my heart that wanted to stay locked up tight to protect him and myself. He wiped his slightly callused thumb across my cheek and kept his eyes locked on mine.

"You know if I'm caught with you, they'll kill me, but you're worth the risk." He whispered to me as he gently pulled some of my hair behind my ear.

"I would never let that happen to you. I'm not worth it Toby." I took his hand in mine and held it between us. I couldn't help but notice how perfectly his hand fit into mine.

Toby smiled softly, "You'd save the world if you could Ember. That's what is so incredible about you. And I'd risk my life a thousand times in a thousand lifetimes if it meant one more moment with you."

I exhaled slowly as I fought back the desire to kiss him. It didn't seem like a fair thing to do knowing my emotions were all over the place and I wanted to be sure of what I felt so that I wouldn't risk playing with his heart. "Maybe we should just run away then." I saw Toby's eyes light up in surprise as he bit his bottom lip for a brief second and considered my offer.

"And where would we go? Ember, we'd always be on the run. You deserve a better life than that." He placed his hands on my waist and I could see the look of sadness hit his eyes as we faced the reality that we'd never get to live a normal life. Not like this anyway. I looked down to help steady myself as the reality of the situation fell on me. "Maybe, I could help you escape for a little while. If you'd like?" Toby's excited tone lit up the otherwise dark moment.

I looked up and saw Toby smile uneasily. "How?" The idea of running off with Toby, even if just temporarily, excited me beyond words.

"You just have to trust me. I mean after all I'm the one risking death." He chuckled lightly and I couldn't help but return his smile.

"I trust you. Lead the way." He took my hand and we walked towards the back exit of the underground dwelling. He opened the door and let me walk outside first. The sky was just beginning to show hints of light as the sun was slow to rise in the sky. Toby closed the door softly behind him and then looked at me as if he were calculating his decision very carefully.

"You can trust me, Toby." He smiled and nodded, "I know. Turn around." I turned my back towards him and he placed one strong arm around my waist pulling our bodies as close together as they could be sending a sharp wave of electricity through my veins. Then he covered my eyes with his other hand. "What are you doing?" I asked curiously and feeling a surge of nervous excitement run through me.

"You've asked me what my ability was and I'm going to show you. Hold on." He held me tightly against his body and suddenly I could feel my feet lifting off the ground. I grabbed onto Toby's arm tightly as he released his hand from my eyes and placed it tightly around the other side of my waist. We were about 10 feet off the ground and climbing higher.

"You can fly?" I gasped as I watched the world grow smaller and smaller below us.

"Yes, I can take you anywhere you want to go." His lips were right against my ear as he spoke and despite the wind hitting us, his voice sent my heart beating faster and faster as we climbed higher and higher.

He continued to hold onto me tightly as we flew around just under the clouds. The view was unlike anything I had ever seen before. For the first time in my life I knew what it felt like to be truly free and if we could just keep flying and never touch back down again, I'd be okay with that. The sun continued to rise illuminating the city below us and with every second the sun climbed higher in the sky the city became more alive. Off in the distance I noticed the sky was remaining dark and no amount of sunlight was able to penetrate through it. "Toby, what is that?" I pointed towards the darkness that fell like a dark shadow over the city.

"I don't know. We'll land and see if we can get a closer look." Toby veered downward and toward one of the larger city buildings. We landed gracefully on the top of a high rise roof. Toby didn't let go right away and that was perfectly fine with me. We stood there together looking out toward the sky that continued to remain untouched by the light.

"I think it's...moving." Toby said softly in my ear as we stood there watching the light being snuffed out by this dark cloud that was slowly sweeping over the city.

Before I even had a chance to think about what was happening or how I was all too familiar with Shadows I crumpled over holding onto Toby's arms, that were still around my waist, for support. I moaned in pain as my body was reminded of the forces that sought to take me down.

"Ember, what's wrong?" Toby spun me around to face him and I buried my head in his shoulder. Tears filled my eyes as the pain moved through every nerve and every vein. My head was throbbing and felt as if it would explode into a million tiny pieces. I had no control over myself or my abilities. I forced myself to look up at Toby, "Home." It was the only word I could manage to speak. Instantly and without pause he lifted us into the air and flew at a speed I didn't know was possible. The further we got away from the Shadows the more control I gained back but I knew with the size of what we were seeing I wouldn't be able to run from them or force them away this time. As we flew over the city we could hear the onset of screams and saw buildings beginning to fall and crumble. People ran for their lives as dust began to fill the air. I wanted to close my eyes and pretend that this wasn't happening but it didn't seem fair to look the other way. Innocent people were going to get hurt, just as they had with every other Bender attack against them. They were causalities of a war they didn't even know existed and because people like me and Toby lived, their lives were being interrupted or ended far too soon. I watched as the waves of hysteria began to sweep over the city and people tried to outrun what was coming.

We got back to the underground compound in what felt like no time at all. Toby placed me gently on the ground and we quickly got inside to find that everyone was awake and preparing to fight back. Toby quickly let me go but remained by my side. Aden ran over to me and threw his arms around me hugging me. I didn't return the hug but didn't push him away either.

"Where have you been, Em? Why did you run off with, *him*?" He pointed to Toby and I rolled my eyes pushing Aden away.

"Now is not the time for jealousy, Aden. We were just getting some air and then the attacks began." I saw Mikey and Romie heading over quickly and at that Toby disappeared into the crowd but still maintained a close proximity to me.

Romie walked up first and had an eager fire in his eye to attack back but he was calculating his movements first and wasn't about to attack without having a plan. "Ember, what did you see?" He pulled me down the stairs and into the common area, as a parent would do with their child.

"This is what we were warned about. The captured Benders who are being used by the government." I said trying to regain control over myself as I felt the Shadows growing closer. Romie sighed and looked at Mikey giving him a single nod. Mikey ran off into the distance without a word.

"You can't fight this Romie. None of you can. They want me. I started this and now I have to end this." The room erupted into cries of anger, lust for war and outrage. The outrage mostly coming from Aden, Toby, Jade and Dylan. "You know it's true. I've always been The Guild's secret weapon and I think somehow they've always known the time would come when Addison would want me back and I'd be your sacrificial lamb."

Romie's eyes narrowed and he held out a hand that instantly silenced the room. "You're just one girl. A powerful girl, yes, but enough to appease the Statics in this war? I don't think so. They've taken our families and friends and they won't stop until they have it all."

I nodded, "That is all very true. Except for one point you're missing. They raised me and I know more about how they work than any one of you ever will. Addison confirmed it when we rescued Aden. These rogue Benders, the Shadows, are a creation based on what I can do. Today is not the day to fight this war. The war you so eagerly want isn't with the Statics out there, it's within our own ranks and if you hope to have a world left to rule then you better do whatever is necessary today to ensure that tomorrow." I saw Romie flinch slightly at my words and I could tell no one dared speak to him like that. He wasn't used to having someone else take control and from the flicker of irritation in his eyes I could tell he wouldn't be accepting of it either.

Romie paced slightly as a few hushed whispers floated through the acoustics of the room. "And what exactly is it you propose to do?" He stopped right in front of me and we locked eyes as he challenged me to create a plan better than he could.

I shrugged, "I don't exactly know what I will do except that I've always ran from my past and hoped that somehow if I just kept going I'd out run the pain too. If there is anything I've learned it's that sometimes you have to stop running and face it head on."

I looked away from Romie and into the crowd of people. "I am just one girl who undoubtedly won't even be remembered when I'm gone. My only legacy up until this point is that of rumors and my lineage. You've all believed at some point I was capable of something great, something bigger than any Bender has ever done before. I don't know if you're right or not, but I do know that I am ready to try. And if I can succeed, then wouldn't that make my life worth at least something? Isn't it worth giving up one life for all the other lives we'll save?"

Looking around the room I saw people glancing at one another as if they didn't want to make that decision. Lucky for them I already had made the decision for myself. Romie moved closer to me as if we could actually have a private conversation with all the people surrounding us.

"Why would you ever give up your life for Statics? All they've ever done is try to destroy us and hurt us. I am not as excited about bloodshed as I appear to be, but I also know that something has to be done for our kind to be free. What good will sacrificing yourself to the Statics do? It will only encourage them to keep coming after us. This won't end with one life being lost."

I nodded, "Maybe. But think about it, you chose me to join your ranks for a reason. You seem to think, like everyone else, that I can do something extraordinary. I've seen glimpses of what I can do since I've come here and I am willing to make you a deal."

Romie's eyebrows raised and he rubbed his chin. He motioned his hand in front of me, like a royal would to their subjects, to continue. Before I could speak again the ground began to rumble beneath us and we all knew the Shadows were getting closer. Time was not on our side anymore.

"Let me try things my way. If I fail you can wage your war. But if I succeed you hold off on the fighting." I held out my hand for him to shake in agreement. He narrowed his eyes as he considered the offer and then reached out to shake my hand. "Deal. I'll send some of my people with you to report back to me what happens. God sped, Ember." He released my hand and walked away.

Romie wasn't about to fight in a war that meant saving Static lives and thus losing Bender lives in the process. He was all too ready to concede to my plan because while he wanted me to fight with him, he wasn't prepared to sacrifice his people. I stood there watching him leave with a sadness in my heart. I hoped I could succeed, not just for the Statics but also for Benders like Romie. He had lived his life being brainwashed that all Statics and Lost were the same and that they only wanted to use us or destroy us. Losing his mother changed him but there was still hope that he could see things differently. His bloodlust wasn't really about power it was about revenge. A deeply, personal, revenge that could never truly be satisfied. My only hope was that I could succeed today and buy him more time to consider other options. To see that Statics and Lost were worth fighting for too. I watched as a majority of the people left in Romie's wake and I looked around at the all too familiar, disappointed, faces before me.

Aden rushed to my side and grabbed my hands, "You can't be serious, Ember." I looked at him as tenderly and gently as I could and nodded my head to let him know I was all too serious about this plan.

Dylan, Jade, and Toby joined him as they surrounded me. Their thoughts were loud and piercing in my mind and I didn't need them to speak to tell me that they were against this idea all together. I inhaled to steady myself and was thankful that while I was getting my feelings back I still could push them aside in times like this. "I wouldn't blame any of you if you chose to stay here and didn't join me."

"There has to be another way, Ember." Jade finally spoke with her eyes pleading me to stay. I smiled softly at her and Dylan.

"You both saw my death. I read your minds on our way to Washington. I'm sorry, but I had to know what you weren't telling me. I know that the future can always change and that what you see isn't always exactly what will be, but what choice do we have? I may not be the girl everyone thinks that I am. I may just in fact be the girl who wanted to be loved and in my pursuit of that love got caught up in a mess far beyond my understanding. Or maybe this all had to happen so that I could help those people out there and around the world. I know what it feels like to lose the one you love, to feel as if you don't matter anymore and to wish someone would stand in the gap for you. I never want anyone to feel that way again." I looked at Toby as I continued to speak because I wanted him to hear this next part most of all, "No matter what we are capable of we are still human beings. We all came into this world the same way and we all go out the same way. Everyone is capable of the extraordinary and who are we to say who gets to experience that and who doesn't? We've made a lot of bad decisions as Benders thinking that we had to protect ourselves but I think we got it wrong. I think we were given this birthright, these abilities, so that we could be the protectors of the world. We may remain in the Shadows and never be known for what we did, but the lives we help or maybe even save will be enough of a legacy for me. Will it be enough for you? Let today be the start of true change. Let it be the start of a true future alliance between Statics, Lost and Benders. We don't have to remain divided and segregated. I know I sound like a dreamer and I suppose I am, but this dream is one I am willing to give my life for."

Aden appeared to have tears welling up in his eyes as I spoke and I suppose he realized I wasn't going to back down from this decision I had already made. When I looked into his eyes they were pleading me not to go. He looked like a man consumed by inner demons and the reality that he had no way of recovering this relationship and in the process no way of stopping me now. I touched his arm sympathetically and then looked to everyone else, "Shall we?"

CHAPTER SIXTEEN

As we left the Opposition compound and entered the early morning streets of New York, we found what looked more like a war zone than a typical Tuesday morning. The destruction that surrounded us was unimaginable and indescribable. This city had become my refuge and now somehow it was anything but safe. I watched a woman run by frantically trying to cover her toddler from the falling debris of the buildings that surrounded us. She was followed by others dressed and ready for work but now covered head to toe in white powdery dust and in some cases blood. These people didn't deserve what was happening to them and worst of all they didn't even understand what was going on. I could only begin to imagine how terrifying it must feel to see the sky darken around you and to feel as though you were about to be consumed with no hope of escape. Some people yelled as they ran by that it was a terrorist attack, others swore it was a freak storm hitting off the coast. Those who called it a terrorist attack were completely accurate except this was domestic terrorism and that was the worst kind. Terrorism in any form was never acceptable or justified but when you attack your own people, on their own land, that somehow feels a million times worse than a foreign enemy holding a grudge.

This wasn't the Statics' war and yet they were quickly becoming collateral damage, innocent causalities, and for what? I looked behind me to see Aden focusing his abilities to try and calm those around us but he could only reach out so far and while he was calming the nerves of those nearby, it wasn't enough. Jade and Dylan were also using their abilities to try and calm the situation down by pushing people out of the way as pieces of cement fell from above as they could see it coming before it happened.

Dylan was tapping into his tech to try and jam the signal that was controlling the Shadows but he was coming up blocked. "Damn, what kind of tech are they using to keep us out?" We had experienced a tiny dose of this back at the facility when we discovered the guards were now immune to our abilities and Addison had been able to block us completely. We never did get a chance to discover how they had achieved that because at the time it didn't seem important. I sighed and turned my eyes to the Shadows that were increasingly covering the city and locking us in a darkness that seemed unbreakable, "You're not just up against tech, you're up against Benders and their abilities, it's impossible to stop that." "Nothing is impossible." Dylan said still attempting to reach the computer systems back in Washington.

I felt helpless just standing there watching people get hurt and dying around us. I did my best to send our a telepathic warning to everyone within a small radius but the chaos and panic was so widespread it didn't appear anyone was listening. I managed to help injured people to their feet and to usher others into safe buildings. My empathy was slowly trying to rear its ugly head and although I was fighting it back into the hole I tried to lock it into, that too felt impossible. All my life I felt defined by what I could do; the abilities I held and displayed. Aden got a lot wrong about us, and me, but the one thing he was spot on with was that I was born to love.

Dylan warned me that taking away my empathy would change who I was meant to be and what I was here for. I didn't see it then because I was being selfish and only looking after my own heart. I didn't care how my actions effected anyone else because to me I was just one person with a broken heart and how could anything good come from me in that state? I was a telepath and that meant that I was stuck inside my own mind and the minds of everyone around me but hearing thoughts and actually believing them or acting on them was another thing altogether. Thoughts were a brilliant technicolor mix of emotions and logic. I suppose it's why I'm also partly an empath because nothing is black and white in this world. We love to believe that we shouldn't let emotions control us and that logic is always right but the truth is they need each other. Without emotions we don't have instincts or intuition to tell us when our logic is faulty and without logic we can't tell if our emotions are right. They go hand in hand and it just requires us learning how to navigate the two together. I wanted to live in a black and white world where it was just pure logic and thought. I believed like most people that emotions were a waste of time and a world without pain would inevitably be the best thing possible. Truth is as much as we want to avoid the pain of life, it's what makes us stronger, it's what makes us realize there is life beyond the broken moments, that there is a will within us thriving to exist. The world can shatter into a million tiny pieces in a moment and it can feel as if ghosts of memories are all that can be found around us, but those ghosts remind us that something waits for us around the corner if we're willing to wait it out. All of this helps us to remember that we've survived 100% of our worst days so far and if we can make it through all of that there isn't anything we can't do.

A child about the age of 4 or 5 ran up to me clutching their dust and blood covered teddy bear sobbing as they tugged on my pant leg. "Have you seen my Mommy?" I knelt down and embraced the child as I looked around to see if I could find her. I sent out a telepathic message and image of the child but no one replied. "Shh... it's going to be okay, sweetie. I know your Mommy is looking for you right now and if you'll let me take you somewhere safe she'll come find you." My heart might as well have been ripped out right then and there as I lied to this child. I had no idea if their mother would come for them or not and this child's life could already be destroyed before they've even had a chance to live it. I knew all too well what it was like to live without parents and this was my breaking point and as much as I could feel myself wanting to just fall apart, it was too late for that. I rushed the child into the closest building I could find where people were leading others to safety in a basement below. As I came out of the building I found Toby landing back on the ground covered in debris himself. He had been flying people as far from the danger as he could but I could tell it was taking a toll on him too. We were fighting a battle that we knew we couldn't win and if we kept fighting we'd just kill ourselves in the process.

I looked back at Aden, Jade, Dylan, and Toby and knew what had to be done. "I know what will make this all stop." They all stopped what they were doing and looked up at me eagerly anticipating the game plan. "Me."

"What are you talking about?" Dylan asked obviously hoping that I had decided against this outcome.

"As we discovered, what feels like ages ago now, I'm responsible for all of this. When we were at the facility and I broke us free from the drugs I realized that if I combine all my abilities at the same time I can cause some type of reaction of devastating proportions. I suppose this is what everyone already knew a long time ago that they were eager to exploit. Commander Addison has always wanted me back and he won't stop until he gets me and the rest of us. So I'm going to give myself up. I'm going to do something good for once and make this end before anyone else has to die." I should have been terrified by what I was agreeing to but I knew, without doubt, it was the right thing and therefore I wasn't afraid of what I had to do.

Despite the chaos that surrounded us there was silence from Jade, Dylan, Toby, and Aden. They held the kind of eerie silence that hung in the air that spoke loudly of the realization of truth mixed with denial.

"There has to be another way Ember." Jade spoke softly but there wasn't much fight left within her. Dylan reached out and took Jade's hand into his and I couldn't help but smile softly knowing that when I was gone they'd at least have each other. Aden grabbed my arms and pulled me face to face with him and the world suddenly faded away around us in that moment.

"Em, you can't do this." Aden's hands were tightly wrapped around my arms and I could see his eyes peering as deep into my soul as they could trying to reach me.

All I could do was place my hand on his chest and push him back. He didn't release me but I couldn't be close to him like that right now. I felt his body weaken a bit under my touch as it always had; the familiarity was nice in a moment like this. Aden was a desperate man and I had to make him see why it had to be this way. If I didn't he would do everything in his power to stop me and that wasn't a possibility anymore. I knew how dangerous desperation could be and I wasn't going to let him go there.

I pulled him aside and looked into his eyes and kept my hand on his chest. "This is suicide, Ember. Please, I never meant for this to become your life. I hate myself for destroying your heart this much that this is all that is left."

I stroked his cheek softly with my hand and although I knew inside he was boiling with frustration, desperation, and pain he would listen to me now. "I'm not doing this because of what happened between us. I'm doing this because I am the only one who can."

As I looked back at the scene of destruction behind us and closed my eyes trying to suppress the pain it caused me. "Do you know why we're here Aden? Here in this very moment right now?" He shook his head painfully and confused. "Because once upon a time you loved me and I loved you. A love so real and true that it could change mankind forever. It sounds like a fantasy or one of those cheesy fairytales we hear as children, but it never was. I know that you felt it as much as I did and that what we had was unexplainable and powerful. We're here because that love that I have for you gave me the strength to discover who I was meant to be. Gave me the courage and bravery to go after what I believe in no matter what the cost or risk might be. Everything I did, leading up to this point was out of my pure love for you. I left on this crazy journey to fight for our love, believing somehow I could bring it back and make you realize you made a mistake. You were worth fighting for and giving everything for, even though you didn't deserve it. I used to look at life and all I could see was Aden and Ember. I somehow missed all these souls walking around me that needed people like us; that needed heroes willing to sacrifice their own chance at a normal life so that they could be safe and free."

Aden let tears fall down his cheeks but he didn't break his eyes away. "But they'll never know what we gave up for them. I'm losing you for them. We're losing each other."

I smiled softly at him, "We already lost each other, remember? It's not their fault that happened. And yeah, they won't know any of this, if I can succeed they won't even remember what they saw. Aden, this world doesn't want to be saved, all it wants is to be loved. That's all you and I ever wanted and for a time we had that and remember how it changed us for the better? Letting go of love out of fear is what destroyed us."

"We can have that again Ember, just stay with me. There has to be another way. This world has done nothing to deserve your love, it's quite the opposite." Aden was resorting to begging and no matter how hard he tried he knew he couldn't win.

"There isn't another way. It's me they want. And no, it doesn't deserve my love. I don't know these people anymore than you do, but doesn't it mean something to know that someone out there loved you enough to give up everything they wanted for you? That whether you realize it or not there is someone out there fighting for you? I did that for you Aden and I would do it again in a heartbeat, now it's their turn. We are here to protect them and keep them safe and we can't fail them now. Our love was meant to show the world what true love really means. True love isn't something you just feel or find in multiple places; it's rare and precious. It's something the world has lost sight of and forgotten. We live and thrive on fear and love is the antidote to that fear. You forgot Aden. You thought you could find what we had with someone else because you forgot what real love looked like, you feared you'd never be truly loved again. At the end of the day I came to the conclusion that if our love couldn't survive, if we couldn't make it work and give to the world what we were put here to do, then the least I can do is this now. Show them what real love means in this one last moment of sacrifice. Love doesn't ask for anything in return, it's just meant to be given freely. Aden you once told me I was born to love and that the way I loved was magical." I smiled at the thought of that conversation we had years ago and how it still made me feel butterflies in my stomach and how he had been so passionate and serious about trying to make me believe this truth that I only just now was believing.

"I remember." He spoke quietly as sadness consumed him. I wiped the tears off his cheeks gently.

"All I've ever wanted to do is help people and love them even if it hurts and doesn't make sense. I wanted to remind the world what love really is. I wish things could be different but choices that were made brought us to this point and I have to go." I held his face in my hand for a moment longer and before he could say another word I turned and took off running with a speed I didn't know I had within me.

The destruction and people around me were now a blur as I ran into the darkness. As I ran towards the Shadows I felt someone following me. I looked up to see Toby flying alongside me. He held his hand down to me and I took it as he joined me in running. "You can't come with me, Toby." I said trying to kept my breath steady. His eyes were glassy and red from crying. "I know. I just can't let you do this alone." I felt my feet lift off the ground as he pulled me into a tight embrace and our lips met passionate and fiercely. He kissed me as if his life depended on it and for a moment I wanted to be selfish and stay with him because the thought of leaving him was too painful a thought to entertain.

As I stayed in his arms flying above the people running on the street below I knew this was my chance to channel my abilities to begin formulating my plan. I had to connect with the Shadows in order to make this work.

I began focusing all my mental thoughts on finding the core of the Shadows and infiltrating the Bender's minds as if they were computer systems that I could shut down with a virus. The heat began to rise in me like a supernova that was about to explode and I could feel my heart racing and empathy overflowing through my veins as it resurfaced within me. I heard Toby groan as I sent a shock through his body and he placed me back on the ground but continued to follow above ground. I could feel my mind pushing everything away from what would soon be the epicenter of this event.

I was seconds away from the moment of impact and feeling the exhaustion coercing through my body and every part of my being. It felt like I wouldn't make it, but I kept pushing myself to the breaking point. The darkest point of the Shadows was right in front of me now and I felt myself lift off the ground and I was flying, without Toby. Under normal conditions this would be a dream come true but right now I knew my abilities were in control and I was losing control. Toby continued to follow me and I knew he had no intentions of holding back. He was going to be with me until the end and I couldn't bear the thought of anything happening to him. Thoughts were flooding into my mind from the Bender's that were trying to fight back against me and I could feel darkness taking over me. With what little control I had left within me I held out my hand to the side and pushed Toby out of the sky and back onto the debris covered street. I wasn't able to look back to see if he made it without injury but I took comfort in knowing that he was alive and I was able to protect him, even in this small way.

As I was about to explode with energy, literally, I forced one last burst of thoughts and feelings to everyone around us that would hopefully make them forget any of this ever happened. I let them believe this had been horrible, freak storm that swept through off the coast. I sent out a feeling of calm and peace to let them know it would be okay and they'd be safe. I made sure that any memories of what they had seen of the Bender world were erased and that Aden, Jade, Dylan, Toby and I, didn't exist in their memories at all either. I reached the exact epicenter of the Shadows and I could feel my body collapsing as light began to flood out of my body like angelic flames and then as if the

heavens exploded into stars everything went to a
blinding white and it was over.

ACKNOWLEDGMENTS

God: There isn't a language in existence that will ever contain the proper words to express how extraordinary You truly are. My faith in You drives everything I do and all I can hope for is that everything I do is a reflection of You. Thank you for this glorious life. You have my heart and soul for eternity.

Mom & Dad: Since I was born you've been a consistent source of love and support. You taught me to always go after my dreams and to never give up! You've always gone above and beyond to see that I have only the best this world can offer and there are truly no words I can say to express how much you both mean to me. I wouldn't be who I am or where I am today without either of you. Thank you, for being the world's greatest parents and always believing in me. I love you to infinity and beyond!

James (aka: Chookie): I love you immensely and always will. I hope that one day, when you're a bit older, this book will be a source of inspiration to you. I hope that it will encourage you to always remember you can and will make your wildest dreams come true.

Zoe (My little girl): This book is for you. It's been a long time coming and you've been by my side through it all. May this be the start of a bright and amazing future for us together. Thank you for the endless cuddles & kisses. I will love you forever and beyond.

Linkin & Phoebe: You bring me endless amounts of joy and I love you heaps!

Uncle Dave & Aunt Val: From the moment I began this venture you helped me create my pen name and it will forever keep a part of you with me in all that I do. Thank you for all your love and support. I love you!

Grandma: You have always shared with me your love for all things creative and have always supported me in my creative ventures. You are truly special to me and I am so blessed to have you as my Grandma. I love you more than you know!

SPECIAL THANKS:

-**All my friends at R345:** You've continuously supported me and believed in me. I can't thank you all enough! "Here's to the crazy ones…"

-**Romie Celestino:** I will always remember when our paths crossed over a lunch break and you requested to be the "bad guy" in this book. You are far from a "bad guy" and truly an amazing person. Thank you, for your constant enthusiasm and excitement for this story.

-**Mikey Whitson:** You're an extraordinary person and a source of inspiration everyday. Thank you, for joining forces with Romie in this book and giving me yet another source of inspiration and encouragement.

-**Book Reviewers:** Tami Abbas (@agreatbook), Kaelea Bearwald (@bibliomanicgirl), Sarah Dubien (@Lovvlybooks), and Gillian Mancock (@michaelareads). Thank you for your excitement about the book and your honest reviews!

JENNIFER CAZEY DANIELS

When asking family and friends how they would describe Jennifer, they would say, in a word, quirky. Jennifer's quirky personality has continued to fuel her imagination and child like spirit over the years driving her passion to share her stories with the world. In 2009, she graduated with her B.A. in Film Production, allowing her the opportunity to take story telling to the next level. The years following, she worked as a freelance script reader for, theSCRIPTgurl, and has written countless screenplays and stories. When she's not writing you can find her reading with her fur babies, Zoe, Linkin, and Phoebe, swooning over Apple products and Owl City, or roaming the aisles at the local bookstore.

INSTAGRAM: @happylilrainclouds